Stewart Home is the
and cultural comme....
Pity, and *Neoist Manifestos/The Art Strike Papers*. His novels, *Slow Death* and *Come Before Christ and Murder Love* and the edited collection, *Mind Invaders: A reader in psychic warfare, cultural sabotage and semiotic terrorism*, are also published by Serpent's Tail. He lives in London.

SUSPECT
DEVICE

A reader in hard-edged fiction

Edited by Stewart Home

Library of Congress Catalog Card Number: 97–81174

A complete catalogue record for this book can
be obtained from the British Library on request

The right of the individual contributors to be
acknowledged as authors of their work has
been asserted by them in accordance with the
Copyright, Patents and Designs Act 1988

Copyright © 1998 of the individual contributions
remains with the authors

Compilation copyright © 1998 Stewart Home

First published in 1998 by Serpent's Tail,
4 Blackstock Mews, London N4
website: www.serpentstail.com

Set in 10pt Sabon by Intype London Ltd
Printed in Great Britain by Mackays of Chatham plc

10 9 8 7 6 5 4 3 2 1

CONTENTS

INTRODUCTION

Regrettably compiling a fiction anthology requires compromises. One is expected to accept as a given genre distinctions between fiction and poetry, literature and pulp. On the basis of these and other arbitrary differentiations, selection procedures are established. I took avant-bardism as my starting point then refined things. Obviously from this perspective conventions such as 'style' are completely unacceptable. Therefore what follows does not delineate a movement or tendency within contemporary culture – it is just an unrepresentative sample of what is 'out there'. As things fall apart and what was formerly projected as the centre ceases to retain its stranglehold on 'literary production', all the mystifications concerning the 'marginal' and the 'mainstream' fall away. The 'marginal' is the foundation upon which the 'mainstream' is built. The literary establishment is now in retreat. Having conjured itself up through the expedient of treating what became the 'marginal' as an excluded Other, the defenders of 'sweetness and light' have finally embraced this 'base' in a last-ditch attempt to save a culture that is dying on its feet.

Just as the Celts of old sacked Rome and Delphi, so following in the footsteps of the Arch-Druid Karl Marx, the avant-bard will – 'metaphorically' at least – vandalise the street lights of Hampstead. The meaning of the term culture is anything but fixed, as can be seen from its heterogeneous use. It is derived from the Latin word *cultura*, which was primarily applied to agriculture. It should go without saying that the avant-bard sees nothing wrong with rearing cattle in the evening. Having fished in the morning and hunted in the afternoon, the individuals whose work has been gathered here are determined to criticise after dinner. That said, this is not the voice of a generation, abstractions do not speak. When stories by *NME* journalist Steven Wells and the philosopher Roger L. Taylor are placed side by side, intelligent readers shouldn't require an explanation of the relationship between them. Instead, they'll use the gaps to open up their own 'north west passage'.

To the extent that the literary establishment is able to embrace writers such as James Kelman and Irvine Welsh, it does so as the leading representatives of a Scottish literary renaissance. The avant-bard has no country. For us the desig-nation 'Celtic' simply represents the process of cultural cross-fertilisation and continuous becoming. Scotland, like 'England', does not exist. Paul Gilroy suggested in his book *Small Acts* that there: 'is a reductive, essentialist understanding of ethnic and national difference which operates through an absolute sense of culture so powerful that it is capable of separating people off from each other and diverting them into social and historical locations that are understood to be mutu-ally impermeable and incommensurable ... It is therefore necessary to argue against the rhetoric of cultural insiderism and the narrow practice of ethnic nationalism, whatever their source.'

In compiling this anthology I have tried to avoid making it a round-up of the usual suspects. The best-known names are those of journalists such as Tommy Udo and Steve Beard, while some of the other contributors have had very little published. I have avoided the throughput of idiots who predicate their 'precious' identities on being novelists – such a one-sided approach fails to create books that will interest those who have developed a critique of literature. The gift of metaphor is much better served by the prosaic activities of everyday life, from the persistence of the commonplace to the ephemeral inventions of fashion. Treat what follows for what it is; demanding metaphysical 'truths' is a demand for religion, hierarchy, division of labour and alienation – it is the rallying cry of those who wish to defend class society.

Stewart Home

BLIND DATE

Hilaire

It was like a sleeping bag, but tighter. As he heard the zip squeeze shut right up the length of his back, Darren remembered that as a kid he'd liked to sleep in a sleeping bag inside his bed, the zip pulled up to his neck. His mother had worried that he'd choke in the night. If she could see him now.

He tried to wriggle inside the body bag. His left hand was tingling. But he really couldn't move. A flap opened, uncovering his buttocks, and it was at that precise moment he suddenly wondered what he was doing, but it was too late then. He was trussed up, immobilised, and he would have to take whatever was coming to him.

The restriction and panic were part of it. He slowed his breathing down, savouring the whiff of rubber he got with each inhalation. While one compartment of his brain was rapidly listing the traumas which might befall him, there was a still, central part of him which was awestruck. That he had stepped into the car at the agreed pick-up point, shaken hands with Tom (if that was his real name) and been driven here, to an address none of his friends, not even John, knew.

It was early evening. Suburban streets had glided past, kids twisting their bikes in and out of the traffic, making those awkward, jerking movements up on to the pavement and back down into the gutter. The car radio was on low, tuned to Jazz FM. Darren let everything happen; the journey was one long liquid moment of relinquishment. Tom had touched his knee briefly when they were stopped at traffic lights, a gesture of reassurance. He was older than Darren. *Old enough to be my father*, but he squashed that thought down. His hair was short, peppery, and, Darren noted thankfully, he was clean-shaven.

Fingertips brushed across his arse cheeks, then a thick finger was drawn firmly down his crack. Darren's heart raced. His pulse pounded in his ears. As soon as they were inside the flat Tom had eaten his face, to make it clear that he was in charge. Darren loved that urgent lust, when you felt the other person would devour you in one go. He was eager accomplice to his willing victim.

Through his nostrils the intoxicating smell of rubber; and now the slow opening of his arse, the application of lube to his sphincter, in his blindness and bondage trying to sense how many fingers. Beneath him his cock stiffened; a pocket of his brain registered surprise that there was room for this, but it made sense.

Tom had offered him poppers but he'd declined. He wanted to do this all on his own. A sudden, deeper jab caused a rush of panic, his muscles tightening and squeezing out the digital intruders. His cock went limp. Tom's hands stroked his buttocks, circling, the way his mother had soothed away the terror of a nightmare, her hands rubbing rhythmic circles on his back. *It's okay. Deep breaths*. The night light glowing pinky-orange.

This was all part of it, he told himself, the seesawing between arousal and fear, controlling the doses to intensify the experience. In the same way, over the course of a weekend, he would judge and measure his drug and alcohol input, building up for the final binge at four o'clock on Sunday morning. He pulled himself back from the edge of panic, in his mind conjuring a picture of the scene, his bound body face down on the floor, the older man introducing his fingers once more to Darren's arse, and excitement flooded through him again.

He remembered the letter he got from Tom, after he'd responded to the ad. Tom had described what he wanted to do to Darren, and he'd read it quickly, in amazement, before setting off for work. But the images, the words, had kept flashing through his mind and he'd had to jerk off in the toilet, his back against the cubicle door, swallowing his breathing in case someone came in and realised what he was doing. And now those things were happening to him, something hard and pointed was entering his rear, pushing it wider, splitting him apart, until his arse closed around it, the buttplug lodged deep. What a mindfuck; it felt as if his brain was about to flip inside out.

All of a sudden he was being pulled up on to his knees. He felt dizzy, disoriented. He tried to remember the layout of the flat, whether Tom had deadlocked the front door, as if he was in any position to make a run for it. His mind galloped ahead; how did he know there was no one else here? Someone gripped his shoulders, steadying him, stemming the panic.

Hey, I'm meant to be having fun, Darren reminded himself. The zip which held his mouth shut unpeeled tantalisingly, tooth by tooth, and a finger outlined his lips. Darren teased himself with the thought that this could be someone else, Tom sprawled on the sofa watching the action, dandling his cock.

A warm, yeasty smell tickled his nostrils, and then his mouth was full, crammed, he was trying not to choke and he felt tears sticking to his eyelids, trapped by the rubber mask. Instinctively he jerked his head back but there was a firm hand there, and the cock kept thrusting in his mouth, he couldn't breathe or swallow. Once when he was little he'd been playing with a plastic sword. He liked putting things in his mouth, so he plunged the sword in deep, pretending to be a sword swallower, but it had jabbed his soft pink palate. It made him cry, he felt sick, but he wouldn't tell his father what had happened. Somehow he knew it was dirty, wrong.

For a moment his mouth was empty and he gulped down a huge lungful of air. The cock rammed into his mouth again but this time he was prepared. Darren sent his mind over to sit next to Tom on the sofa, to take a mental video of the scene which he would be able to replay at his leisure. Now his body, emptied of its mind, got down to the business of its pleasure, sucking down this piece of meat, getting its taste, learning its ridgy veins with his tongue, while his arse bulged and strained with its fullness, and his cock twitched and swelled and ached.

It was quite amazing, to be so intensely inside his body and yet at the same time way out of it, off on another plain. The various illegal substances he had consumed over the last couple of years had never given him this sensation. In the far distance of his brain a little warning triangle flashed up: *This could get addictive*. But the next cock-thrust extinguished it. Spittle bubbled out of the corners of his mouth. The cock pounded in and out and Darren worked it hard, willing it to come, feeling nothing but this shocking intimacy, a stranger's cock fucking the soft and wet insides of his mouth.

The cock withdrew abruptly and Darren strained forward, mouth open, suddenly bereft. He wanted to be filled up, in every orifice, and now the dummy had been torn from his mouth. Briefly the man plunged his fingers in Darren's mouth. He sucked at them. They were sticky with lube and the juices of his own arse, tasting sweet and forbidden. Then his lips were shut and the zip drawn gently closed.

His eyes, though shut, blinked under the mask. He sucked his cheeks in, ran his tongue around his teeth, *licking the plate clean*. The main course was yet to come.

Tom eased Darren back down to the floor. He flexed his kneecaps cautiously. God knows what his body would feel like tomorrow. With tiny movements he adjusted himself as best as he could, his hips digging into the floor. His mother was always nagging him to put on weight.

She was banished from Darren's thoughts as soon as Tom began twisting and coaxing the buttplug out of his arse. He contracted and then relaxed the muscles holding it in place. A protracted disgorgement, veering between agony and bliss and back again; subliminal images flickered beneath his eyelids: a woman in labour, sweating and straining to deliver; his mate John bent double on the toilet, squeezing his stomach in as if he could force out his constipated guts; a rubber fist he'd seen in a catalogue. Then with a soft squelch it was out, leaving Darren to enjoy the after spasms.

Behind him he heard the familiar rustle of a condom being unwrapped. His brain went into overdrive. Usually he didn't like getting fucked face down; with a lover, he'd want to kiss him and put his arms around him, not be a passive object. But this was precisely what he had chosen in this situation. Deep down, the idea of being used, of being in someone else's control, with no emotional attachment, was immensely, outrageously, exciting. And yet, with the aural sign Tom had given him, with that one gesture which meant he could cross off the item at the top of his risk list, he felt something which could have been the beginning of love.

Tom hoisted Darren's hips slightly off the ground, his left arm hooked strongly beneath him. The cold tip of his rubber clad cock nudged at the puckered sphincter and then pushed in. Darren sighed. It felt as if he could never get enough. His eyeballs rolled back inside his head, as if he would then be able to see Tom. His hips were clasped firmly and Tom was thrusting into him. He must be half squatting, half standing, a leg each side of Darren, fucking him like an insect. The sense of being desired overwhelmed him briefly. He thought he was going to black out. It had happened once before, after a strenuous weekend. He'd passed out under the shower but luckily John had brought him round. Now he bit his lip, tasting his own blood dissolve in his saliva.

There was a sharp slap across his buttocks, then another. His skin tingled. Darren's cock felt as if it was about to burst. He was being ridden like a horse. The muscles in his stomach were stretched tight, his neck ached, his body was in such a contorted position, but he could do nothing about it. He tried to concentrate all sensation in his arse which was being alternately pounded and stroked, Tom's balls smacking against his buttocks with each thrust. He'd be walking like a cowboy for days; he'd be feasting on this experience for months, years to come. His arse was raw and the fat, long cock continued to plough into him, digging a deeper furrow of pleasure.

Darren's body dropped back to the floor as Tom withdrew his cock. After a few moments something spattered over his backside; exhaustion flooded through him, every muscle in his body suddenly relaxing.

When he woke he had no sense of how long he'd been lying there. Water was running somewhere in the flat, the pipes groaning. For a second or an hour he drifted back to sleep. He was five years old and he'd fallen asleep beside the lavender bush in his nanna's garden, safe and sound, bees hovering nearby, the sun warming him.

He was still drowsy as Tom unzipped him and peeled him out of the body bag. *I've run a bath*, Tom said, and led the sleepy boy through to the bathroom. Darren stretched out in the hot, lavender scented water and glanced at Tom. He had almost forgotten what he looked like.

Tom was now dressed in worn-out jeans and a red shirt, the sleeves rolled up above his elbows. He sat on the edge of the bath and dipped a flannel in the water. Then he began to wash Darren carefully, remembering all the secret places dirt gathers, in the bend of the elbow, behind the ears, in the soft parting of the buttocks. For Darren, this too was a form of relinquishment.

As Darren towelled himself dry, Tom said: *I'll give you a lift back.*

—*Okay, thanks.*

Once he was safe inside his own flat, the door double-locked, the answer machine flashing at him, Darren sensed a kind of shock, a dim awareness beneath his brimming excitement that he had experienced something akin to unconditional love. He knew enough to grasp that it would be unwise to seek it out again, that the memory would have to suffice. The details, the pornography, he could play out with John.

Darren switched on the lights in the empty flat and pressed play on the answer machine.

VEGAN REICH

Neil Palmer

Tina Hay dressed and made a mug of tea before ringing Chris, her business partner. Together they were running *Phentasm*, East Anglia's summer music festival. It was looking good. All the bands had confirmed and ticket sales had already put them into profit. Most of the promo work had been supplied on the never never, as the top-flight acts they'd conned into appearing boosted the confidence of their creditors. Tina rolled a cigarette as she spoke to Chris on her mobile. They were staying on site overnight but she needed a lie-in tomorrow morning, while he'd be up early attending to anything that needed sorting.

Since the Yanks had packed up their weapons and gone, the region had felt the pinch and was coming round to the idea that a rock festival might bring in some extra wedge. In the music press the flat Fenland location of *Phentasm* had been compared unfavourably to the green hills of Glastonbury. Tina put this idiocy down to the fact that most rock hacks were New Londoners, eager to display their urban consciousness by adopting a city-idealised vision of 'the country' as a big farm, a landscaped park or an empty space.

Tina had been living and working in London for ten years and she'd met Chris at a party to launch some worthless product. She'd worked for a record company at first but got bored, then tried her hand at various media jobs, settling on publicity as the most bearable. PR work was easy if you could arse-lick. Tina was from North Cambs originally and had lived on the edge of the Fens till she left home. It was the only place she had ever seen, apart from the sea, where the sky was the main feature of the landscape. Of course she was free to romanticise because she no longer lived there. Moving to London she'd rented a small flat in Hackney which overlooked a main road, busy day and night. Tina had watched Cambridgeshire change from being predominantly rural to mainly suburban in the last fifteen years. City culture was engulfing rural England. She longed for peace and quiet, unaware that this rural ideal was simply a commodity she was being sold.

Chris Fitt shoved his mobile back into his shoulder-holster and pulled gingerly at his slacks, releasing the material stuck to the end of his uncircumcised cock. Two nights ago he'd been out to a club in Shoreditch and some teenager had picked him up. He took him back to his place and the little spunker had kept him up all night. The youngster had a nice tight arse and a mouth full of sharp teeth, and the double assault on his prick had left it red-raw. Tina had woken him up and he needed a cup of filter coffee. He was well shagged-out before he got here and getting up at sparrow's fart would do him no good at all.

Some months ago Chris had agreed with Tina that there was nothing further to be gained from their sexual relationship so they decided to call it a day, but continued to work with each other professionally. They'd decided to locate *Phentasm* in Cambridgeshire after arguing the pros and cons of Norfolk, Suffolk and Essex. There hadn't been an event like it in East Anglia for years and although initially there had been some local opposition, this subsided after Tina had emphasised the economic benefits. The music press had doubts too, they equated the countryside with hills and derided the idea of a festival in the Fens, but thanks to the line-up they'd put together things were working out.

Chris had wasted his 'yoof' listening to records and producing DIY fanzines. This had been enough to get him a job as a staff writer on a rock weekly in the mid-80s. In the early nineties he'd jacked-in an editorial position to become a club

DJ. He became famous for his eclectic mix of house, techno and funky sixties and seventies tunes but his background was a bit of a mystery to his colleagues. It wasn't hip to say you came from Lowestoft, so Chris kept mum. Eventually he'd discovered many of his colleagues in the business actually came from this part of the country too. It was strange the way people in the music biz were almost ashamed of coming from East Anglia, unlike the mancs, scousers and fake-cockneys who all shouted about their roots. Maybe it was the general lack of recognition for the regional accent. When he'd arrived in London everyone thought he was from the West Country. His cultural awareness didn't awaken any dormant regional pride, it merely confirmed Chris's suspicion that concentrating on the regional origins of rock music was a divisive sub-nationalistic tendency. He hated football for the same reason.

Wilf Hobson changed his name to Dog when he was sixteen. Going to gigs dressed up in bondage strides, painted leather jacket and hair spiked with glue didn't fit with the name he'd been given. That was back in the early 80s. He'd bought a van in the mid-80s and had been travelling since then, parking up wherever he could, living off the land. He was forced to visit towns in order to pick up his fortnightly benefit cheque from the government. He figured it was better for him to be happy wandering about rather than stuck in some poxy room in a city, poverty-stricken, on hard drugs and robbing old ladies. He had a swig of Tennant's Super and sucked on the end of a joint. He fucking loved his skunk!

Dog met up with people every year at festivals. There was a brilliant community feeling about the whole lifestyle. The way that straights were always ready to point the finger at him and his kind made him sick. Alright, so he didn't have a bath every day, so what? He might have a crusty arse but his conscience was clean!

As a Dark Green anarchist, he was proud of his grass-roots political convictions. The straight world had fucked the planet up and the Great Mother was about to wreak havoc in return. The seasons were fucked. The trees were dying. Cities were spreading like cancer. Cars were belching out poisonous gas and choking the environment. He'd tried to use unleaded petrol in his van, but the engine was too old to take it, anyhow, his was only one vehicle out of millions used by the straight world! It was only people like him that were making a difference at the moment. The rest of the country deserved to die, squirming in their own vomit, as the cities poisoned themselves to the point of destruction! The Great Mother would protect her children, of course, and he and his kind would be saved! No consumer scum would survive the coming holocaust!

The Dark Green activist network was made up of two magazines and the odd meeting. Dark Green didn't go in for public actions, they just claimed other people's activities as their own. Since non-hierarchical organisations were too easy to infiltrate, the core leadership of this communal movement had decided to remain incognito. The Dark Green network was causing a lot of trouble to the authorities. Thanks to their superb line in hyperbole the mass media had credited them with halting the progress of more than a dozen road-building schemes up and down the country since the start of the previous year.

Their organisation was well underground. They were intent on returning Britain to its true state – an agrarian society organised around self-governing feudal communities. Dark Green was going to give the fat, bloated System a gigantic heart-attack! But destroying civilisation was not for the faint-hearted. As Intelligence Chief of Eastern Command Dog was well aware that Special Branch were monitoring local groups while MI5 was co-ordinating the surveillance.

Dog and his mates were making a proper nuisance of themselves. He'd heard tales from some of the city-based activists that their phones were tapped and they'd been followed by plain-clothes cops and their own offices were always being raided. The spooks were on their case. Walking into the village, he saw the headline on a board outside the newsagents: 'Festival Boost to Local Economy', and scowled. *Phentasm* would make a packet for the promoters, ruin the land and rip off the punters. If he didn't get an invite to the event from the promoter he'd be going over the wall as usual.

Derek Folds, singer and frontman for Shelf-Life, was doing an interview with Jill Carter of the Music Mail. He'd agreed to this person accompanying his group on their mini-tour of Britain after his management had instructed him to cultivate a good press image. This was vital to the ongoing viability of his career after an outburst in which he belittled his fans as morons for consuming the pap he produced. Derek was expending a great deal of effort attempting to break out of the pop-star mould he'd spent six years getting into.

He was bored with the scene. The music biz was full of cretins. Off stage most groups could hardly string a sentence together and practically none of them had read a single word of modern literature! Every chance he got, he talked about the books he was reading and how he was writing poems and stories. With the connections he'd cultivated he would soon be in a position to have some of his stuff published. He'd been reading everything he could find by Will Self and Charles Bukowski. These were true individuals, just like him! They walked it like they talked it! The way they wrote about dollybirds was refreshing in the face of all the PC bollocks around the pop scene. Even his girlfriend Sheila, the singer with Gussette, liked them, so they couldn't be anti-women. What people needed were examples of how to live, written with style.

'Actually, that's the good thing about pop music,' he drawled, 'you can be an individual and show people alternative ways of living.'

. Jill nodded to show she was paying attention, despite the fact that the rock bore was sending her to sleep.

'You can learn as much from books and art as you can from music. That's what Shelf-Life are about . . .' Derek droned on, 'intelligence and individuality. We're the epitome of eclectic postmodern life. Our career is, like, a series of media situations.'

Jill changed the tape over and pressed 'record'. She sneaked a glance out of the window at the passing fields. The pint-sized jerk stopped talking long enough to take another dab of coke and offered the bag to Jill. She rubbed some of the white powder on to her gums. Initially she'd been delighted to tour with Shelf-Life, the intelligent face of English pop, but it had quickly become a drag.

'Are you looking forward to the festival?' Jill enquired, virtually defeated by her pretentious subject.

'Yeah! It'll be interesting to see how it goes. The organisation's been really good, despite the line-up wrangles!'

'Have you visited the Fens before?'

'Well, a few of my friends went to Cambridge, so I know the area fairly well, obviously.'

Derek now wished to be taken seriously. He'd recently told the press about his privileged family background and this was received warmly by the Sunday magazines. Initially his upper-middle-class roots had been kept a dark secret. Like most people in the supposedly classless music world, he'd feared that he'd scare off a potential audience who required street authenticity. He'd done music, now he wanted to be a novelist like Will Self.

Dog had given up going to see indoor concerts years back. That was just after he'd got into anarchism. He'd read a lot about it from the record sleeves of bands, like Crass and Conflict, but never did anything until he heard that a few anarchos he knew were regularly attending hunt saboteur demos. This was his introduction to the bloody world of revolutionary politics. He'd been hospitalised by a hail of fists, truncheons and flying boots, wielded indiscriminately by his father's hunting friends and their blue-uniformed lackeys. The second time he'd got wise and gone tooled-up. The pigs had sussed that he wasn't soft and left him well alone, settling on arresting a middle-aged lady and a kid.

You couldn't get near a hunt meeting now for police cordons and hired muscle. This was the reason Dark Green had de-targeted hunt-sabbing two years back. Soon after he'd stopped, though, he'd met up with some old mates who'd put him on to the eco-activists. He'd been impressed by their dedication and initiative in taking credit for other people's actions. Dark Green was a trained guerilla force, not some bunch of one-issue animal-lovers. They were committed to bringing an end to the current system and replacing it with a network of rural communities run on feudal lines.

Dog gulped his Golden Pippin Ultra 12% Cider and finished pasting-up July's newsletter. It was a restricted document for command staff only. Alright, so he wouldn't win any media awards, but the point was that he'd produced it himself. There would be no earth-raping corporate hardware in their new system of self-governing agricultural communities! He was making a statement by using craft-skills he'd taught himself. The headline read: 'Smash the Music Money Makers!', and the text dealt with the facts about the takeover of free festivals by businessmen, followed by a call for more direct action.

Music should be free and live, record shops should be boy-cotted, community drumming workshops should be set up to teach people the value of living in tune with earth-rhythms. For years now the capitalist controllers of the music industry had been infiltrating festivals. Dog had just finished reading *Triangular Extortion*, seditionary shaman Gary McMara's breathtaking critique on the subject, in which he exposes the ways in which the Vatican and the pop industry have been infiltrated by the cult of the all-seeing eye.

The last Glastonbury had been marred for Dog and his cadre by the vast uniformed presence and the threat of plain-clothes operators. They'd set up a sound-system without permission and had it confiscated before they'd got fifty punters dancing. They'd lost a packet on the impounded PA. This time they weren't going to be denied their legitimate right to express themselves freely. It was time for Dark Green to do more than simply take credit for other people's actions, they had to do something themselves.

He rolled the A4 sheet into a cylinder, put an elastic band round it and passed it to Justin Sinclair, a new recruit. Dark Green needed street-tough kids who had nothing to lose, but all they were getting through the door was drop-outs from sixth-form colleges and universities. He had to admit the lad had a taut arse and a terrific-looking cock pressing against the inside of his combat trousers. But such thoughts were forbidden! In a post-urban civilisation it was every healthy man's duty to procreate on demand to strengthen the community's chances of survival. The future depended on strong, fine children who would live free from pollution and consumer gimmicks. He must ignore his deviant sexual urges and concentrate on the common good. If that meant fucking birds, then so be it!

After instructing Justin to run off ten copies and get them in the post before dinner-time, he scanned the year-planner. He had a two-thirty appointment with the local print co-op to negotiate a price for 200 copies of the DG paper *Flagless Nation*, and he had to ring HQ. He got up and locked the door of his bedroom-cum-office. Flipping his cock out he watched it stiffen and inhaled its heavenly perfume. A swift wank wouldn't hurt the revolution.

Tina was due to meet the bands in their tour buses as they arrived. It was all part of the arse-licking expected by rock groups these days. Part of the festival contract required the bands to arrive the night before they were due to play. She was proud that she'd managed to arrange a dawn photo-shoot for all the bands who turned up. She knew that there would be absentees, but she'd planned to maximise her pay-off for *Phentasm*. However it worked out it would look good in the press and add to her reputation as a fixer.

The Celtic angle had been her idea. She'd become interested in Britain's ancient cultural legacy, which had been suppressed by Rome and Christianity. She'd recently had a Celtic band tattoo done on her left arm, the sinister member. This limb represented a symbolic opposition to Christianity, which always alluded to the right-hand side as holy and its opposite as the reverse. She'd also become interested in the work of an underground movement that was protesting against the increasing urbanisation of Britain. This cause was something she passionately believed in, especially since she'd decided to move back to the country. The last thing she wanted was to spend a fortune on a decent property in a pleasant location and then find herself face-to-face with the sort of traffic conditions she'd paid good money to leave behind in London. However, as long as she was far enough away from a bypass not to be able to hear it, she couldn't give a toss what the road-builders did.

Tina had invited representatives of the Dark Green Network to *Phentasm* so she could show them her usefulness as an organiser of large-scale events. They'd erected their teepees a couple of days before the main event, then decorated the main stage. Activists were given space in which to organise recruiting, a drumming space and a tribal culture workshop which would detail how the forces of 'civilisation' from the Romans to the EC were intent on destroying the naturally anarchic spirit of the Celto-British tribes. Tina hoped to gain their backing for a full-scale campaign to halt development in her chosen part of East Anglia.

Chris disagreed with her, but he was already a lost soul, a city-convert. By choosing to reject his roots he had forfeited his right to a place on the cultural presidium proposed by the Dark Green executive which would make the final decisions about the carve-up of land throughout the country. Tina was determined she wasn't going to be left out. She could see the split with the EC only months down the line and that would lead to the destruction of the Norman-dominated British state.

She had done some research and found that Dark Green had contacts in very high places. Of course, she gave no credence to the filthy-arsed anarchos who chose to put themselves on the front line. But by making her position clear she hoped to get an 'in' with the shadowy figures backing the movement.

Ray Musgrave, a rock god with genuine working-class roots, scratched the side of his nose. This was the signal for his driver to fetch the big bag of Charlie. Ray never carried more than a quarter and he'd done his little bit of 'personal' earlier. The site was all but deserted with the festival due to kick-off in less than twenty-four hours. Part of the contract had been for all the acts to turn up early in order to take part in some poxy photo-opportunity. It was an unusual clause for a festival, but they were paying £££s so he'd gone along with the demand.

Up on stage technicians were installing the lighting rig. Ray sneered at the mock-Celtic images painted on to the sides of the main stage. By utilising this puerile pagan imagery the promoters hoped to tap into some authentic culture-stream that the kids viewed as preferable to Christianity. The Celts were just one of countless ethnic groups who held a claim to the genetic and cultural ancestry of Britain. What about the Anglo-Saxons or Romans, Danes, Friesian pirates, Bronze Age nomads, Jews, Huguenots, Normans? The list was almost endless.

The sun was going down and the sky was darkening. Hippies were gathering around smoky fires. The shriek of tin whistles annoyed the fuck out of him, and the drums were doing his head in! Ray didn't mind the original hippies, in fact he was currently earning obscene amounts of wonga ripping off tunes from late-60s rock groups, but he hated their latest filthy, whingeing incarnation. He flicked away a fag-end and shook his head in disgust. He sprinted back to the tour-bus wondering if it was all worth it.

Chris guided the flat-bed lorry carrying half a dozen portable kazis into position. He didn't mind doing the donkey-work. Tina was far better suited to the flesh-pressing side of things. But he was pissed off about Tina's involvement with the underground eco-bores. She reckoned that London, like all cities, was dying. Cities were cancerous tumours eating up our island race. What a load of cobblers!

He'd looked into the fringes of the ecology movement. Behind their championing of environmental issues Dark Green were proposing vast social reorganisation along feudal lines. They publicly stated that they were fully committed to the immediate abandonment of city culture and a return to what they termed 'traditional' society. Their literature was ominously silent about how this earth-saving social miracle could be brought about. They glossed right over the obvious fact that a population of sixty million could never be squeezed into tiny hamlets of roughly a hundred people in such a limited space as the British Isles. Their grasp of race issues and sexual politics was also primitive. Their magazine, *Flagless Nation*, spent a great deal of time stressing the efficiency with which Mother Earth seemed to deliberately control her excess human stock by inventing continually more novel ways to rid the planet of dangerously high numbers of people: plague, TB, cancer, syphilis, AIDS, ebola, all were featured and eulogised as other fanzines extolled the virtues of particular celebrities.

This ghoulish delight in gross human suffering sent a shudder down Chris's spine. The gap between this crew's caring façade and the viciously misanthropist implications of the imposition of a neo-rural society seemed clear to him . . . nothing short of rapid depopulation would suffice! The answer could only be some form of genocidal programme.

Chris spied Tina wandering across the field and called over to her. She heard him shout, and moved towards him.

'Are you sure about these eco-arseholes?' Chris nodded towards some hippies huddled around an open fire.

'Look, this is my decision, right? If you've got a problem with my organisation then let's hear it.'

'This is bollocks!' Chris bellowed. 'Dark Green are fucking you over! I dunno what you reckon you're getting out of the deal!'

'Why don't you relax, Chris? Don't hassle my guests, right? Chill out.'

Being told to chill out really pissed him off. When he was DJ-ing and he responded to some drugged-up tosser giving him a hard time he was told the same thing.

'How can I relax? I've got a living to make!' he barked. 'You seem to be telling me those cunts are more important to this festival than me.'

'Don't be stupid, Chris! All I'm saying is, this event was always about people coming together,' she paused, 'about issues . . .'

'You keep on like that and you'll start fuckin' believing it!' Chris shot back. 'These shit-stains are not only giving me a king-size headache with their fucking bongoes, they're also a vicious bunch of creeps. I've read their paper. They want to liquidate the cities! They'll ship me and the rest of London off to a fucking death-camp!'

'You've got a big problem. I can't talk to you when you're like this.' She turned and walked off.

This was a common strategy Chris had noticed in 'new age' types. When faced with a different point of view they invariably tried to turn any adverse dialogue around so that their questioner became the intransigent one.

Duncan Oade was the chairman of AgriSolutions; during the last four years he'd built the business into a multi-million pound operation. His company offered development capital to businesses involved in the food production industry. The last couple of years had shown him that there was a niche for a political organisation which offered the people of Britain a way to control their own destinies. He had developed a network of powerful allies in industry and politics through extensive lobbying and attendance at tedious, but necessary, committee meetings of local and national business interest groups. These rich, short-sighted mugs were putting up the cash which would facilitate the social change he envisaged, simply to gain medium-term economic advantages from Britain leaving the constraining economic policies of the EC.

Oade had become convinced that the only way forward was to establish growth-limited, self-sufficient rural communities based around hamlets connected to a regional centre. Britain must abandon city-development. Britain, as a political and cultural body, must cease to exist and would be replaced by a network of independent rural bodies. Excess population would first be excluded from the life of the newly-established mini-states and then liquidated. The environment must be saved from the cancer of urbanism at any cost!

On the dawn of the next morning the underground movement known as Dark Green would be transformed into Green Age, a genuine political force! Oade and his associates had gradually taken over the leadership of various groups of disaffected youths. By proliferating as a grass-roots organisation, they had become aligned with the anarchist movement. Oade was happy with that if it brought in new blood. His propaganda focused on the menace of fascism, which gave it an acceptable radical face that appealed to solemn young anarcho-activists. These kids were relatively easy to control by emphasising the individuality and creativity of activism. Likewise, they were quick to embrace ludicrously reductive political and social dualities: rich/poor, fascist/anarchist, technology/craft.

The first blow was to be struck in East Anglia. For years national politics and the public had refused to accept this area as anything more than a featureless aberration. Apart from a couple of First Division soccer teams, Oade was willing to bet that the only exports most people outside the area could name from this glorious region would be Cambridge University and certain turkey products! He was continually annoyed at the public perception of East Anglia. The apparent emptiness of the place, based on its flatness, was always cited as the antithesis of the professed spiritual richness of hilly areas like Glastonbury.

Devolution was a fact now in Scotland, Wales, and even Northern Ireland had its own independent assembly. The lack of obvious linguistic differences between the Eastern Counties and the rest of Britain was no reason to oppose cession! Let the West Country keep her Tors! Let Scotland swing the mighty Claymore! Let Londoners map out their squalid psychogeography! But let the East reclaim her destiny! Dark Green would strike here first. The vile results of city expansion and enforced rural decay would finally be overthrown! Duncan Oade would lead the return to the soil!

Just before dawn Dog made his way to the *Phentasm* site in Dark Green East's brand-new Transit. Up and down the country well-trained cells of committed activists were poised to assault symbolic and material targets and claim victory in the name of the New Green Dawn. In Glastonbury and at Stonehenge squads were ready to seal off the Tor and stone circle. In London vital traffic arteries were to be blocked to cause road chaos, a symbolic thrombosis from which the City would never recover. Dog and his crew were on site at *Phentasm* to bring the message home to tribal youth. The skinny eco-maniac drove the van up to the service entrance and flashed his pass at a security guard. Other members of the team unloaded the sound-system that would herald the New Dawn.

Jill got up early to take in the sunrise. Dawn was spreading its violet palms over the lightening sky. She was still buzzing from last night and needed some fresh air away from the bollocks being spouted by the rock élite. She made her way round the perimeter fence and ended up at the main stage where all the action seemed to be. By her watch it was 5:00 a.m. A rasping fart echoed over the field and she looked behind her to see a gathering crowd of pasty creatures being shepherded by a small posse of more self-possessed human beings. It was the stars being taken to a photo-shoot.

'Attention! You are now subject to community law!' a voice bellowed.

Jill worked out that the voice was coming from a massive sound-system behind the stage area. The wasted musicians stood still staring around them, wanting their managers to work out what was going on. A wiry shape leaped from the stage and made its way toward the celebrities. Other figures moved into view. They were all carrying weapons.

'All band members are to prostrate themselves face down on the ground! NOW!'

A smattering of applause broke out from the press pack surrounding their meal-tickets. They seemed to think it was a joke. The chief gunman grinned at the powerless dolts in front of him. He had nothing but contempt for them and their decadent kind.

'If you follow my instructions I probably won't have to shoot anyone,' the lean gunman roared.

He motioned to a fat woman in ripped purple tights who waddled over to him, followed by a mongrel puppy weaving in and out of her legs.

'Sandra, watch them for me while I tell 'em the score.'

'This is futile! Anyhow, we're all socialists and most of us are vegetarians. You can't do this!' Derek Folds blurted out a sudden protest which Dog ignored, except to return a disgusted grimace before grabbing the wretch's cheeks and squeezing tightly.

'You've all had your chance to make a difference and none of you have taken it. You are guilty of planet rape and compliance with a system of social slavery. All of you are gonna be put back in your coaches till showtime . . . none of you are gonna make an appearance till then.'

'What about the hospitality area?' Tina darted out and whispered urgently, 'The pop press will expect some celebs. It will look odd if no-one shows, these ponces would never pass up free booze!'

Dog stiffened and then pushed her away.

'In that case, march the scum to the hospitality bar immediately,' the eco-activist growled, 'but no-one's talking to anyone, right?'

'No-one said anything about guns,' Tina whimpered once separated from the other prisoners.

'Course they didn't! You wouldn't have let us in if they had, would'ya?' The wiry eco-rebel shook his head in disbelief. 'This whole show *was* about lining your pockets, but *now* you're gonna be making a very large donation to us! OK?'

Chris Fitt finished wandering round the site checking fences. He went over to the catering area to see if he could get a spot of breakfast. He was still uneasy about the soap-dodgers. The last thing *Phentasm* needed was some kind of Altamont-style scenario going down. They'd never get their security deposit back from the local council and their insurance company would shit itself.

Walking out of the back-stage café, he'd noticed Tina huddled on the grass. She was sobbing and sitting beside her was a hunched figure Chris recognised as Dog, one of the Dark Green activists that Tina had befriended. As the filthy shape reached forward to ponce a fag off her, Chris saw the automatic stuffed into the belt of his trousers. He backed away immediately. There was no doubt left in Chris's mind that the eco-fascists had staged a coup.

Sound-systems were chucking thousands of Ks of bass into the morning air and the smell of frying meat and onions wafted about on the breeze. *Phentasm* was nearing capacity. The crowd was gathering in the best spots to see the bands, watching the contents of a flat-bed articulated trailer unloading. Some hippies were busy erecting a pre-fabricated wooden-framed structure made from criss-crossed batons. It looked like a massive pair of legs. Then they added a new bit, on top of what they'd already assembled. The on-board crane was lowering this part into position as Chris watched. It made a torso joined to the legs below it. Arms were bolted on either side and finally a head was mounted above the rest to top-out the ghastly edifice. There was something terribly familiar about the way it stood astride the earth like a DIY colossus. But Chris was already on his way out of the site.

Stakker's 1988 electro-smash *Humanoid* roared out from the enormous PA on the main stage. Recognising the pre-arranged signal, Dog dragged Tina to her feet and pointed toward the Wicca Man.

'You can't! Not in front of thousands of people! It's monstrous!' Tina spluttered.

'These islands haven't seen the spectacle of the Great Ritual for nearly two thousand years. This scum don't deserve the honour of being the first to be offered!' Dog thundered.

He gave orders for the prisoners to be assembled immediately. The sight of the Wicca Man brought a lump to his throat. This was the symbol of their culture of resistance. This was the symbol which opposed the waste and greed of consumer capitalism. He drained the gaudy can of Hawk Optimum 8% Perry. They would find newer and increasingly more grotesque ways of punishing those who sought to perpetuate the disease of commodity-culture. Dark Green would bury eco-criminals alive, up to their necks, and let the miscreants rot in the very earth they'd helped to destroy! This was the last push towards unstoppable social revolution. They would fight mass society by offering a series of autonomous actions by networked groups. This was the first step to establishing the self-governing, self-sufficient communities which would be needed as the state lost control of the planet. Britain was coming home!

A minibus passed through the guarded perimeter. Inside was Duncan Oade, his partner Teri, and other top members of the

Dark Green Network's Eastern Co-ordinating Committee. Dog greeted Oade with a wry grin. The businessman returned Dog's handshake.

'Congratulations! Your troops have pulled off a major success here today. This is something we can all be proud of. With the publicity gained from hijacking such an important youth event we'll force a nationwide discussion of our political role. National dissolution will follow.'

Dark Green's executive applauded and Oade motioned with his hands for them to cease. He stared straight ahead.

'That looks interesting, what is it?' He pointed to the giant Wicca Man.

Dog told him and laughed at the surprise his answer registered.

'B-but that's ridiculous. The whole point of this exercise is to get people involved in the creation of a New Albion, not assault their senses with m-mass b-bloodshed!' he stammered, 'besides, it's against my orders!'

'The revolution is here, there is no chain of command. From this point we have devolved all due process to the community,' the gaunt street-politician paused to study the faces of the astonished businessmen, 'any questions?'

Oade was speechless. He'd gravely underestimated the ability of this street-tough eco-veteran. But the first blow had been struck effectively. At the very least, the brutal response this armed gang would attract from the police and security forces would move public opinion in their favour and help mobilise youth interest.

'Dog, I suggest you continue with your plans. The show's all yours!' Oade announced.

'There's thousands of our fans out there! There's no way they'll allow our ritual slaughter, we're contemporary cultural icons!' Derek Folds, the singer with Shelf-Life, sobbed.

'Yeah!' sneered Ray Musgrave, raising his arm in a clenched-fist salute, 'we put our trust in the people! Consumerism is the ultimate democracy because people are free to negotiate positions of cultural power!'

Dog shook his head in disbelief. These fools were quite convinced that their antisocial actions were morally vindicated by their economic success. This scum represented a tide of darkness that was rolling over the whole planet. The world was festering under waves of manufactured music, deodorants, plastic, people and concrete! The earth was threatened by scientists, junk and poisons. If it wasn't for networks of devoted activists opposing the filthy hordes of consumerism the very solar system would be swamped in human filth! How he hated his inherited genetic material because it linked him to unpure elements! The rock stars' whining only hardened Dog's resolve to offer their wretched carcasses in human sacrifice. His body stiffened and his face contorted with berserk rage.

'At last I claim my birthright! I pronounce my true name without shame! I am Wilf of Anglia, son of Trevor! Take these symbols of social decay to the sacred place!' he shrieked.

The eco-fascists ignored the celebs' pitiful mewling and shoved them on to the main stage. The crowd went barmy. From habit the seasoned performers grinned in appreciation. Wilf Trevorsson bellowed a curt speech.

'This is the Green Age! We stand on community land. The relationship between human and earth has been reestablished. The consumption-cycle has been broken by an audacious act of revolutionary force! These people are no longer your property! You are no longer their subjects! You are all free to choose life in extended family units, unfettered by the compulsion to consume! Let us celebrate our ancient Eastern Motherland and the true meaning of festival!' Wilf raised his can of Valu-Mart Xtra 9% Lager and poured a libation to the Mighty She, then downed the fiercesome brew with one superhuman gulp.

Sandra Keats and her gang of specially-trained wimmin herded the consumer-fodder off the stage and into the enclosure that held the Wicca Man. She showed no mercy to her snivelling prisoners as they marched to certain death. Britain would learn that the Great Mother enjoyed the taste of the warm blood of her defilers. Proudly, she waited as Wilf Trevorsson signalled for kindling to be placed at the foot of the monstrous vertical oven.

The pop stars were shrieking with fear. Unable to escape from the blasphemous wooden beast, they fought one another for space. There was just room for arms, legs, heads to protrude from the interior of the massive abomination. As the flames licked at the ankles of the fearful pagan icon the crowd grew silent. Smoke rose up the legs of the Wicca Man and caused panic among the sacrificial victims inside. The stars were screaming and clawing at each other as their will to survive drove them to inhuman lengths to cheat death. Lower down, in the thighs of the beast, the thick fumes had already choked several well-known dance acts whose bodies were charred beyond recognition, bursting like sausages in the flames. In the belly of the Wicca Man the sacrificial fire had turned the pop élite into a bunch of dribbling maniacs fighting for their lives. Ray Musgrave strained to break free, vainly stretching out his arms, as gobbets of flesh melted and dripped down his lean body. Derek Folds was howling in agony, scorched beyond recognition as the flames leaped around him then, suddenly, his eyeballs burst and he fell, tearing at his burning skin. The rock gods were being torched like BSE-infected cattle.

A voice rose above the crackling fire and the screams of the doomed celebrities.

'No to human sacrifice!' Jill Carter yelled at the top of her lungs.

As much as she despised the wretched ideological vacuity of most pop entertainers, she couldn't stand by and watch the ritual slaying of fellow human beings. The crowd murmured uneasily. Groups of fans surged forward. They recognised the reality of the situation.

'If they succeed we'll be plunged into an age of imposed pseudo-folk tradition!' Jill bellowed.

The crowd hissed with rage. Groups of fans started to invade the stage but were held back by security guards.

'Rock music will die without electricity!' Jill yelled.

The crowd thundered its response and massed to the attack. The stage was taken. The music fans were incensed, but as they fought, their idols were incinerated in front of them. They were unable to save the lives of their gods, but someone would pay dearly for the void tickets!

'Storm the free bar!', 'Take all complimentary catering for hungry fans!', 'Claim all music equipment as due recompense!', 'It is the masses who will serve as the shock troops of the moment and oust the tyranny and degeneracy of anti-technological ruralism!' 'We demand that all our demands are met!'. Slogans like these, plus many others, were shouted as the stage was looted.

The eco-fascists were not prepared for a full-on riot. Despite their basic training in neo-Druidic martial-arts the initiates of the New Green Dawn were no match for the incensed festival-goers. Most were beaten senseless immediately, caught off guard by the furious mob. Some were trampled as they regrouped to counter-attack, others were caught and bashed remorselessly by the angry mob as they tried to get away. Dark Green's van was overturned and torched as the Wicca Man collapsed, still burning, showering charcoal and crackling onto the horrified crowd. An anarchist video-art collective did its best to record the extreme violence, but disorder undid them and they and their cameras were trampled beneath thousands of feet. And above the noise of battle emanated the ugly sound of massed voices howling a single protest against the end of the illusion of fun.

Wilf had misjudged his audience. Who'd have thought they'd actually want to save the cowardly scum who imposed themselves through a corrupt media? As he slipped backstage, Wilf spotted his Green Age supremos celebrating the moment of communal victory with a sex-session.

Duncan Oade was doing some rectal expansion on Pete Harris, an electronics expert from Fakenham, grunting and sweating over the kneeling figure in front of him. The small-businessman gasped as Oade's hard prick stretched his arse-hole. Outside he could hear the sound of smashing glass and shouting, but all he wanted was his arse filled up with hot cum. Tina Hay had protested her innocence of earth-crimes and was rescued from burning by Oade, who introduced her to his partner Teri. Blood-curdling screams emanated from the Wicca Man, but the wimmin were intent on grinding. Teri exposed her funky twat to Tina, then worked several fingers into herself before pushing Tina on to the grass. It wasn't long before Teri slipped out of her pregnancy smock and shoved her tongue up Tina's pulsating snatch. Tina felt her yoni swell and moisten at the touch of the fecund womun's expert tongue. The knocked-up bitch smelled fantastic. With her back on the grass and the fertile womun licking her, Tina could feel the spirit of Mother Earth inside her. The crowd roared beyond the confines of the hospitality bar.

Wilf was repulsed by the sight of decadent sexual abandon in the face of counter-revolution. He fired one round into the guts of Duncan Oade, who shot his wad instantly. The back-stage entrance collapsed under the weight of unauthorised intruders. He made good his escape.

The rioting fans burst through stage security. What they found was a dead man still joined by the penis to the arse of a naked, sobbing middle-aged tosser whose sphincter had contracted with fear, and a bunch of naked people scampering around looking for their clothes and a way out. The fury of the mob was all but spent by the time it was confronted by this sorry sight. A rumour spread that several armed-response vehicles were entering the festival space even as the crowd's anger was subsiding. Having stripped the stage and immediate area the mob dispersed. The looters were escaping with their haul of booze, food, and expensive music equipment. When the police back-up arrived the crowd had retreated, leaving only certain well-known local business-people for the authorities to question. The cops imposed a cordon to contain the situation. Meanwhile, the looters were escaping with the spoils of riot.

Jill's medium-term security was assured. Not many rock hacks were bright enough to make it out of the weeklies. She'd rung several national newspapers on her mobile after the riot started and was currently initiating a bidding war for her story. She'd also got some dynamite pictures which would be worth a mint back in the smoke.

Wilf had stolen a motorbike and was on his way to join the earth-tribe hordes at Stonehenge. The Green Age would revere him as a hero for what he had achieved. As he rode he imagined the article in praise of him that anarchist elder-statesman, Gary McMara, would compose in his honour: 'Wilf had a duty to stay alive. He was one of a select band of activists who were all that stood between society and its immersion in a new age of fascist barbarism.' The stolen bike burned up the road and took Wilf Trevorsson in the direction he wanted to go, dreaming of revolutionary glory, skunked out of his brain, travelling at dangerously high speed on the wrong side of a country road . . .

Tina Hay stroked the hair of her lover Teri, who responded in kind. They had both made separate statements to the local CID which, while unusual, revealed no obvious basis for criminal charges. Teri was still a little upset about Duncan's sudden and violent death, but Tina whispered to her that they would be alright. If she could hang on to Teri she would soon be the partial recipient of a multi-million dollar legacy and a sizable country estate in Suffolk.

Chris Fitt had cut his losses and scarpered. He was hitch-hiking to Peterborough where he would catch a train to Cambridge. He had a job lined up DJ-ing the Judas College May

Ball. He'd get decent-sized helpings from the buffet, and free booze, though the rich punters were all a load of putrid shit. But under capitalism everyone was forced to make a living.

THE SUICIDE NOTE

Ted Curtis

It was on a freezing-cold weekend lunchtime that I decided to do it properly, without all of the fuss and talk. I had been at least vaguely suicidal for most of my sad and sorry life and the only thing that had really kept me from it for thirty years or more had been this strange kind of a gut guilt feeling about a few people who might possibly miss having me around; but then, not one of these people had ever been able to find it within themselves to take me seriously or to accept me, completely unconditionally, for what I was and at purely face value. It appeared that I was never much of a prospect in any sense of the word in the cold light of day. Also there was the little matter of whoever it was discovered upon and thus found themselves having to deal with the responsibility of the mess of my corpse. A dead human body is one fuck of a thing to see, especially when you once knew its inhabitant. Even after it has been tarted up in order to spare your feelings a little bit, its pallid and yellowy-leathery-skinned finality stops the world: except of course that it doesn't, which is somehow much much worse. With death, as with life, it apparently all meant nothing. I consequently now felt none at all of this prescient guilt but instead only a generally saddened and sickening contempt for everything that had ever existed. Sitting upright in my bed on that afternoon, shaking away to myself madly, there came to me in a sudden blinding flash the instant and glorious realisation that my remains need never even be found. All kinds of people managed to disappear and start new lives all over the world so it must surely be possible for me to do this and go unnoticed when not even performing the most basic of motor functions. As to those who might miss me, I felt no remorse for my passing from their occasional grasp: this was not bitterness, however, but a strange and airy vacuum of insentience coupled with a deepening sadness and disappointment at the world. I felt it to be an ugly place and that everybody in it was innately and irredeemably rotten and yet I nonetheless still harboured a profound and stirring love for a few people and for what might have been, that which now never could be. In my mind it was all over and my body would surely soon follow these sweeping thoughts.

I had the initial idea of swallowing a quantity of some kind of barbiturates – sleeping pills or whatever – and then drinking as much from a bottle of low-quality whisky (for the maximum damage and the speediest pass-out) as was possible before losing consciousness; then, at that crucial optimum moment I would dislodge a prelocated manhole cover and crawl into the sewer mains where I supposed that I might afterwards be eaten by the rats or the alligators or whatever. The first part of my ostensible masterplan I had gleaned from listening to the final deliberations of Kate Aldridge in *The Archers*: she had boyfriend trouble. I didn't have boyfriend trouble and pretty damn soon I wouldn't have any other kind of trouble either. The rest of it was that which had come to me in my flash of blinding inspiration that very morning whilst languishing lazily upon my bed of nerves. It was simply a matter of securing the pills, taking a room in a part of the city where they obviously didn't maintain the sewers and the drains particularly well ('simple', I figured to myself), and the rest was plain sailing. A week or so previously an old junkie friend had accosted me on the street where I lived, attempting to sell me Temazepam and Valium: on this occasion I had politely declined but I now knew where *he* lived. I had first met him some years previously and now every time that I happened across him – which was relatively rarely – I was always a little bit amazed that he was still alive. This seemed to be an unfortunate thing for *him*, from all appearances.

It turned out that purchasing ropy supplies from the gritty and earthy street-level drug-dealers of Hackney would prove to be an unnecessary inconvenience, and one that I wouldn't have to subject myself to: during my last drinking bout I had seriously injured parts of my digestive system, apparently during a fall which I could not recollect, and after five days and sleepless nights I crawled my way along to the doctor's surgery. Despite numerous cracked ribs – and perhaps some other ailments too – I had not visited the general practitioner's in some time: my usual sympathetic medical ear had apparently taken a couple of years off in order to breed and I didn't seem to get along with the others there one little bit. Now she had returned and I was really quite glad. She bade me lay down on the couch: I hoped that she hadn't turned into yet another pop psychologist during our mutual absence. She commenced feeling me up.

'How is the drinking coming along now?' she asked me.

'Same as ever, honey-pants!' I answered.

'Did you fall?' She dug hard into my injured side with her powerful physician's fingers.

'Probably,' I replied.

'Hmm.' She smiled down at me benignly from on high, at least from where I was laying it seemed that way. It was hard to work out exactly what the smile meant, though. Coupled with the angle and the grey sunlight filtering through the dusty Venetian blinds, it was in any case an ambiguous kind of an expression.

'Would you pull down your shorts for me?' she asked.

'I beg your pardon?'

'Loosen your shorts. I need to feel your pelvic girdle!'

I sighed and then something else sank too. I did as asked

and she dug those fingers around the top of my pelvis, feeling its contours and checking that it was still there. You could never be sure. You could never be sure of anything.

'Any pain?'

'All the time!'

'OK, what I mean is, is anything new?'

'No.'

'Alright, you can get down from the couch now,' she said, making her way back to her desk. She began writing on something. Something official and medical and, hopefully, something pharmaceutical too. She was the doctor. She was Emily Crippen, midget and professional temptress. And who was I? I was just nobody. Damn. I got down from the couch.

'I'm going to give you some codeine tablets: you're obviously in quite a bit of pain. But it's very strange, you don't appear to mind.'

'Oh, I mind.'

'What are you going to do now, Englebert? Do you want to stop drinking?'

She always addressed me by my real name. It was more than a little irritating but I kind of let it slide. We had this nice professional relationship.

'Well, I suppose I ought to but it's difficult. It's very hard. I don't really know how to do anything else,' I told her.

Her computer printed out the prescription, groaning away as if it were giving birth which of course it really was. We were all just machines of varying complexity. She handed me the prescription. I took the prescription.

'Come back and see me in two weeks whatever happens,' she told me. 'I'd like to see how you are.'

She was Emily Crippen, midget and professional temptress.

In a matter of two weeks I had moved out of the area and secured a dank and lonely bedsit in Poplar, E14, and so naturally I couldn't make my doctor's appointment. The rent was quite reasonable and the room was freezing and there in the middle of January I could see what was left of my breaths in the room quite clearly; there was also this green mouldering wallpaper which was nailed to the green mouldering walls but, in the interests of modern decor, somebody had sprayed the curtains a quite indescribable shade of pale pink and there was also a filthy stinking sink in the corner. One of the curtains was barely hanging on to its rail which in turn was barely hanging on to the crumbling plaster, and that itself in turn was just about hanging on to the rotting brickwork of the 5000-year-old building and thence the cruel and savage world outside. I liked it, it was a nice place. It was getting me used to the sewer mains which would constitute my final breathing-place. If you wanted to piss or shower you had to walk down the hall and so I didn't bother: I pissed out of the window when I thought that nobody would notice, ceased washing (the sink helped) and pretty much stopped eating as well in order that I wouldn't need to shit. If you brushed a section of the sea of condensation from the grimy windowpane then you could just about make out the docklands-light-railway trains taking the failed yuppies to and from their joyless jobs at the nearby Canary Wharf at the appropriate times, if time had any meaning at all to them in their parallel universe: it certainly didn't mean much in mine. My clock stood still and an egg-timer in which the sand had been taken out and replaced with the black, viscous amniotic fluid of the sparse remains of my excuse for a life was slowly and yet somehow determinedly dripping away. And yet this was a very happy hiatus: and I did not tire of it.

After I had been fully ensconced in my new place for a couple of days I took the 277 bus to Tower Hamlets town hall in Bethnal Green to take a look at the Borough's sanitation department plans: and just as I had hoped, there were none.

'Sorry, mate,' a stupid bald guy at the reception informed me. 'The department moved back in '73 and a lot of stuff got lost. Then there was a fire back in the eighties and the whole place had to be completely refurbished. Something to do with a group called the "Ken Livingstone Commando", I dunno. Anyhow, there's no overall record of the sewers anywhere anymore. You a student or something? Some sort of college project you're doing, is it?'

'No,' I told him. 'So how do you maintain people's drains, then? Do you just not bother or something?'

'Oh, we bother,' he assured me. 'Well, sort of. What happens is that if there's a specific complaint from somebody then we look into it and then eventually we see to it, usually. But there's no overall programme or anything. We just deal with things as and when they crop up. You see?'

I saw.

'Thanks, mate,' I told him. 'You've been very helpful'.

'My pleasure!' he beamed, closing his ledger.

'Hmm.'

I wasn't quite sure as to the precise relevance of the book that he was closing. Probably it was an album of his pornographic holiday snaps that he had wanted to show me or something. Anyhow, the matter was now settled for my mind. No overall programme for the maintenance of the sewers of Tower Hamlets.

It was all that I needed to know.

I had just gotten through a tape recording of *A Taste of Honey*, a play by Shelagh Delaney, when it occurred to me that my days here were finally over. I had not taken any of the codeine pills to alleviate the pains in my insides, believing instead in 'deferred gratification', a concept that I had first heard of during a sociology class back in school a long long time ago. There had been yet greater pains inside of me since before even then and these concerned me more, and so I waited. Now it appeared that it was time. I alighted from the damp and stinking mattress, put on my coat and headed out of the housing block and for the off-licence.

*

On my way there I walked past the ubiquitous old bums on their benches, shaking, cursing, freezing, angry, drunken and paranoid. I wondered just why they bothered to hang on for as long as they did: perhaps they were afraid to die. I turned the corner and the off-licence was still there and I walked on in.

I peered up at the spirits secreted behind the counter, squinting. They were quite near to the cigarettes: dealers in death. Yes, of course.

'Um, I'd like a bottle of Claymore please. Oh, and twenty Lambert & Butler as well.'

'£10.69 please.'

He placed the stuff into the bag and then he pushed the whole thing across the counter, away from him and at me. These transactions were always embarrassing for everyone concerned: we were both very glad when it was completed. Swinging the stripey-blue carrier bag that barely seemed able to take the weight of its contents I rushed back to my stinking room. I was by now, needless to say, very excited.

The first gulp of the whisky proved a little difficult but I pushed it on down as its poison shook my body. By the third swallow I had once again attained the power of flight but I instinctively knew that I would never be flying anywhere again: when you died your heart stopped and the bacteria moved in and that was that. All else was contemptible fantasy. I had no illusions, especially not now I was so close to death. I rested my head against the sopping wet wallpaper and smiled, letting the rot and the decay and the confusion of the world fall away. The rest was easy. I peeled the cellophane from the packet of cigarettes, pulled one out and lit it, flicking its dead ash around me with careless abandon. Then I unscrewed the cap from the pill bottle, spilled about half of its contents into my open palm and threw them into my mouth, hurriedly washing them down with more Scotch. I stood up to sing something, and the room suddenly began to spin violently. I collapsed back on to the mattress and a cloying blackness rained down on and into me like the sick rains of Hiroshima and Nagasaki.

When I next awoke a short time later my head was pounding away to itself like never before. I felt my guts heave and I summoned my remaining strength to keep inside me my long-awaited ticket out of here, and that worked so well I quickly took an extra big swallow of Scotch in order not to break with the beautiful cycle. The dirty amber fluid was an incredible thing: its corrosive taste seemed to burn away all of the hurt and the remorse and the doubt. I noticed that about a third of the bottle had gone and so I took another enormous gulp. I felt at this stage that it was important to persevere, to have ambition and some kind of a purpose to one's life. The room was spinning again but I kept with it and made it on through. I gathered up my things into a sports bag and lurched towards the door, making for the manhole cover situated in the alley outside.

It took me around fifteen minutes to hook up and dislodge the drain cover. I had to keep taking breaks from my grim determination in order to breathe. I sensed that my strength was beginning to fade very quickly now and so I made one last mad, desperate and powerful attempt: and off it came with an almighty clang and a clatter, echoing down the alleyway after slightly bruising a couple of my toes and simultaneously scraping a little of the skin from my right shin. The stench of the nation's shit and used tampons and condoms and Christ alone knew what else came up at me from some vile subter-ranean netherworld just then, and once more I had to fight to keep the pills and the whisky down. I grabbed the torch that I had brought with me, flicked it on and climbed on in, pulling the cover back over me as I went. I was on the home straight.

One of my earliest memories is of playing on a building site. This would have been during the early 1970s. The builders had gotten as far as putting in some of the foundations for the housing, the access roads and drives and the as-yet virgin sewage system. I had heard from some young roughnecks standing around on a street corner smoking chair-legs that it might perhaps be an interesting thing to see, and so one desperately dead and lonely Saturday afternoon without even telling anyone that I was going out I ventured over there to check things out for myself. Looking back on this, I could see distinct parallels with the end of my life. As now, I – aged, I think, six – tugged and wrenched obsessively at the drain cover until some time later, it finally gave in and went with my mighty and superior will. That first time, I was not thrown back with the sudden surge and thrill of release but instead forwards and headlong into the yawning chasm of the unfilled cesspool, knocking myself out in the process. I awoke several minutes later nursing a large bump on my head, in what appeared to be a grey plastic foxhole near the frontlines of the third intergalactic space war: I was a big *Dr Who* fan and such images came easily to me. The inside of the thing was clean if a little dusty and, much like myself, it did not appear to be connected to anything at all. I looked up toward where I had been told the sun burned constantly and saw nothing: my prison, my new home, was about eight feet in depth. Being still very young and naive, I began to call for help but there was nobody around: I suspect that anyone old enough to help me was out drinking Watney's Red Barrel or Worthington E on football terraces in the pissing pouring rain or watching old black-and-white musicals on television sets with aerials that didn't work properly. After a short while I gave it up. I have since heard that calling for 'help' as such is a patently useless exercise because nobody is ever interested and that you should yell 'fire' instead, which is something to really get things moving. Either that or 'raid'. After it had gotten dark, a search party consisting of several responsible and compassionate adult members of society set out to look for me. Eventually these heroes found me and hauled me out of the hole. I had been down there for about eight hours without food or water and so I looked upon the experience as being some kind of a crash course for long spells of solitary confinement whilst in prison during my later years. The entire time that I had been stuck down there: down there in the hole: I hadn't been able to find one single little thing to do, there was nothing at all to capture my interest, so the episode differed little from my ground-level existence. Being trapped for an indefinite length of time in a sewer was simply ordinary life in microcosm.

I got to the bottom of the drainage shaft, which seemed to have shrunk since my last visit, either that or I had grown. I went down on to all fours and, biting hard on my lower lip, crawled for a quarter of a mile along a tiny cramped shaft. The stench was pretty bad and getting steadily worse but you couldn't expect miracles. People had been puking, pissing, shitting, wanking and menstruating into here for hundreds of years now, and in any case it wasn't really much worse than that in my room. There was also the small matter of vermin, unsolved murders, bizarre scientific experiments gone wrong and a number of other things which were best left unimagined if you didn't want your mind to snap right there and then. Oh, and tea-leaves. I once shared a house with somebody who emptied his teapot down the toilet. Disgusting. And all of this had gone completely unregulated since 1973. At the end of my crawl there was a little more space to move one's limbs around but I found that I needed it less and less: I was very tired now.

I shone the torch downwards and observed a much more manageable space, a down-tube about three feet in diameter equipped with this handy metal stepladder which was bolted to one side of my dark and welcoming pit. Slinging the sports holdall containing my final comforts over my shoulder, the pills and the whisky and a small transistor radio, I brushed some stray faeces from my mouth and the left side of my face with the sleeve of my sopping wet jacket and climbed on to the top of the ladder. But where are the flies? I thought to myself. Maybe the rats and the alligators had consumed them all. Taking one long deep breath of stale and rancid air, I negotiated the thing and began to descend.

When I reached the bottom of the shaft shortly afterwards I found myself in the main part of the waste disposal system for Tower Hamlets. It was about eight feet high and a few rats ran about my feet sniffing and squeaking. The flow of sewage was at this point surprisingly shallow and slow and I began to walk; there was a slow and persistent drip-drip-dripping all around me but other than this I was not disturbed. I must have been walking for about fifteen minutes when I came across a relatively dry alcove in the sewer wall just before the flow bent off to the left and continued to wend its way further on downhill: I decided that this was to be the last resting-place of the damned. I settled down, pulled the whisky from my bag and took a good long swallow. Then I necked the remainder of the codeine pills in about two or three handfuls, taking the utmost of care not to drop any of them into the shit and general effluvium that was swimming around my feet. I felt that pulling them from the sewage and eating them might possibly prove a little unhygienic. I turned on the radio and that evening's episode of *The Archers* was about to begin. Perfect. Other than that my only thought was, this is very strange, there is no fear. I did once consider the vague possibility that death might be worse than life, but this soon passed from me as the remainder of the cheap whisky warmed me. It had been a good life now that it was over.

I lay back and waited for that.

ST ANDREW'S ARENA

Bertholt Bluel

Up off the pavement and on to the low wall which runs along the chapel yard; the gable end of the Hide and Skin Market looms high above. The well-kept lawn adjacent is paved with memories of mourning. *Alexander Johnson, Presbyter. Precious in the sight of the Lord is the death of his saints.* A crow breaks the calm, screaming for attention from the roof of the empty Tent Hall to the north. *Richard Curtis, Musical Instrument Maker.* The elaborate tomb purchased by his father trumpets itself from the chapel wall. *Arthur White, Merchant in Glasgow. Died 1796.*

Climbing on to the corner window sill, I reach up and rub away the grime from a faded plaque: *The Queen's Theatre, which stood on this site from 1843 to 1860, was built by James Calvett. The theatre owned its prestigious name to a royal visit. Calvett, and later George Parry who ran the theatre from 1854, specialised in gymnastic displays, acrobatics, music and variety entertainments. It was also used for panoramas, including an exotic journey to Egypt and India. The theatre was especially popular with local young people and grave concern was expressed that it was teaching them the ways of idleness. The building was bought by a rich evangelical who turned it into a centre for mission work. This did not last long and the building soon became part of the Hide and Skin Market.*

Below the two-storey arch at the entrance of the building: *Professional Boxing. 12 × 3 minute rounds at 8st. 6lbs.* I wonder if, when STEVE WOZ ERE, he too had glimpsed the watchman through the hole in the wrought-iron gate, sitting watching TV in his portakabin – or if he had contemplated the pronouncements of undiluted bygone teenage love which now bore his signature. Confirming that the watchman is pre-occupied, I prise away the loose panel at the bottom of the gate and edge carefully inside.

The rooms on the ground floor are strewn with the remains of illicit use; piss-stained blankets, used condoms, broken syringes, discarded rizlas and torn girlie mags. The walls no longer talk of unrequited love but FUCK THE IRA and PROVOS sprayed on UVF. At the foot of a staircase to the upper floors a door, whose broken padlock shows signs of having recently been forced, now stands ajar. Climbing up to the first floor, a missing handrail pressing me close to the wall, I emerge from the gloom of the stairwell into a long, narrow room. Startled by the noise of a dozen or so pigeons, their wings beating the air, I duck instinctively as they fly over my head and out through the broken windows.

Regaining my composure, I begin to absorb the qualities of the space. Sunlight dissects the room, casting shadows on to dusty timber floorboards. A single wooden window frame, surrounded by glass, lies in the middle of the floor – picked out by the light of the window from which it has fallen. A row of cast-iron columns begins at the tip of each of the glowing squares of light illuminating the floor, dividing the room into equal, opposite halves. The rhythm of dripping water seeping from the rotten ceiling accentuates the silence, the smell of pigeon shit hangs in the air. I walk into the centre of the room to feel the warmth of the sun on my face. My eyes close and my heart swells. Relishing the effects of this place I remain motionless for nearly fifteen minutes; entranced by the perfect balance sought and found by that single window frame.

Leaving the building by the same way that I came in I take a left to go eastwards along Greendyke Street towards the tall crenellated tower of an old military depot. The windows of the administration wing are barricaded with fading shutters and rusting security bars. Walking slowly up Lanark Street, along the West wall of the depot, I notice some of the window bars have been wrenched out of place. The shutters behind are rotten, and after climbing up on to the sill, it becomes possible to kick at them with sufficient force to make an opening wide enough to squeeze inside.

The floor of the upper storey has collapsed, floorboards and plasterwork hang precariously from the remaining structure. Everywhere is damp, the smell of rotting timber is over-powering. This room had clearly once been used as a cloakroom or mailroom. An orderly line of hooks is still affixed to the wall on my right. The timber framework of old pigeon-holes, now lying awkwardly across the room, still contains some remnants of personal possessions; a comb, an empty pack of Embassy No. 1, a sodden notebook, some keys. Scattered over the floor lie a number of plastic signs, some only half complete. I pull away at the upper layers – CLYDESDALE BANK, MACDOUGALS GARAGE, FIRE EXIT – to reveal a beautifully overlaid cutting backboard, its thick white perspex yellowed with age; a number '3' template still taped to the top right-hand corner. Obscured beneath a layer of caked-on grime a thousand letters and numbers overlaid in such compositions as to confound forever Isou's lettriste system for the future construction of poetic substance.

This was too good a find to resist. I pull open my collecting bag and lift up the board; but there, underneath – sign of signs! A broken blackened template. Only two letters still remaining, S.I. Turning it over in my hands, its underbelly reveals the reversible connection, I.S. These are surely the moments from which the dérive is fuelled. My adrenalin finally calming, I notice that at the rear of the cloakroom a half obscured doorway leads to a much larger, darker space. Walking cautiously through the half-light I almost stumble over a huge orange teddy bear, about three foot long – the type usually won at fairgrounds for mastering bent dart flights or dodgy air rifle sights. It is lying face down in the dirt by a bricked-up fireplace. Someone, in their wisdom, has decided to dress the bear in a blue and white schoolgirl pinafore.

Stepping over sleeping beauty and around a pile of collapsed roof timbers I make my way into the larger, lighter space through a small arched opening in the wall ahead. A carpet of ferns lies draped over the opposite wall, their leaves glistening with surface moisture. A slowly undulating patchwork of light and shade struck by sunbeam diagonals from morse code glowing in the gaps between the timbers above. Advancing further into the room, neck craned back to trace the curving portal superstructure, I am jolted suddenly by the crack of breaking glass beneath my feet. A flurry of beating wings as yet another flight of pigeons express their indignation.

The main hall could have been declared a Treasure Trove of indifferent reversions. Lying everywhere there are objects and ensembles of every hue and texture. I consciously allow myself to be dragged around the room by their aura. On my right more signs lie scattered over the floor – WILLIAM RENNIE GLAZIERS, PROPERTY OF ALLIED BAKERIES. Steel rods hang at intervals from the ceiling structure above. There must be over thirty of them; their ends twisted away from the vertical, terminating in foot-square metal plates. An image – thirty single sculptures, composed of debris from this room, each connected to its own stem, merging into a single structure – forms itself in the space above me. I manipulate the image and its components, selecting from the catalogue strewn across the floor. CARAVAN SIGNS MADE TO ORDER.

I find myself in a lobby off the central section of the West wall, a painted notice has been fading above a servery – TO THE OFFICERS MESS, SERGEANTS MESS,   UB ROOM, SH   NG HALL   ING & EQUIP'T STORE. ORDERLY ROOM. An arrow points down a flight of stairs; at the foot, around a corner, a massive steel door bars the way. Yet it gives, without a sound, into a pitch black tunnel stretching, or so it appears, some distance underneath the lane outside. I need a torch; this will have to wait another day.

The East side of the depot, opposite the administration wing, is littered with objects of every description. Clearly the building is being used by local builders as a free skip. Yellowing bags of tenement horse-hair plaster stand in the far corner; rotting lathwork has completely filled the vehicle inspection pit. Two enormous timber cable spools, over two metres in diameter, lie in the centre of the room, reverted almost beyond recognition. A number of discarded water heater switches, the old ON/OFF type, are scattered in such a way as to suggest some form of code; a set of instructions even? Yet no translation is available and so, after collecting some ten to fifteen of them, I begin a relocation; positioning each of them alongside one or other *psychogeographical* element to which I have been drawn. A blackened poster peeling from the front wall. The freshly painted dayglo purple STOP THE BNP. Two broken – headless – barbie dolls embracing. A crushed Heinz tomato soup can below THE LISTENING BANK. Empty cider bottles lying across the *Scotsman*'s photograph of Thatcher. Half-buried Hush Puppies obscured by moss.

Jumping back out of the window, I catch my footing on one of the broken bars. I fall forwards, my arms outstretched, landing with a painful jolt on the cobbled lane. I lie there for a few moments, much to the amusement of the children playing in the park across the road. The contents of my bag have been scattered. My knees and left elbow hurt like hell and I've grazed my hand quite badly. What a prick! Eventually I lift myself up, reorder my collecting bag, vigorously rub my elbow and set off North along Lanark Street. My attention is drawn back towards the Hide and Skin Market. In the middle of the wasteland of bricks and rubble separating the lane from the remnants of the market, a petrified forest of twisting, re-enforcement bars stands memory to a previous devastation.

I walk across the rubble, past the remnants of the electricity substation behind which, months before the demolitions, we had unexpectedly prised open the doorway to a wide shaft, descending down an echoing steel stairway three storeys into the arena's depths. The door at every landing firmly barred. Was the tunnel from the depot, leading to the officer's mess, once connected with whatever lay behind those doors? The bricks which litter the forest floor are surprisingly intact. I bend down for further inspection, admiring the texture of their surfaces; browns and blue-grey, a predominance of terracotta; a lonely piece of toilet wall, its white ceramic glaze now fading grey. THE HEADINGLY BRICK AND TILE MANUFAC-TURING Co. DARNGAVID ACCRINGTON No. R8 CALANDER BARROWHILL 1917. PATRICK. R. BROWN. PAISLEY CLEGHORN TERRA COTTA Co. Ltd. GLASGOW.

The bell in St Andrew's Churchtower peals two dull strokes. Looking up, I notice that the sun has now risen over Basil Spence's condemned towers on the other side of the river. The area has suddenly become very still. A quiet has descended over the square which is unusual for this time of day. Paddy's should still be in full swing and yet there is very little activity along Greendyke St. A council cleaner walks past, I hear him whistling. But as soon as he has left that uneasy feeling returns. The ambience has definitely begun to change. I bend down again to re-examine another brick, turning it over in my hands, annoyed by the passage of a cloud obscuring the sun. It passes and the sun strikes the brick again.

Immediately another shadow. Voices. Footsteps. Two lads, early twenties, jeans and bomber jackets, dead scruffy – I can smell the sweat – pass right behind me. I freeze. Are they stopping? No. That's it, keep walking! They move towards the scorched circles of copper wire casing burnings at the heart of the arena. Crossing back over to the lane I sense an impending melancholy. I am conscious of having deliberately waited until the two men had moved out of sight before resuming my activity. I still feel angered by this reaction. I've been on my own, without talking to anyone for over five hours now, and it shows. I decide that no matter who it is, I will instigate some form of communication with the next person or persons to enter this ambience. My fascination with the surface topology is beginning to get the better of me.

I climb on to the high fence separating the long-abandoned buildings of St Francis' High School from the lane. This place is now so silent every single sound is amplified. The school buildings are heavily boarded. Riveted aluminium panels obscure the lower openings and wire grilles prevent the upper windows from being broken by flying stones and bottles. The fence from which I'm hanging is topped with rusting razor wire; there is no possibility of entry. I console myself with the knowledge, recently narrated to me by a Sally Army resident, that the building complex was being regularly patrolled with a view to redeveloping it as a business park. I had no reason to disbelieve him; a few weeks earlier I had caught a glimpse of binoculars reflecting sun flashes in the upper storey of the Killespie Kidd Koia annexe. An appropriate residence for a policing operation!

At the top of Lanark Street I peel back part of the wire mesh fence which blocks my route. FUCK THE SYSTEM sprayed across a bricked-up, boarded doorway draws me left along Charlotte Lane. Here the boarding is of damp plywood, bolted into the masonry surround at irregular intervals; fixings half protruding through the worn surface of the timber. A less menacing atmosphere begins to descend upon the square. The silence of foreboding has been replaced by disquiet. A bird is singing away to my right and a van driver crunches his gear change somewhere along The Gallowgate. The cobbles here are all obscured by moss and grasses, only in a few places do I manage to make them out. A young elm has taken root in the base of the FUCK wall while about two metres further down the lane a much larger sapling, nearly a storey high, is already in full bloom.

A rusted can resting on the pathway of blown-over diagonally braced hoarding catches my eye. All traces of paint and graphic have been eroded from its sides; it has totally decommodified itself. Now these mottled orange surfaces simply are. The dream they sought to peddle is just a memory; a temporary assignment whose only significance now is its absence. With a well-placed right foot I send the can bouncing down the lane; it crashes and tumbles, finally coming to rest against a rotting sofa-bed waiting at the gate to the back court of the John Turnbull Street tenements. I follow the can down the lane. To my left an *enchanted garden* inhabits the exposed basement of what used to be Nos. 10–15 St Andrew's Square. In the early nineteenth century these buildings formed the most exclusive residences in Glasgow, constantly guarded by the merchants' private guards. Their richness today in psychogeography brings the reversion almost full circle. Only wanderers and navigators now patrol these lands.

The melancholy of the last half hour begins to lift, but a longing still remains. To have had the opportunity to walk these absent streets while their histories were formed. To have witnessed the smell from the open sewers in the miserable back courts behind the Saltmarket drive the merchants west. Away from St Andrew's perfumed tobacco palaces to the iron regime of their new gridded city. To have bid farewell to the last bank. To have watched the Square slowly turn its back on the growing leather industry building up around it. To have seen the stonework tanning in the acrid air. To brush past cartloads of coal being dragged over these cobbles, drawing up by the doors to the old smithy which stood here for over one hundred years. Steam emerging from heavy double doors and the slits in ventilated roof lights. A moist autumn evening; the furnace glowing in the centre of the room, the rhythmic thump of the hammer.

When a building, in its old age – like one of us – becomes

a place of knowledge, of experience, its discordances and reversions having allowed it to settle, the presence of its absences becomes so much more overpowering. The qualities which it had the potential to release become absorbed by the surroundings, and as long as they remain, the essential backward sighting in time will continue to empower the navigator.

The superimposed double gable at the foot of the lane – the imprint on the City Orphanage of the demolished north wing of the square – transfixes this locale. So many signs still exist. Its memory haunts the air above. A collection of fireplaces, in varying states of disrepair, some whose grates are even still intact and surrounded by floral wallpaper, cling stubbornly to the wall. Imprints of cupboards, once heavily secured reflect on blocked and plastered doorways; smooth against exposed rubble party walls. Dressed and naked ashlar contrast – a stand-off either side of the ridge line. Peeling paint traces one floor level to another. Skirting boards are held by joists whose presence is marked by a row of small, neat, rectangular holes running from one side of the gable to the other. The amputated stumps of front and rear elevations protrude sufficiently from the orphanage to demonstrate the reveals of the old window bays.

The details of the buildings which once occupied this place still exist in such depth that its memory emerges from the gable, reaching beyond the previous boundary to drag any suggested new mass back towards the limits of present surface. I begin inhabiting this captive void with structures amalgamated from the many objects strewn around these hunting grounds. Dismembered washing machines. Broken lathwork and reverting cable spools. Window frames, felled by enemy fire, MIA. Re-bar connecting wire and cavity butterflies. Ripped up mesh fences and corroded cans. Plastic bags; empty, stolen wallets and odd left shoes. Bricks awaiting resurrection. Pages torn from the *Book of Psychogeography*.

Tracing my steps back along Charlotte Lane West, I decide

to turn towards the church itself; its East wall beginning to loom above the hoarding to the right of the lane. The cobbles here are clearly recognisable, fixing the perspective focal point which vanishes past the church, high up on the wall of the Hide and Skin Market beyond. Each cobble is of a different cut and shape. Initially I am surprised; I suppose that it had never crossed my mind, having been conditioned to a world of standardisation and regular components, that the 'cobblers' cut each stone right here, to suit the ground and path.

As the lane emerges into what used to be St Andrew's Square proper, the East gable of the church looms above. Its presence has dominated the character of the entire quarter, almost since the moment I first came to this arena. Yet unlike the signifying structures telling tales of absence which inhabit this place in such numbers, the mass of the church, the relative domination of its weight and position, veil it in an inverse emperor's clothing. Hard to grasp at first, it is its enormity which conceals its presence. I ponder whether such psychogeographical landmarks only operate effectively when in dialogue with smaller, less grand surroundings. Could it be that once the mass of the surrounding square had disappeared, instead of revealing the church in all its glory – its unveiling to the eye – its public nakedness – caused embarrassment and the church shied away behind a curtain of glare?

To the left of the gable, one of the few pre-war streetlights still remaining in this part of Glasgow is still alight, casually blinking away, its fading orange glow a symbol for the drunken promiscuities of St Andrew's evening occupants. The sun has become much warmer. I lift my face, warming my skin, my eyes closed. A powerful sense of freedom. Memories collide, reverberations envelop me in the immanence of my surroundings. Time slows down and I hear the sun begin to speak.

PROLETARIAN POST-MODERNISM OR FROM THE ROMANTIC SUBLIME TO THE COMIC PICTURESQUE

'Stewart Home'

The Stewart Home Project was launched on 24 March 1979 by the Celtic bards K. L. Callan and Fiona MacLeod. The idea was for diverse individuals to produce a body of work that would be credited to a fictional author called Stewart Home. Under a variety of pen names Callan and MacLeod were simultaneously involved in a propaganda campaign attacking Home and 'his' work as a means of creating media interest in this phantom novelist. Unemployed actor Tony White agreed to play the part of Home whenever public appearances were required.

Due to disagreements between Callan and MacLeod over what might constitute an appropriate introduction to this anthology, it has been decided to reveal that Stewart Home is a collective pseudonym. As well as the introduction at the beginning of the book, we offer here two phantom introductions that given their placing in this short story collection might be read as fictions. They have been arranged in two different columns, one on the left and one on the right. The prose in one column is satirical, the writing in the other column is serious; it is up to the reader to decide which is which. Anyone perplexed by this strategy should consult Iain Sinclair's introduction to his *Conductors of Chaos* anthology and Swift's *A Tale of a Tub*, since both are fine examples of recalcitrant prose that operate within the same discursive field as the work in hand.

Introductions to prose anthologies are supposed to pull everything together, rather than fly off at a tangent. This may account for the fact that the explanations editors give of their selection procedures tend to annoy me. Anthologies are usually put together using the same principles that structure those tiresome 'Best Of The Year' space fillers which appear in the arts sections of newspapers soon after the winter solstice. Everyone knows that these lists are really a map of the compiler's social network. Editors of prose and poetry anthologies usually have more space in which to cover their tracks than Fleet Street hacks. Wantonly ignoring the fact that time itself is an epistemologically questionable construction, anthologists often claim to have discovered some new cultural trend. What's actually going on is considerably more sordid.

Writer X will have been included because s/he has shagged the editor, while writer Y will be there because the editor wants to get into his or her knickers. Editors are also predictably biased in favour of those helpful individuals who put them up when they visit New York, Berlin, Delhi and elsewhere. It can be an amusing pursuit working out how many of those included in a collection have written favourable reviews of the editor's previous books, or included the editor in their own anthologies.

The absence of Iain Sinclair from this anthology may be taken as an indication that I don't suffer from run-of-the-mill literary vices. The first time I ever laid eyes on Sinclair, he was standing behind a suitcase on the Bethnal Green Road flogging that fabled novelty item known as Leaping Panty Hose. I'd spent most of the morning and what remained of my unemployment benefit seeking mystic inspiration in a bottle of 100

It may appear strange that I should advise readers to skip this introduction and turn directly to the stories that make up this anthology. In many ways this is a strategy that has been forced upon me. The fictions that follow are not difficult to read but the editor pressurising me to piece together a justification for the choices I have made won't concede that the type of dialogue he is urging upon me is a form of violence against the effects I wish to produce. I am not interested in philosophic discourse and I find Platonic dialogue particularly problematic in this context. Lyotard has observed that the poet is not concerned, after his statements are made, to enter into a dialogue with his readers to establish whether or not they understand him. Unfortunately, I have to deal with an editor who imagines that he has been arguing with me about whether or not I can 'access' the 'mainstream'. For those of us who live in a world of proliferating margins, there is no 'mainstream' to 'access'.

The stories collected together in this anthology were written neither within nor against the various canons of English literature. I do not wish to establish yet another canon and I have no interest in the mythologies of literary undergrounds. While the writers represented here all have some connection with the British Isles, the hybrid nature of their work is very much the product of transnational cultures to be found throughout the Atlantic littoral. As Paul Gilroy has explained in works such as *The Black Atlantic*, the image of a ship travelling between Africa, the Caribbean, America and Europe is central to an understanding of these hybrid cultures and the claims they make on (post-) modernity. Clippers not only carried slaves and manufactured commodities west, while raw materials were brought east on the return voyage, the men and women who travelled onboard these ships sustained ever evolving cultures

Pipers. One of the advantages of blended Scotch to those wanting to open up their inner eye – other than the fact that it is considerably cheaper than malts such as Laphroaig or Talisker – is that by the time a typical booze hound has reached the bottom of the bottle, they are virtually unconscious. People often ask me why the characters in my early novels always drank 100 Pipers. This is a question that I'd previously put to the now deceased pulp hack James Moffatt. He generously explained the notion of placement to me. Moffatt had experimented by dropping the names of different booze brands into his books and quickly discovered that the makers of 100 Pipers were more generous than any other whisky producer. They sent him a crate of Scotch every Christmas.

'Watch them jump!' Sinclair was calling as I staggered into the Bethnal Green Road.

Attired in his customary patched-up secondhand book dealer's suit, Iain Sinclair was pitching to four or five gawkers. A familiar street scene in the Brick Lane area on a Sunday. As luck would have it, the item to which Sinclair referred was his latest novelty sensation – Leaping Panty Hose – an ingenious device made of soft, flexible, flesh-coloured plastic in the shape of a tiny pair of pantyhose that lunged and flopped wildly at the end of a miniature air tube each time the rubber bulb concealed in the costermonger's hand was squeezed. The crowd was staring in rapt, hypnotised fascination and only Sinclair noticed as I grabbed a black doctor's bag that was wedged between his feet. As I stumbled away through the threshing crowd, pandemonium broke loose. Six meat wagons descended on the market traders and Sinclair was amongst those seized.

Having made my way to Christ

in the face of degrading and inhuman conditions.

One of the peculiar features of literary canons is the way in which those individuals and institutions that pursue this form of closure exude an exaggerated sense of their own cultural superiority while simultaneously laying claim to some mythical humanising essence that after Matthew Arnold might be designated by the phrase 'sweetness and light'. I have little interest in either individual works of 'literature' or the institutional systems erected around them. Literature is just one fictional genre among many others. Characterisation and obsessive attempts at replicating a quasi-Platonic system of grammar are of no concern to me. Likewise, there are times when I find genre distinctions between 'fiction' and 'non-fiction' more of a hindrance than a help.

What the writers gathered between these covers share is a range of concerns that will be incomprehensible to individuals who believe 'English literature' is a culturally and politically neutral subject. While familiarity with novels like *Negrophobia* by Darius James or *Cast In Doubt* by Lynne Tilliman will assist readers in their navigation through this anthology, an appreciation of the texts collected here requires more than a mere acquaintance with modern fiction. This can be illustrated by way of reference to Neil Palmer's story *Vegan Reich*. The background to this piece clearly lies in the emergence of the modernist conception of Europe. After atheism won acceptance as a viable form of intellectual discourse, new negations took shape and fought for a favourable reception. However, negations such as anarchism were simultaneously bound up with positive assertions about the world. The anarchist critique of authority was and still is grounded in an acceptance of the ideology of the aesthetic as a mode of internalised legislation that generates a white,

Church, I sat down on the steps of Hawksmoor's masterpiece and examined Sinclair's black bag. It contained some bloody medical implements and a lot of hardcore pornography. Several weeks later I ran into Sinclair at a literary event and he thanked me for helping him evade the bust. He didn't seem to realise I was a thief and when he asked me to return his bag, I arranged to meet him in a pub on Fieldgate Street. Sinclair bought me several drinks and didn't seem bothered that his wank mags had become badly stained while they were in my possession. I had no use for the bag or medical implements and since seeing a video featuring an actress giving a donkey a blow job, I viewed Sinclair's porno glossies as a little too tame for a man of my tastes. I gave Sinclair copies of all my novels and not long after a very positive write-up appeared in the *London Review Of Books*.

As well as Sinclair, another name missing from this anthology is that of Doctor Al Ackerman, from whom I have stolen shamelessly during my long and distinguished career. Even if it is not very instructive, it will at least fill some space to reproduce what the good doctor wrote about me in his introduction to the 'Ling' section of *Blaster: The Blaster Al Ackerman Omnibus*: 'I was told there was a deranged fellow in London a few years ago, a sort of penny-dreadful pornographer, who created an unpleasant scene in the Charing Cross Station early one morning by spilling what he called his "genetic wealth" on a basket filled with skinhead gear, old pieces of laundry, dead pea fowls and artificial limbs – all this while dressed in a pillowcase hood and claiming to be "Young Ling." That is almost enough to make a person more careful about how he handles his scissors.'

Immediately after I'd written the bourgeois, able-bodied, male subject.

Like the other writers whose work is collected in this anthology, Palmer's modus operandi is self-consciously intertextual. He reworks and rewrites earlier fictions to create a narrative space where he can investigate the Eurocentric idealism that produces the illusion of a transcendental white male subject which is then pressed into service as a model for the subjectivities of all people, everywhere. Among the more obvious precedents for *Vegan Reich* are Simon Strong's *A259 Multiplex Bomb 'Outrage'* and my novel *Pure Mania*. Even the name of the piece ironically undercuts the titles I've given to my books, many of which are appropriated from punk songs of the late seventies. *Vegan Reich* is the name of a particularly reactionary Californian straight-edge band who advocate the physical liquidation of smokers and meat eaters in *I, The Jury*, a song whose title is lifted from a right-wing thriller by Mickey Spillane.

While Palmer revises the regional setting of my writing, his relationship with East Anglia is sufficiently critical to make him doubt whether there is any longer a meaningful distinction to be made between the country and the city. The dubious use of the terms country and city as rhetorical devices in the outpourings of a number of eco-activists is one of the factors that structures the critical parody of *Vegan Reich*. As well as attacking anarchism, Palmer uses *Vegan Reich* to mock East Anglian separatism, an ideological trope that has close connections with the libertarian creed. While in purely political terms the demand for East Anglian independence is currently a marginal phenomenon, its entanglements with other totalising cultural formations make it something that is worthy of attention. One of the stalwarts of the East Anglian regional cause is the Cambridge based ley spotter and rune magician Nigel preceding paragraph, my seventeen-year-old girlfriend Poppy stumbled in from turning a few tricks on Wentworth Street and then using the money she'd earned to feed her dope habit. After bawling me out for blowing the rent on several dodgy crates of Four Roses bourbon bought from a market stall trader who was introduced to me by Iain Sinclair, Poppy observed that I never made any dosh because I was constantly writing new introductions to a fiction collection for an editor who rejected everything I did. Poppy might be a runaway and a crack addict but she isn't stupid. She observed caustically that pretty soon there'd be enough rejected introductions to *Suspect Device* to be turned into a book in their own right. This reminded me that another voice excluded from the anthology is that of Ben Watson. Out To Lunch – as Watson is known to the readers of his 'underground' pamphlets such as *DIY Schizophrenia* – sprang to mind because he writes at the beginning of the book *Art, Class & Cleavage: A Quantulumcunque Concerning Materialist Esthetix*: 'My publishers tell me that they fear the book's "unorthodox" political assumptions will render its thesis incomprehensible . . . They advise me that upfront exposition of its tenets would make Materialist Esthetix more effective . . .'

Watson is confronting a problem that anyone who credits their readers with the possession of critical faculties is likely to encounter when dealing with British publishers. The average editor wants work that is pre-digested pap. I'm told that I have been producing 'anti-introductions', some of which have been criticised for being too difficult, while others were rejected as too flippant and all of which – it is alleged – will 'turn readers off'. Rather than allowing readers to make connections for

Pennick. A rune that particularly fascinates Pennick is the swastika, and as long ago as the seventies he was using forums such as Stuart Christie's *Anarchist Review* to propagate his peculiar views about this symbol.

While satire disperses meaning, critics often experience difficulty with this process unless they have some knowledge of the subject that is being dissolved. While readers do not need to be familiar with the writings of Nigel Pennick in order to enjoy Palmer's text, they will blind themselves to the extraordinary fecundity of *Vegan Reich* if they look for psychological insight or characterisation. Those who seek the tropes of realism in satiric fiction rarely realise that they are simultaneously transforming themselves into figures of fun. Readers of this type will not derive much satisfaction from Palmer's prose unless they happen to be masochists. Since there is much humour in repetition and doubling, those who are able to hear what is being (un)said are generally happy to find themselves lost in the text. At least one commentator has claimed that in decrying 'the night in which all cows are black', Hegel ended up making a joke at his own expense. Likewise, it is not always possible to separate writing from reading or speaking.

Jonathan Swift in his introduction to *The Battle of the Books* observed that: 'satire is a sort of glass, wherein beholders do generally discover everybody's face but their own; which is the chief reason for that kind of reception it meets in the world, and that so very few are offended with it. But if it should happen otherwise, the danger is not great; and I have learned from long experience never to apprehend mischief from those understandings I have been able to provoke; for anger and fury, though they add strength to the sinews of the body, yet are found to relax those of the mind, and to render all its efforts feeble and themselves, I am being pressurised into explaining everything in advance. While this may be the manner in which the pod people of PR hype are processed, it is not something that interests me. I could, of course, argue that most English literature has been shunted on to a privatised railway sideline whereas the work I've gathered together represents a continuation of the trajectories to be found in the modernisms and post-modernisms of the Atlantic littoral. However, my editor really doesn't want to hear this and since he is the gatekeeper I have to get past, I'll just have to provide the explanation of my selection procedures he is demanding.

Ben Watson would have been included in this anthology if he'd mailed me his story in which I appear as a major character prior to my final selection of pieces for *Suspect Device* being agreed with Serpent's Tail. I'm also a great admirer of Barry MacSweeney's work but in taking on this commission, I reluctantly accepted the imposition of genre distinctions between poetry and prose. Likewise, I thought Christopher Petit's novel *Robinson* was fabulous but this author was excluded on the grounds that he used Sting as an actor in his road movie *Radio On*. A cardinal sin in my opinion. In many ways the selection procedure for this book was quite arbitrary, I threw away all unsolicited manuscripts and refused to read stories from friends that were submitted in spidery handwriting. Next, I went through the covering letters that accompanied the submissions. Seven would-be contributors were rejected for making references to their 'art', twenty-four for mentioning writers I don't like and one for using the word 'caveat'. I was able to eliminate another two authors because of their posh double-barrelled surnames and a

impotent.' Satire dissolves character, and so it is comic writers who are most likely to be peculiarly misunderstood. A widespread appreciation of Swift's oeuvre has certainly been retarded by popular caricatured portraits of the satirist which depict him declining into misanthropy as he aged.

My fiction was, and to some extent still is, generated from a self-consciously comic reading of the entire output of various 'trash' authors as a single nouvelle roman. Palmer, in his turn, productively (mis)reads my novels as an interminable medieval romance. Such readings are simply one of Palmer's procedures for dissolving a regional identity he critically rejects. There is a considerable body of writing devoted to tracing the 'origins' of modern drama – and thus through the influence of playwrights like Shakespeare, all contemporary literature and culture – to East Anglian mystery plays. In conversation, Palmer expresses amusement about the fact that many of those embroiled in this discourse are academics working at Cambridge University in East Anglia. Palmer's response is to use medieval texts and the imaginative recreation of medieval ways of reading texts as a means of writing himself outside the bourgeois culture imposed upon him during the course of his working-class schooling in rural Cambridgeshire.

It would be a mistake to view Palmer's modus operandi as a return to tradition, or indeed, a rupture with it. A critical response to modernity does not necessarily make a writer a primitivist – even when, as in Palmer's case, they openly proclaim their interest in medieval prose. It is worth recalling here what Marx had to say about the English and French revolutions in *The Eighteenth Brumaire of Louis Bonaparte*: 'In these revolutions, then, the resurrection of the dead served to exalt new struggles, rather than to parody the old, to exaggerate the given third for being called Martin. After twenty minutes' work, I was left with the selection of pieces you hold in your hand.

The Suicide Note by Ted Curtis and a number of other stories collected here feature characters who are devotees of serious drinking. Reviewers often experience difficulty in distinguishing a writer from the fictional characters that populate his or her works. I am often asked by journalists if I am an alcoholic. My standard reply is that if someone who smuggles industrial quantities of duty free booze across the English Channel for their own consumption has a drink problem, then yes, I am an alcoholic. If someone who drinks at least one bottle of whisky a day has a drink problem, then yes, I am an alcoholic. If someone who spends as much time as possible boozing down the pub has a drink problem, then yes, I am an alcoholic. What I can state without equivocation is that as someone who repeatedly drops the names of various class brands of whisky into my prose, I deserve a few free crates of Laphroaig and Talisker.

To sum up, the writers collected together in this anthology tend towards the occult, mathematics and philosophy, particularly Frege and Gotthard Guenther. Their work represents a turn away from realism into the infinite depths of self-referentiality. These crazy writers are a quarrelsome bunch of uptights who can be divided into two antagonistic factions: either they are gay and suffer from an excess of the fraternity spirit, or despite reaching middle-age they are still to be found fondling runaway teenagers with drug problems; they are either excessive beef-eaters or strict vegetarians, uninhibited posers or bashful theorists, and usually both at once. All the writers represented in this anthology are acting out a surreal

task in the imagination, rather than to flee from solving it in reality, and to recover the spirit of the revolution rather than to set its ghost walking again.' Derrida's 'enlightening' commentary on this trope can be found in his book *Specters of Marx: The State of the Debt, the Work of Mourning and the New International* (Routledge, New York and London 1994).

While, like Palmer, I try to avoid over-determining meaning in my prose and readers can read my texts any which way they like, each individual has to live with the consequences of any reading they choose to make. While I do not wish to impose a single monolithic meaning on my fictions, the fact that I am frequently misidentified with my subject matter demonstrates not so much that I've been successful at avoiding closure, but that many 'critics' no longer know how to read, or indeed, how to write intelligently. I'd imagine that most of those represented in this anthology have experienced or will experience similar problems. In saying this, I am not suggesting that everything collected here should be read as satire. I have made *Vegan Reich* the focus of this preamble precisely because no useful purpose would be served by indulging in generalisations about the texts that make up this anthology.

Obviously it is didactic to state that the compilation of anthologies, even anthologies of previously unpublished fiction, has a long association with pedagogical discourse. While certain readers may view what follows as reproducing or even parodying such revisionist cultural forms, I do not wish to promote the work collected here as delineating a movement or tendency within contemporary culture. As things fall apart and discourse is endlessly reconfigured, what was formerly projected as the centre has lost its stranglehold on 'literary production' and those who once made an unconditional defence of modernity find the values existentialism. This consists of living in run-down apartments, drinking day and night, cross-dressing or wearing clothing from the nearest Salvation Army shop and reciting J. H. Prynne's *Brass* several times a day while standing bollock naked on whatever balcony affords the greatest audience. Anything less would be unacceptable, since I am not interested in the processed prose of show-business sell-outs. If anything is anything, then rock and roll is the new rock and roll, while writing fiction is something else entirely.

they previously upheld transvalued. Since I credit readers with the wit to realise it is neither possible nor desirable to explain everything, I have always but not already said too much.

ZYKLON B. ZOMBIE

Simon Ford

Ted Glass stirred: 'Wall of Sound' by Throbbing Gristle blared into his ears from the CD alarm clock next to his bed.

'Time to get up!' he said to himself as the sonic abuse pounded his eardrums.

The blonde girl sharing his futon groaned. It was only six o'clock and she was still recovering from last night's sex magick rituals.

Ted was up early because he was off to Exeley on a trip that promised both business and pleasure. The success of Luther Blissett's Industrial tribute band – The Australian Whitehouse – had finally spurred him into action. Whitehouse had always been a mere comic parody of the one and only, truly industrial noise terrorists, Throbbing Gristle (or TG as they were known to initiates).

Ted had been a fan of the group from the first moment he heard the excruciating tones of *Second Annual Report* in 1977. At last he'd found something that could approximate the alien-ation he felt from late capitalist society. TG's disbanding in 1981 had caused him real psychic distress and created a lack in his life that he was still finding difficult to come to terms with. This was all, however, about to change. The idea of forming a TG tribute band was just so perfect he wondered why he'd never thought of it before.

Ted had always been complimented on how much he looked like the electronics expert of TG, Chris Carter, and he'd recently come across the spitting image of TG's sampling supremo Peter Christopherson at a sleazy disco in Soho. All that remained now was to sign up a duo that could pass for the kinky couple themselves, Genesis P-Orridge and Cosey Fanni Tutti.

This is where Alex and Kim, currently residing in Exeley, entered the frame. Ted had known them for years. They had all been fellow TG Control Agents and hardcore Terror Guards back in the hey-day of Industrial Records in 1978. Ted had talked to them recently on the phone and after he'd explained his plans to them they were just about ready to sign up for the band. Ted's mission was to get their signatures before they changed their minds.

'Time to get up!' Ted said aloud this time.

Ted was already up and running. Lay-ins were anathema to him, excess sleep meant less time for life and Ted now had a real lust for life. He grabbed a towel from the nearby radiator and made his way to the shower. The pulsing white noise of the water reminded him of the 'Wall of Sound' that had just awoken him. He allowed the cacophony to envelope him, closed his eyes and assumed power focus. The will to power was Ted's gospel, what he did not control worried him, discipline formed a coda to his every thought and action.

He pulled himself back from his reverie and began to wash his hair thoroughly. The day was going to be long and he wanted to look his best. Finally, after every square inch of his body's surface had been scrubbed clean of the night's excesses, he reached up and stemmed the flow of the shower. For a moment he stood still, letting the water drip from his now glistening body. He looked down at his penis and contemplated its enigmatic powers.

'There are no answers,' he thought, 'in the end we all die.'

On this deeply profound thought he pulled back the shower curtain, wrapped the towel around his waist and returned to the bedroom.

'You still not up?' Ted was getting angry.

'OK, I'm going.' The blonde emerged from beneath the black

duvet. Normally Ted would have invited her to join him in a few pre-breakfast rituals but today was special and Ted wanted to keep his elixir potent for whatever eventualities lay ahead. Besides he also had a coach to catch!

As the girl pulled on her now dishevelled khaki T-shirt and camouflage-patterned trousers, Ted gathered together his kit for the mission ahead. He reached into the dark interior of his wardrobe and pulled out a black shirt (with TG lightning-flash patch), a pair of black para-military trousers, black boxer shorts, and a pair of black socks. He dressed methodically, taking particular care with packing his survivalist kit into the bulky side pockets of his trousers, before sitting down to pull on his heavy black combat boots.

The greatest dilemma that faced Ted that morning concerned suitable reading matter for the journey. This particularly occupied Ted because he was a librarian, a librarian with a difference; Ted was an Industrial Librarian. In 1979 he had taken literally P-Orridge's statement that 'Real total war has become information war' and immediately given up the beginnings of a lucrative career in the art world and enrolled on a librarianship course. Most of his friends thought he was crazy but Ted considered if information was to be a weapon of the new world order then librarians were to be the storm-troopers to operate it.

Ted finally selected Colin Wilson's *The Outsider*. Although Wilson's theories were simplistic, and his books often based on unreliable research, the original 'angry young man' had been satisfying Ted's appetite for sensationalist subject matter – murder, sex, and the occult – since his early teens. Since then Ted had increasingly identified with the alienated and the 'outsiders' of society.

The girl looked around the room. She had never seen so many books. Her original attraction to Ted had been purely physical, now she caught herself wondering about his mind. She was about to say a few words of farewell, but Ted obviously didn't want to be disturbed. She saw the concentration on his face and the precision of his movements as he dressed; this was a man-machine that was going places.

Ted waited at Victoria Coach Station to board the 501 National Speed service to Exeley. He could have taken the train but found the thought of five hours amongst cars and articulated lorries on England's finest autobahns strangely compelling. For Ted the bleakness and monotony of motorway travel in post-industrial Britain constituted the height of aesthetic experience.

The stewardess lingered as she checked Ted's ticket. The librarian before her exuded a pagan sexuality. Her husband, a former childhood sweetheart, had neglected her sensual demands for weeks now. The barriers that held in check the floodwaters of her desire were in constant danger of fracturing; the librarian could be the one to burst them.

Ted made himself comfortable at the back of the coach. By looking suitably aggressive he had managed to discourage the other passengers from sitting within five rows of his staked-out territory. Ted did not like being disturbed by screaming kids, personal stereos, and nattering holidaymakers.

As the coach crawled through the congested early morning traffic of Hammersmith, Ted watched the masses going about their daily commuting rituals. Ted believed man had stopped evolving with the passing of the Industrial Revolution. Since then Civilisation had been progressively alienated from the shamanic potential at the core of its industrial self.

As the coach hit the motorway, and its engine settled down to a steady drone, Ted began to feel the vibrations pulsing through his body. The internal combustion engine vibrated at a frequency that activated genetic codes deep within his brain. This archaic industrial language was translated by the librarian into a throbbing hard-on. Ted shifted to ease his cock's transformation from passive softness to active solidity. It was at this moment that the stewardess began to move down the aisle towards him.

The swaying vehicle only marginally hindered her progress. Ted saw her approaching but did nothing to hide the straining member making a tent out of his black combat trousers. The stewardess soon realised that because of their position at the back of the half-empty coach, she and the horny librarian would be invisible to the rest of the passengers. She had been taking orders for light refreshments, now she was in search of some for herself.

The coach swerved suddenly and the stewardess dropped her pen as she reached for a nearby seat to steady herself. The pen hit the floor and rolled under Ted's seat. The librarian's and the stewardess's eyes met and each instantly understood the other's craving for relief. The stewardess sank slowly to her knees amongst the discarded sweet wrappers and empty cans.

Ted stared out the window at the banal landscape. If the individual is to free him/herself s/he must cast off all restraints, everything was permissible. The stewardess's fingers found the buttons of his fly and proceeded to release his 'manhood' from his black boxer shorts. The industrial librarian felt a veil lift from his consciousness as her hot breath tickled his cock. As her lips tentatively closed over the end of his penis, the doors of perception were cleansed and Ted saw things as they really were. As the girl sucked him deeper into her mouth and began working his length, he walked through the doors into the landscape of the imaginary.

Ted reached under the stewardess's uniform and located her moist centre. Like her mouth his fingers spoke the language of liberation, the promise of eternal play, the ecstasy of annihilation. As his fingers caressed her creamy slit, she joined him in the realm of the imaginary and they roamed the landscape together, marvelling at its wonders. The colours they saw were intense. But before they could comprehend where they began and where they ended, they were momentarily engulfed by darkness before bursting through into the blinding light of cataclysmic ecstasy.

The stewardess rearranged her uniform and dusted down her knees. Using a Kleenex she wiped the white and sticky fluid from around her mouth and strolled back down the aisle. As she walked past the other passengers they wondered what had happened to their tea and coffee; the stewardess wondered what had happened to her psyche!

Ted sipped his soya milk whilst Alex and Kim ate their vegan meal. Ted hated soya milk but he would drink anything, even his own urine, to ensure TG's successful reincarnation.

'How's Exeley then?' Ted asked to break the silence.

'Crap,' replied Alex in disgust. 'It's full of morons.'

'Yeah,' agreed Ted. 'I had a look around town earlier and couldn't find a single light engineering works. What's an industrialist meant to do for entertainment around here!'

'Exeley is and always will be a mindless shit hole,' said Kim. 'We're looking forward to getting out of here. I think we're too big for the provinces. London is the only place large enough for ambitious couples like us to fulfil our potential.'

Ted was glad to hear of their dissatisfaction, the TG tribute band required their total commitment.

'Sure,' he said, 'I can see us going a long way. With your outrageous stage act and my marketing skills, we'll form an unbeatable team.'

The two performance artists returned to their ideologically correct fodder. Ted had already got them to sign the contract, so now he could relax. He emptied his soya milk and opened a can of lager. Ted was bored and felt in need of alcoholic refreshment. To the librarian drinking was a fine art. Whilst others treated it simply as an aid to breaking through repression, Ted drank for drinking's sake. It was one of the few pure things left in his life.

As Ted had planned, his visit to Exeley coincided with the day of the local art college Degree Show. Ted, Alex and Kim saw the show as an ideal opportunity for causing trouble. An excited crowd of recently graduated students, their loving parents, plus illiberal doses of alcohol would provide the perfect brew for a demonstration of auto-destructive art.

By the time Ted had drained two more cans of Stella Artois the industrialists were ready to hit the road. Because of its useless public transport system, everyone walked in Exeley, it was a pedestrian city in more ways than one. The route to the art college was long but uncomplicated. Ted continued drinking. He realised that to get free wine at these events you had to arrive early, but as everybody knows that was not cool. Ted was determined to be late for his own funeral.

The industrial librarian switched to Tennant's Super, it was to be alcoholic quantity over quality for the time being. He passed the cans around to his new business associates and opened one for himself. The frequent pulls were a fitting accompaniment to the grey and banal landscape through which they passed.

Exeley School of Art had gone through many changes since its founding at the turn of the century. During the 1970s it changed its name to Exeley College of Art and Design and moved out of the city centre to its present site at the end of a leafy cul-de-sac lined with large semi-detached houses. In the 1980s, after being swallowed up by the Thatcherite Plymouth Polytechnic, it had become known as Exeley Faculty of Art and Design. Its latest manifestation was as Exeley College of Arts and Crafts. The title clashed with the architecture of the college, which was closer to that of a 1970s hospital than a rural retreat, but Ted had come to find the design apt, especially considering the emotional cripples it housed.

The change of name had consolidated the college's position at the head of an arts and crafts revival that was currently making the blood boil of all true industrialists. The students' work reflected the college's idyllic location in the middle of the West Country, with everybody busy making ceramic pots or wicker baskets. It was as if the Vorticist Wyndham Lewis had never blessed England in 1914 as an 'Industrial Island Machine'.

Ted blamed William Morris and his middle-class socialist followers. Ted believed that taking pleasure in an idealised rural culture was a sickening betrayal of England's status as the first industrial nation. For the industrial librarian, true art took the form of aggression against culture, the only way to change everyday life was to alter matter at a physical level. He'd realised long ago that it was only high culture that possessed the ability to transform the fact of its disappearance into exchange value.

In addition to these crimes against inhumanity. Ted's hatred of the college was fuelled by his having been a student there, along with Alex and Kim, in the mid-1970s. Their lack of interest in rural matters set them apart from the rest of the students. The tutors, embarrassed by their inadequacies in the face of such conceptual rigour, left them well alone. Their graduation had been a formality, their teachers had been so intimidated by the sheer physical presence of the extremists that they didn't have the nerve to fail them. One of their works was to form a performance art troupe, the Excrementalists, advertising their flat as a venue open twenty-four hours a day. Anyone who came to see them perform was tied to a dentist's chair and forced to listen to the group denounce them. They were only allowed to leave after they had also renounced pre- and post-industrial culture. Ted's art college years had been fun but like the rest of society, they still owed him.

'Let's go through the back entrance,' Ted said as they approached the college. 'It's probably best if no one knows we're here.'

The industrial librarian reviewed his resources: a few friends, a knowledge of the college layout, and a desire for noisy destruction. His mind pondered the irreducibility of corporeal phenomena: instinct had a funny way of telling us to do things our conscious minds would never contemplate.

*

For the show, the building had been converted from studios and classrooms into a rabbit warren of makeshift display boards. The college authorities knew how dangerously combustible the large wooden screens were, but the money was not available to replace them. Instead they'd paid a contractor to paint the boards in fire-resistant paint. The contractor was also suffering financial problems and fire-resistant paint cost the earth. The cowboy firm immediately saw an opportunity to increase their profit by using ordinary emulsion. No one would know the difference and besides the possibility of a fire was minimal. However, a visit from a pyrotechnically inclined industrial librarian had not entered their calculations.

Ted turned to Alex and Kim as they toured the show.

'Our mutual desire for destruction will soon be satisfied,' he said. 'Tonight we will be striking at the heart of the arts and crafts movement, tonight we'll do our bit for urban culture.'

The stench of country life singed Ted's nostrils. Only a semi-rural post-industrial state of repressive tolerance could subsidise such silage. The sooner the crafts men and women of Exeley were on the dole the better.

'This is so depressing,' moaned Kim. 'Let's go on to the party at the Double Locks Pub and drown our sorrows in some liquid engineering.'

But Ted had other plans. He noticed the door to the student canteen had been left open by the catering firm handling the hospitality contract.

'I'm just popping in there,' Ted said, pointing to the kitchen. 'Cover the entrance and don't let anyone in for a couple of minutes, then get out of here quick. I'll meet you round the back of the college on the path to the Double Locks.'

'Can we do anything to help?' asked Kim.

'This'll only take me a minute,' Ted replied. 'It only takes one person to light the fuse of a second industrial revolution.'

Ted left Kim and Alex and disappeared into the darkness of the kitchen. His eyes soon adapted to the dim light. Outside the darkness was broken only by flashes of lightning; a fitting apocalyptic backdrop to the 'last degree show'. The electric blue light illuminated the stainless steel surfaces of the kitchen equipment. Ted went round turning each of the gas stove burners on. Soon the room stank of the escaping gas. Ted picked up one of the paper towels lying nearby and carried it with him to the window. He opened the window and pulled himself through. He then took a lighter from the survivalist pack in his trouser pocket and attempted to ignite the paper towel. The wind and the rain hindered him but it eventually flared into life. He threw the lighted towel into a pile of other towels just inside the kitchen. He then closed the window and ran like hell!

He didn't look round as the first explosion pounded against his back. The kitchen was located at the back of the college and at first the fire spread slowly. The visitors had been alerted to the danger by the explosion, which was fortunate because the fire alarms didn't work. The startled students and their guests had just enough time to get out and assemble in front of the college to watch the towering inferno.

Ted decided to call this particular work *Exorcism of Shit*. The awed crowd felt some kind of sublime terror in front of the destruction but were too blind to see the compulsive beauty before their eyes. 'But is it art?' many wondered.

Ted caught up with the others as they walked to the pub. They had observed the auto-destructive spectacle from the path and were suitably inspired.

'What a mind snap!' exclaimed Alex.

They all felt relief at the art college's demise. Its existence had been a continual reminder of their wasted youth.

The path to the pub led them through two muddy fields. The rain continued to pour as Exeley experienced its most violent thunderstorm for decades. Up ahead they saw the headlights of the flash cars belonging to the posh scum who'd assembled for the degree show. Rather than dampening the enthusiasm of the crowd, the explosive show had whipped it into a frenzy.

Why the Double Locks had become so popular, Ted found difficult to answer. It was situated a good three miles out of town on a strip of land between the canal and the River Exe. It was the most inaccessible and poorly designed pub Ted knew. Ted and his fellow TG fanatics were soaked through by the time they reached the packed and steaming bar.

'Three pints of Foster's,' Ted shouted as he caught the barman's eye.

'We're out of glasses at the moment,' replied the flustered barman.

'Well get a bucket then!' The industrial librarian was losing his temper. He lived in a consumer society and wanted to consume, what was the problem?

He was just about to explain the finer points of Tony Blair's Citizen's Charter to the barman, when the glass collector turned up with a fresh supply. Ted scooped up the three pints of the amber nectar.

'And a pint of Bishop's Tipple,' he added.

The barman turned and pulled the extra pint. The bitter was difficult to draw and by the time he'd finished the librarian had disappeared.

'Shit!' A wall of thirsty punters confronted him, waving money, demanding drinks. He would be lynched if he tried to pursue the drink thief rather than serve the thirsty punters.

Ted did not usually go in for such petty scams but the pub's uncaring attitude to its paying customers angered him.

'Cheers,' the three esoterrorists bellowed as they raised their glasses.

The industrial librarian and his friends stood back and surveyed the scene. People were gesturing and shouting. Ted didn't know what they were saying and didn't care. He was looking for something new, something different. He relaxed and let his eyes drift out of focus. The scene became a blur and he retreated into his subconscious. The sound of the crowd became dull and Ted began to experience inner peace. With his ego separated from his id, he swam amongst the crowd, drawing on the energy the group dynamics were generating. Ted probed the throng and waited.

Ted came back to reality with a jolt. His eyes and mind instantly focused on a girl three tables away. She turned round slowly and Death smiled. The industrial librarian did not look away, instead he absorbed her penetrating stare. What was she seeing; salvation or annihilation?

The girl eventually looked away. Ted felt uneasy. He'd got this far in life by persuasion, when he could no longer convince people to do his bidding he was dead.

'I'm just going out for some air,' the disturbed librarian told Alex and Kim.

Ted was having doubts about his scheme. TG had not been an ordinary group, maybe he was unleashing something beyond his control.

Ted sat in the rain on the river bank, staring at the angry water. His drenched cropped hair clung to his fevered skull like a helmet. The girl from the pub approached him from behind.

'Let's fuck,' she whispered into his ear.

Upon hearing these words the industrial librarian instantly dismissed his melancholy thoughts. He held the girl's hand as she led him away from the lights and noise of the public house to a spot further down the river bank. Sheets of rain pounded the earth as the river rushed maniacally on its way to the sea. The two nymphomaniacs quickly undressed. The raging torrent, mud and storm provided an ideal setting for the dirty fuckers.

The lightning flashes periodically illuminated the girl's pale skin. Her brown nipples stood out like ciphers and Ted had no difficulty interpreting their meaning. The rain acted as a lubricant as their bulks collided and rubbed frantically together. They did not feel the cold, just a liquid warmth as their bodies were united and became one. His balls slapped against her ass, churning up and mingling with the rain, mud and love juice. As they approached orgasm, Ted suddenly realised that he was sliding down the bank toward the river. Soon, his feet were in the water. The overwhelming feeling of *jouissance*, however, blocked out anything he could do to stop what now seemed inevitable. Ted felt the current tugging at his legs. If he could only hold on for just a couple more thrusts . . .

As he came Ted's world shrunk to a point of pure light. He was unaware of the water that surrounded him. The white noise of the raging river engulfed him as he shouted:

'EE-AH-OH, the mission is terminated.'

TRADESMAN'S ENTRANCE

Barry Graham

Ronnie Towney was as perfect an example of a closet faggot as I ever expect to encounter. Like many latents, he was disgusted by any reference to homosexual behaviour, and he pursued women with an obsessiveness I've never seen in anybody else.

But cunts revolted him. He could hardly bear to stick his cock in one, and if any woman ever asked him to lick it, he probably got dressed on the way out the door. He quite liked hand jobs. He really liked blow jobs. But what he liked more than anything was sodomy. He fucked some of his girlfriends in the ass so often that they had to plug their asses with tampons to keep the shit from just dropping out.

So you'd think he would've known what to expect.

About a week after he met his dream girl, he called me at one in the morning. I was in bed but still awake.

'Scumbo, do you know where I could get some valium?' he asked me.

I thought about it. 'Don't think so. Not unless I can get my mother to sell you her prescription. How come?'

'I'm fucked up. I mean it. I'm having nightmares. I've hardly slept for the past week. I'm really fucked.'

Now I could hear it in his voice, the strange, brittle tone. 'Do you want to talk about it?' I asked him.

A long pause, then he simply said, 'Yeah.'

'Okay. When.'

'Tonight,' he said. 'But not on the phone.'

'Do you want to come over?'

'No. Let's meet somewhere.'

I didn't feel like getting dressed and going out. 'It's late,' I said.

'The Cooler'll still be open.' This was true; the Cooler stayed open all night.

'Okay,' I said. 'I'll meet you there in about an hour.'

I got there fifteen minutes early, but Ronnie was already there, standing at the bar. He looked as bad as he'd said he felt. His hair hung lank and oily over his white face, and his eyes were red and unfocused.

He gave me a twitchy smile when he saw me. 'Hi, Scumbo. Thanks for coming out. I had to see you. If I don't talk to somebody about this I'm going to go fucking mad.'

'It's okay,' I said, putting an arm around his shoulders. He shrank away; Ronnie never could stand to have men touch him. It got him too excited for his liking.

'Want a drink?' he asked me. He already had a pint of something.

'Yeah. Suffer in Comfort.' He got it for me. Then we went looking for seats and didn't find any. As other bars closed, just about every pisshead in town had converged on the Cooler. We found a tiny space of unoccupied floor and sat down on it.

'So what's the problem?' I asked Ronnie.

'I'll tell you,' he said. 'But you won't understand. You can't imagine what it feels like.'

I realised he was crying.

He told me about Lucy.

He met her at a party. She had silky black hair and pale skin with lipstick the colour of arterial blood. Or so Ronnie said. He immediately went up to her and introduced himself. That was Ronnie's style; it was his policy to try it on with every woman he met, reasoning that the sheer law of averages dictated that they wouldn't *all* tell him to fuck off.

And not all of them did. Lucy certainly didn't. He asked her what her name was and she smiled and told him. Then she asked if he had a light for her cigarette. He gave her his lighter. As she used it, he saw that her hands were trembling slightly. With a numbing sense of disbelief, he realised that she was even more excited than he was.

They didn't see the end of the party. They gathered the stashes of booze they'd brought with them, said their farewells to the friends they'd arrived with, and got a taxi to Ronnie's apartment.

He asked if she'd like some coffee. She answered, 'No, thanks. I'd rather suck your cock.' As they went to his bedroom, Ronnie thought he might be able to share the Judaeo-Christian belief in a loving, benevolent God.

She gave him head until her jaw was slack with exhaustion. Then they began fucking. Ronnie tried to hide his distaste, but the thought of that wet, oily, hairy cunt squelching around his cock was too awful.

Lucy saw it in his face. 'What's wrong?' she panted.

'Nothing,' he said.

To his relief, she pulled herself off his cock. 'Tell me!' she said.

'It's just . . . I don't really like it this way. I like it up the back end.'

She broke into a beaming smile. 'Me too! You should've said.'

Ronnie looked at her. 'Are you sure?'

'Yeah! I love it up the ass. But some guys won't do it.'

'I will,' Ronnie said fervently. Lucy turned over, lying on her side with her back to him. Ronnie looked at his cock. He didn't reckon he'd need any lubrication; he was already wet from her mouth and her cunt.

Lucy moaned as his cock probed her ass. Ronnie held her by the hips and thrust hard. He couldn't believe how easily it slid into her. There was hardly any tightness at all. It was even easier than entering a cunt, and the feel of her sphincter around his knob told him this was no cunt. This was the kind of fucking he loved.

He closed his eyes and fucked harder and harder. Lucy screamed with delight. Ronnie felt a wet splash on his cheek. He ignored it. Then he felt another on his chin. Thinking it must be sweat, he wiped it away with the back of his hand. Something about the texture made him open his eyes.

Smeared across his hand was a patch of brown substance. Even before he'd looked, something inside Ronnie, something deep and primal, had already known.

As he stared at his hand he carried on thrusting, and felt another splash on his face. He looked down at his body and saw that the hot, sticky wetness between his stomach and Lucy's lower back wasn't sweat. It was steaming, liquid shit. Each time he pulled back for another thrust, more of it leaked out of her.

Ronnie lay very still.

'Ronnie! Ronnie! Don't stop! Fuck me! Fill my ass! Stuff it up me!' howled Lucy. Then she felt a thick, burning liquid splatter her shoulders. It was Ronnie's vomit.

I tried my best to counsel Ronnie, and so did the two or three other friends he confided in. But he never really got over it. He couldn't sleep in his own bed, even after he'd changed the sheets and turned the mattress. He moved to another apartment. Not long after that, he blew town and went to live in London.

I haven't heard from him since. A mutual friend who lives in London tells me Ronnie crashed briefly with his sister, who'd lived there for a while. What Ronnie didn't know before he arrived was that his sister was a dyke. She was sharing the apartment with her girlfriend. Ronnie couldn't handle it and moved out after a week. That's what I heard, anyway.

STAR PITCH

Naomi Foyle

Being the Second Part of the Adventures of the
Raven's Orphan Sister

Finally crazy because she knew she was nothing but an abortion, she conceived the most insane idea that any woman can think of. She vowed to kick the habit of loving. In this manner she would put herself in situations so perilous the glory of her name would resound. But first, she had to find her own name.

The first text the girl learned how to read with her ash-coloured eye was part of a manifesto written by one of her foster mother's more intellectual friends. It was taped to the refrigerator door, next to a Far Side cartoon, and a big scratch 'n' sniff picture of roses.

'Neoism is opposed to Western Philosophy,' the manifesto declared. 'Logic is the road that leads to nowhere, or at the very best, madness. Neoism has never claimed to resolve anything, Neoism simply is. No more than a sneeze, or rather hollow laughter, Neoism is undefeatable, self-refuting and incomprehensible.'

She liked the sound of that last bit. And thus Neo Fight the Pirate Girl was born, christening herself in the privacy of the bathroom, with a goblet of melted rum and raisin ice-cream.

Neo grew up into a tall, strapping young woman, never seen

without a black velvet eyepatch. She kept her hair cropped short, and except when government inspectors visited the house, wore bright crimson lipstick and the golden earrings Kait had saved for her from Raven's shell.

She was forever running away from home, because she hated the way Kait's girlfriends patronised her for sleeping with men. Those ignorant bull dykes had no idea how much she loved the subtle communication between the tip of a penis and the rim of her lost eye. If she took in the whole head and cried, the man would lose his mind with pleasure. Then a sympathetic response flooded her entire nervous system like huge chocolate icebergs melting to Byzantium and back. Neo just couldn't see the appeal of deep-socketing a dildo. Just because Kait had long ago given up on the unfair sex, didn't mean she had to.

But Neo was not one of these people who, when they have an affair, expect something. People who always approach 'casual sex' in this way – IE not casually, are missing out on something really important. In so-called casual sex she found a meaninglessness so deep it sucked her in. When two people come together in this way, every moment is a temporary eternity. A 'one-night stand' can offer total fulfilment, total passion, total war, total freedom, total love.

Rejecting her suitors, or, likewise, being rejected, affirmed Neo's deeply ingrained belief that love was nothing more than the anonymous monotony of endorphins breaking on a harsh and stony shore. Certainly nothing to which to shackle one's undying allegiance.

Occasionally, however, she would extend the duration of a liaison, if she felt confident that mutual exploitation was the only bond likely to develop between the participants.

The seventeen-year-old cock-eyed pessimist's latest romance cast her in the role of dominatrix to a legal aid solicitor. Reginald Cush had defended Neo and her best friend, Donna, Ragga Queen of Mango Dreamin', from charges of assaulting a police officer at the Notting Hill Carnival. It was true the girls had deliberately lured the copper down an alleyway by flashing a baggie of oregano as if in mid-transaction on the street. Any witnesses could not have honestly denied that the two girls had then twisted the state-paid gangster's limbs around his beefy torso as easily as Celtic dreads, then tattooed PIG FUCKER across his forehead with a rusty needle. Chanting 'Who gave you de warrant to kill? Choke on puke as de ladies trill', they then kicked his teeth in with steel-toed boots, laced up with yellow, green and red ribbons. But many ethically minded individuals would argue that this was a bold act of retribution, the only recourse of the hunted, a singular blow for justice in a corrupt, brutal police state.

As those types of free thinkers do not populate the upper echelons of the legal system, however, Reggie decided to present a rather different defence. He arranged a private consultation with the judge, for Donna and Neo to convince His Lordship that their dedication to only the consensual infliction of pain was complete. Back in court, the girls were quickly declared the victims of wrongful arrest.

Neo was working part-time as a courier for various coke, smack and ganja dealers, flying in and out of Amsterdam or just biking across the city with the stuff stashed in a moneybelt strapped across her groin. In this, the prime of her youth, she didn't give a shit about the future. She lived for moments of violent intensity, knowing that, with a snivelling, subhuman partner, these moments could be stretched into hours.

Reggie was perfect because, having a reasonable income, he stocked up her cupboards with the ultimate in top-of-the-line S&M gear.

The night of the victory in chambers, the triumphant bandita chose a black, silver-tipped whip. With a twitch of her arm, she sent a savage blow whistling against her lover's spine. She cracked the whip a second time and once again it cut into Reggie's quivering flesh. The action was repeated again and again and again. Rivers of blood poured from the weals that now peppered the bird-brained bottom's badly bruised back.

'Capitalism is pornographic because it turns individuals into ciphers, representations of the human potential it inhibits,' he thundered in ecstasy.

Reggie had wanted her to read the Marquis de Sade aloud as she tugged sharply on the chains connecting his nipples, scrotum and foreskin. But like all Labour Party hacks, community 'arts' workers and associated red scum he couldn't understand why oppressed peoples weren't interested in 'improving' themselves through exposure to 'serious culture'. She soon found she had too much contempt for his puny pretensions to allow his cockhead anywhere near her eyehole. That night she left him writhing on the piss-drenched rubber sheets, and met Donna for a roti and deep-fried plantain feast, washed down the hatch with Red Stripe and tingly ginger tea.

'I don't know what de fuck you doing wid all dese cowboys,' Donna remarked. 'Seems you de slave just as much as de other way around.' She was dressed loud, rude and gold, ready to rotate her hips to the ground to a fresh Jamaican sound, and let her backbone slide deep into the small small hours. She and her beautiful black sisters graced the long road to freedom with righteous pussy motions, night after glittering night. Until they got pregnant, that is.

When the babies arrived, the young women were no longer able to hold down their crap fast food, retail and London underground jobs. They became financially dependent on males who those without historical consciousness might blithely call vain and trigger happy. These men could easily wind up deported, jailed or permanently silenced in a gangland raid. So the young black mothers would grow to embody feminism in its most atavistic form – sharing their meagre material and ample emotional resources in proud defence of the next generation.

But Donna didn't think of the hard, maternal times ahead as she gyrated her tight needle eye that night. She and her bespangled girlfriends were too busy enjoying themselves, laughing about the uptight folk, black and white, who had clubbed together on 'Devil's Advocate' the night before. Darcus

Howe's popular audience participation programme had raised a few hackles by questioning whether or not Shabba Ranks should be banned from commercial radio. But truly, if for the moment certain manifestations of BlacK UnderKlass Kulture were open to accusations of sexism, that was hardly surprising, Donna and her friends agreed. After all these Kultural Artifacts were produced under conditions dictated by capitalist social relations. Sexism and racism being two faces of capitalist oppression, it was inevitable that Kultural creations produced under the boss system would be tainted by at least one of them. And who could argue with the booming bass line that compelled the girls on to the dance floor like a bitch in heat attracts the whole souls of dogs.

Neo didn't join Donna in this metallic marathon of athletic erotics, being too skinny and lippy to attract most of the males present. Besides, she could smell the nappies ahead, and the last thing she wanted was a fat brat to feed, house and clothe. She was even considering signing up to be implanted with the birth control device Norplant. A hormonal contraceptive stick injected into the skin under the armpit, oozing chemicals that leave a woman infertile for up to five years, Norplant had been tried out in 'third world' countries and forcibly given to convicted American women prisoners instead of prison sentences. The British government was now paying large bonuses for women on the dole to offer their bodies as the next testing site.

But Kait vetoed Neo's plans, by refusing to sign the consent forms needed for minors, and tersely reminding her adopted daughter that the council flat could still be snatched from under her if it were revealed that 'Joey', as the girl's mother still called her, were officially revealed to be female.

'Then I'll just have to get a prescription for the abortion pill,' Neo sneered, as if this Kafkaesque situation were all her foster mother's fault. 'You can get it in Britain now.'

'Well, lucky us,' retorted Kait. 'RU 486 is totally dangerous and inadequately tested. One woman has already died in

France as a result of taking it. It is much safer to have an abortion by suction, Joey.'

'I'm not letting any pervert doctor with a vacuum cleaner anywhere near my cunt! If the rubber breaks I'll just get the morning after pill!'

'Don't be bamboozled into thinking there's any magic alternative to common sense and caution, Joey. Do you know how dangerous the "morning after" pill is too? I've just heard of a friend who became sterile after using it and was made so ill and permanently exhausted that she lost her job!'

'Well, if she was a friend of yours she was probably a fat, lazy cow to begin with,' muttered Neo under her breath. She was extremely pissed off at being prevented from fucking all she wanted without the hassle of latex or rank stinking foam. The pill was no good for her because, ever since a close friend had topped himself on an overdose of sleeping tablets, she hated swallowing the little bastards. Having experimented with many a near-lethal cocktail of combustibles in her own line of work, she considered herself quite the Tank Girl, and was positive her system could easily overcome any contraceptive's minor side effects. Also being possessed of somewhat of a death wish, she didn't worry overmuch about the chances of contracting AIDS. The sooner she bunked off this sordid coil, the better, she figured.

But, as it happened, as Neo lost interest in humiliating men – her utter scorn for the weaklings preventing her complete fusion with the sexual dynamic – she found fewer and fewer males willing and able to ignite her insatiable desires. Something about her made those heterosexuals of the masculine gender extremely self-protective, it seemed. Fundamentally depressed by the continuous disappointing effort to achieve physical satisfaction in this world, more and more she turned to politics for salvation, release, and potential suicide scenarios.

No more did she waste her evenings hanging about watching Donna dress and make up for the dance hall. Donna wasn't interested in risking any further arrests. She was all talk, no action now.

While Neo could happily sit all night around a kitchen table with a bottle of whisky and other trenchant social outcasts, she strongly felt the urge to make her discontent a public matter. Far-right skinhead militancy had travelled across the channel that summer, re-establishing UK residency in the form of the BNP headquarters in South East London, and the election of a BNP councillor in Tower Hamlets. But, argued Jax, a hot-wired Scottish anarchist, the general upswing in ultra right wing influence on street level only served to mask the continued ferocity of systemic racism meted out by the police, the courts, hospitals and educational institutions across the country. Those Lefties calling to shut down the headquarters, accepting the State's prerogative to stamp out organisations from the BNP, to the IRA to travellers and squatters, were as thick and self-defeating as lemmings, he declared.

Neo, too, refused to be drawn into such pathetic logic. She and Jax joined forces the night before the volatile Plumstead demonstration, ensnaring two pious, soft-boiled anti-fascists in hair-splitting philosophical battle in a Brick Lane pub, then stomping them into oblivion outside. Right on the corner where the BNP used to sell their papers until similarly despatched by Youth Against Racism In Europe and Anti-Nazi League supporters, Neo noted with delicious irony. She didn't usually like kicking the shit out of other oppressed peoples, but had to agree with Jax that the rhetoric of this right-on mixed race couple was seriously contorted and dangerous to the future wellbeing of the disenfranchised worldwide.

'This country is rotted and rundown, a sea of misery for millions of unemployed and low-paid workers, a place of fear and violence for Asian and Black people, as you no doubt think you know,' Jax ranted as Neo dripped vinegar from little plastic sachets into the blood mush wounds on the agonised face of the Chinese woman. 'To turn to the state, that is, to capital, with the demand to disarm the fascists means to sow the worst democratic illusions, to lull the vigilance of the proletariat, to demoralise its will,' he raved. 'Fascism is what capitalism resorts to when it can no longer rule by its preferred democratic methods: that is, when it is threatened by revolution. In Britain the idea that it will come draped in the swastika and with a straight-arm salute is laughable. It will use the Union Jack and be fronted by "respectable" politicians. Your anti-Nazi rhetoric plays into the dirty hands of British nationalism and nostalgia, completely obscuring the true and horrific scope of the problem all freedom lovers and anti-racists face at this juncture in history. History as well-heeled men have written it for centuries, that is.' And with her metal stilettos, Neo pierced the white lip of the Sussex born and bred young man.

Satisfied that this rigorous rebuttal to the feeble views of the wilfully ignorant couple would long remain ringing in their bleeding ears, Jax and Neo robbed them of their dosh. Pleased to discover that the wallets were full of recently cashed cheques of social worker and school teacher proportions, the voracious victors celebrated with an enormous feast of vegetable curry, onion bhaji and spicy nan, complimenting the waiter on the length of his okra, and tipping extravagantly. They parted at Aldgate East station, well chuffed. Neo rode her bike home to her Stoke Newington squat, to sink into a long, hot Radox salts bath, feeling more alive and self-assured than she could ever remember.

Until the keening strain of an electric guitar solo rose up from between the paint-flaking floorboards, drawn out until time dilated and eternity was defined in terms of water temperature and steam. The beeswax candles in the chandelier above her head flickered briefly, as if the door had been pushed open and someone naked had entered the room, with nothing on his mind but the desire to bring Neo to gentle orgasm after orgasm, by simply pulling on her long brown nipples and whispering *smile*. Someone so familiar with her body he could bring about this immersion in bliss by simply looking at his hands and then deep into her face. Someone who would tenderly slip off the patch she wore even in sleep, as if it were a truly ravishing wig, but he preferred to look at her secret and bald. Then Neo felt suddenly cradled in emptiness. Her scraped, stinging hands were powerless to stop her extended play fall into the grovelling weakness of tears.

In the morning, Neo Fight rose and went about the city in the streets, and sought him whom her soul loved. She looked in record shops, and Camden Lock, in Forbidden Planet and Compendium Book Shop, at the Bad Grrrls film showings at the ICA, in the Crypt at St Martin's in the Fields, in the wastelands of Battersea, and the foxholes of Hackney, at the Greenwich Meridian and in the tunnel under the Thames. Oh she was hot on the trail of him who would be as her brother, he who had bitten off the breasts of her real mother. She knew when she found him he would say, 'My head is filled with dew from sleeping rough on Hampstead Heath, and my locks with the drops of the night. And you, my sister, my love, my undefiled, are one thirsty dove.' And she, in return, would kiss him, and 'Yea,' she whispered to a mange-raddled pigeon, 'I should not be despised.'

But she found him not. Her heart, sick with desire and fastened to a dying animal, knowing not what it was, fast depleted her reserves of adrenalin and vigour. Soon, blood barely moved itself around the spider's mansion of her veins. Unable to set foot outdoors without being overcome by despondency, she found she had recourse only to poetry and music to soothe the sizzling seizures in the secret chamber of her breast. With Jax behind her, a 12-inch crowbar in his hand, she informed the scabrous group of musicians downstairs that if they wished to keep jamming beneath her squat they needed to welcome her as their new lyricist and chanteuse.

Then Neo shaved her head except for one long rope of hair swinging down to her fifth vertebrae, black and copper-orange. Feverishly, night after night, she penned innumerable invasions into an inexorable game of fury, mire and tears. The drummer, guitarist and bass player followed like gale force winds ruffling a serial murderer's hair. And lo, like some misplaced Joan of Arc, Neo Fight the Pirate Girl was blessed with strength, clarity and purpose.

Imagine Bad Religion, Proletariat Descendant, Subhumans, Black Flag, Angry Samoans, Adrenalin, OD, Posh Boy Classics, Toxic Reasons, Germs, Sic Pleasure, No Means No, Noisebleed, Profane Existence, Sharon Tate's Children, 7 Year Bitch, Night Terror Syndrome, None Shall Sleep, Fifth Column, Mourning Sickness, John Cooper Clarke and Patti Smith embroiled in a sweaty contretemps in a half-deserted warehouse, and you have a vague picture of Croaker's first gigs . . .

'This one's called "Flaccid Acid",' Neo introduced the final set to a nearly capacity crowd. OK, so the venue was the size of a midget's shoebox, but the ceilings were high, and she knew for sure a record company scout was underneath them somewhere. National music papers had been raving about Croaker's appearances since their cunt-juice-stained inception. 'There's a Scream Along in the middle, with some excellent words even I didn't know until I wrote the fucker,' she hooted. 'Spoony means "foolishly amorous". Thixotropic means "something that gets thinner when stirred". Thixotropic. Got that? Good . . .'

The guitar sliced in like a chainsaw hitting steel Earth First spikes in old growth trees. Neo made love to the microphone and the mutant daughters of her mind.

'First person present
At the detumescence of the age
I dictate like a peasant
Telling tales is all the rage

Because eye sore what no man can
Acknowledge as the truth
The way the penis disappoints
In so-called maturity and youth

Shit pumps ruling, ape-men warring
Eunuchs making laws
Old men drooling, young men scoring
Lads out killing whores

Because blokes hate their stupid dicks
That jabber mope and flop
They bash the rest of us with bricks
Piss their panties as we drop

The band abruptly lurched into a crazy, loopy polka, Neo urging 'Sing Along Folks!' At first only the odd female voice was raised in answer to the call and response invitation, but by the end of the litany, the chorus was full, resounding and accompanied by the requisite banging of beer bottles, boots, and heads.

Yes, my Daddy's got a thixotropic, microscopic cock
And his brain is such a stunted runted puppy
He really thinks size matters
So he can't even get an uppie
Unless he rapes and beats and batters!

The drummer descended on the cymbals in a demonic frenzy as the guitarist dragged a fistful of knuckle dusters up and down the neck of her red glittery instrument and Neo sank to her knees, to the bassist's morbid, metronomic beat, plunging the microphone up Jax's protruding bare ass. In fact, he was wearing nothing but a spongy, *Spitting Image* Slick Grave mask.

Neo had decided to perform a transmogrifying ritual on her local punkmeister rival. From recent interviews in the fanzine press, he sure sounded as though he could use one. Pissed as a fart the whole time he was, screwing up all his relationships, and still penning songs blaming underage girls for all his spots. Why was the planet crawling with big bad sexy fuck-ups – men, undoubtedly victims of mangled childhoods who overidentified with the perpetrators of their abuse and filled art, literature and the newspapers with intimations of paedophilia and overtly death-clad erotics? Neo knew she had been fatally poisoned by them all. Grave, in particular, was really too much in her face.

Luckily Slick was attractive enough to risk being photographed in the act of purifying his caricature. In facsimile or in person, most self-proclaimed evil beings were far too grotesque for the fastidious pirate chanteuse to consider penetrating up to her elbow while stabbing in the buttocks with the knife she kept in a red leather holster at her hip.

'I am thy beloved, Slick,' she crooned. 'I put in my hand by the hole of thy door, come, let thy bowels be moved for me.'

When the blissfully pampered body beneath her deposited a huge, steaming turd on a golden platter, Neo smiled. She washed the sighing asshole with hot pomegranate wine, then drank deeply from the garnet liquid remaining in the goblet. Pushing her tongue in a huge slow circle around her puckered lips, she sucked her fingers clean, delicious one by one. An underage girl with eight rings in her left ear plucked the shit from the tray, and secreted it in her purse. The bass player kept the pulse, the drummer shimmered softly in the background, the guitarist changed a string.

Finally, scratching Slick's neck and pulling on his hair, Neo spoke again.

'This one's about an endemic epidemic. Polemical, yet tender. Called "Ravenous".'

Her voice a throaty whisper, she gyrated her way through the next slow, hypnotic number, crushing Grave into the stage with her combat boots at the top of his spine. Regurgitated yellow vegetable curry spewed from his lips on to the faces of the dancers squirming too close to the action. Squeals of disgust and delight punctuated the husky ambience of the number.

She's nothing herself
So she's stuffing herself

She's fingering herself
Unfulfilling herself

Eating defines her
Food doesn't become her
She crouches above it
Hoarsely whispers she loves it

Gag reflex
She's automatic
Gut reaction
Why should she stop it

Snarling into the crowd as the musicians ground to a halt, Neo appeared to suddenly notice Slick's puke-stained visage at her feet. Breathlessly, she consoled the heaving bottom.

'Oh, Slicky, your little rubber mouth is all dirty! How disagreeable for you, poppet. Here, allow me to swab the decks of your discerning palate, let me be your crimson cabin girl, and scrub your poop deck clean.'

Spreading her knees, crouching, and reaching up between her hip high black boots, Neo inserted her right thumb and forefinger up inside her rubber skirt, past her silvery g-string and into her rich, engorged cunt. Up against her cervix she grasped and tugged at the string tied tight around the end of a dense, bloody menstrual sponge, and removed the sodden creature in one swift gesture of triumph.

Dangling it in front of the mask, she hissed, 'Now I wouldn't want you to have to smell this instrument of your salvation, precious. Even I am not particularly fond of the aroma of farts and rotting seaweed. And you are being such a good little victim tonight, I think you deserve to have those delicate nasal cavities protected. Phlegm, can you assist?'

Shoving the bass player's chewing gum up Slicky's nostrils wasn't quite secure or dramatic enough a measure to satisfy Neo's theatrical temperament or the curiosity of the crowd. So she drove two hypodermic syringes through the pierce holes each side of his nose, clamping the flaps of skin and cartilage shut by puncturing each plastic drum with the opposite needle. Yanking his long, bluntly cut hair back to open his jaw, Neo carefully polished Slick's teeth and caressed his tongue with the foaming, menses-saturated sponge. When the job was done, and his teeth were like a flock of rusty sheep, even shorn and come up from the washing, she hurled the sodden Dead Sea sponge into the smoky haze of the club.

'NOW thy temple is anointed, oh vain heathen of the penal continent, usurper of my rage. NOW are you fit to be my dais my podium my mercy seat my winged ship of servitude and grace.'

To the building, building rhythm of a James Brown, James BROWN invocation, Donna entered the stage, pelvis first, dressed in gold brocade, twirling black ribbons and a heavy flag in her strong, dark hands, like weapons in an ancient martial art. Neo introduced her as the Queen of Mango Dreamin', High Priestess of West Indian Freedom, and the Devil Sistah of Soul. The crowd went wild at her majestic appearance and she commanded their rapt attention for a full five minutes while Neo kicked Grave's ass around the perimeter of the stage. The High Priestess had oiled her skin and hair with the essence of spikenard and saffron, calamus and cinnamon, with all trees of frankincense, myrrh and aloes. The sweat of her exertion released this heady brew into the venue, like a fountain of gardens, a well of living waters. Finally the pirate girl deposited her booty back in the forefront of the action, and to a crackling backbeat, Donna crisply flicked the ribbons one by one into Neo's red-tipped fingers.

Deftly using elaborate sailor's knots, Neo trussed the writhing doppelgänger, clamping his scrawny knees to his pale chest and his ankles to his wrists, swivelling his torso so that the slopes of his thighs, his shit-smeared ass and his twanging prong faced the adulating crowd. Her skilful work complete, she knelt at Donna's tapping toes, and the High Priestess draped the flag of gleaming ebony feathers around her shoulders. Little silver tokens, of cowrie shells and tree leaves, spaceships and bones, dangled and glinted in two long Vs down the back and front of the cape. From a mojo pouch around her neck, Donna retrieved two golden earrings – two halves of a long broken egg. She put one gently in Neo's left ear, then, slipping the Pirate Girl's eyepatch down around her neck and tightening it like a sexy little choker, she inserted the hollow of the tip of the egg in Neo's eye socket. The shell sucked in the hot concert lights like flames to an inferno. The funk soul mix intensified as the proud, Black British woman gyrated around the prostrate duo, and exited the stage.

In silence thick as lies, Neo rose to her leather-clad feet, blood drizzling down her legs like cream.

'Now I have been anointed, Grave, I am fit to be thy eternal mistress, harbinger of thy desires, flight navigator of the chariot of thy death. I, unspoiled, the only one of my mother, the choice one of she that bore me, I looketh forth clear as the morning, fair as the moon, bright as the sun, and terrible as an army with B-52 bombers and napalm cluster bombs. I looketh through you, degenerate reviler of innocence, bestial prostitute of scorn, to the helpless boy you must learn again to be.'

The band broke into a brief 'Rock Lobster' riff as Neo trod upon the shoulders beneath her, and mounted the perch of his feet and cupped hands. An indomitable pirate girl ascending the mast of a newly captured ship in the midst of turbulence and a fragrant, sweat-infested storm. Yea, verily, it was a miracle that Slick's sweet jism didn't shoot right up through the skylight in the steeple above them, looking, as he was, up Neo's short and slippery skirt, his chest awash in her glorious piss and blood.

'I am no goddess!' she barked, her gaze high-voltage electricity run amok. 'I am human. I have all too human needs!'

The band swelled up behind her in a miasma of bluesy grunge. She sang as low and gravelly as a delta man on his

fifth whisky of the session, just beginning to let his mind slide
into the skeletal-white heart of slavery and love.

> We need to be in bed
> To save our wretched souls
> Give me give me give me head
> Plaster all my leaking holes
>
> We need to fuck all night
> To save the stinking world
> Forget forget forget the dead
> Let your genitals unfurl
>
> I will rob you of your lust
> I will cheat you blind
> We have got each other sussed
> I don't need to read your mind

As she growled the simple, yet so satisfying apex of the evening's aural pleasures, Neo plucked a black silk rope from a
hidden pocket in her cloak and tied one end into a small
hangman's noose, the other around the tip of her long copper
braid. After swirling it around her head, taunting the crowd
and whipping it back to safety, she floated it across her quivering throne of flesh, at last catching it secure beneath Grave's
rock-hard balls, and cinching it tight around the base of his
cock.

'The thread is in the needle, let the gossamer sails be spun!'
she cried, gently tugging at the turgid male sexual organs now
completely in her power.

On stage before a glistering ocean of totally hooked eyes of
stranger upon stranger, the feeling in Neo Fight's body was the
feeling of knowing perfectly how much she was her body, and
how much she was her mind. In so feeling and knowing she
was recognising her mind as the warm, breathing creature
it is beneath the clothing and colour of style. Finding this
harmonious proportion was akin to finding harbour after
threading through a bay studded with ice mountains and

apocalyptic monsters impervious to cold. Not only safety, but a heroine's welcome, a port thronged with friends wanting days and nights of her time, to hear the legends of her travels inveigle the dying light of the stars.

This is what being a cultural worker in the field of popular music promised – this feeling, amplified in every country in the Northern hemisphere, and a privileged few in the South to boot. After this gig, all Neo had to do was sign herself and Croaker to a huge corporate label. She could sing 'Fuck the Pigs' while the money EMI were making off her records went towards making surveillance equipment for the bastards. Like anyone who does this, Neo was fast on her way to becoming one with evil, murdering SCUM.

And, like froth on the first cappuccino of the evening, like mercury on a scorching afternoon, like bread in the oven, Tory votes in a recession, like hackles on a rabid dog, like a penis in the morning, like eyebrows in restrained contempt, like prices in wartime, like the insanity of hope and the shining meniscus on a stone birdbath of pre-Chernobyl spring rain – SCUM RISES.

A kamikaze beer bottle hurtled up from the crowd to the slanted ceiling above the stage, and assassinated the thin pane of the skylight. Thereupon it could be heard rolling down the roof and cascading into smithereens on the bullet-proof windscreen of the record company scout's royal blue Mercedes parked outside the club. A long, chilling whistle of wind skewered the room like a banshee on Dust. Neo's black feathered cape billowed behind her shoulders. As if hoiked by stage wire on pulleys, she began a jerky ascent to the ceiling, dragging the writhing, sinewy body beneath her, still attached by its packet to her string.

'Oh Neo!' Slick screamed. 'Whither thou goest, I will go. Whither thou lodgest, I will lodge.' The band abandoned all aspirations to music, lancing an excruciating boil of white noise. His hands still clasping her ankles, Slick would have made it up to the black square of sky with Neo, intact, were it not for the frenzied attentions of the crowd. A tireless clump of fans lunged at his body as if it were a lifebelt dropped from a helicopter that would only save one person and leave hundreds more to drown.

His slippery sweat didn't save him. Screaming like an elephant caught in the engine of an aircraft carrier, Slick fell to the stage, to be swamped in the boozy grave of his own vomit and shit. With all but the most inconsequential ballast snatched from her clutches, Neo shot like a jagged bolt of lightning, up through the treacherous hatch. One long shard of glass severed the elasticised velvet band keeping her eyepatch in place around her neck. It wafted to the stage and curled up on Grave's groin like a sleepy, newborn snake. A twisted piece of iron ripped her cloak in two down her spine. The ruby-red cock and testicles on the end of her tether flew in one smooth arc to the scarred lips of her cavernous, golden eyehole.

Feeding thus upon the lilies, her withered visions finally blossoming into three unheard-of dimensions, Neo Fight sailed serenely over the time-honoured axis of heaven and hell, on a trajectory no biographer, even the most bitingly poetic, could ever retrace or do justice. To a place without mirrors, or borders, to a place of twilight and echo, of misidentification and inextricable griefs, of genitalia growing together like bunions at the base of a tree. The place language steals away from to bludgeon or bless us. The place music hides when we aren't listening properly, and feeds the breast milk of poetry to words. A place beyond butchery, beyond the family, past opacity and transparency, far over poverty, privilege, gender and race.

Neo Fight is no messiah. She's not coming back to tell us what it's like, or how to get there without leaving home.

HOLIDAYS IN THE SUN

Steve Beard

Delivered from all the signs. El, Phoenician God of Time, Keeper of the Hours, king of the whole ball of wax, is back from the dead. He cradles the sun in his hand like a satellite of love. The earth rocks at his feet.

El is dressed in dark matter. He's got a sense of occasion. His hips snake to the beat of unrecorded stars.

His boys are on the warpath again. Yamm, Guvnor of the Sea, and Baal, Gaffer of the Sky, are fighting over his crown. These two have a score to settle. Who is the Baddest Son?

Astarte, Miss Universe Circa Forever, stands between them with parted lips. She untwists her fuck-me belt and lets it fall from her waist. It spirals down to the town of New Belsen in the land of Ukania and floats on the waters of the Thames. Yamm and Baal descend.

There's an experiment going down in New Belsen. The undead lie nameless in the streets.

El's lips curl in a snarl. He feels the collars of the dead in Wardrobe Place and says the magic words. Some cunt make me an offer.

'Sir' Richard Gresham, Merchant Adventurer, Godfather of the Futures Rackets, makes his appearance. He's got one principle stood him good through all the hard times. Never give a sucker an even break. The deeds of New Belsen are in his back pocket.

Gresham tells El he's got the fix in with the Percy mob, pull in Syon House as the Thamesside arena for Baal and Yamm to have it out. Plus, he's got the name duppies of New Belsen all under contract. All the boys have to do is lift the lid on a boneyard and pick out a suit. He's talking gate receipts, pay-per-view, kickbacks and sweeteners. Crystallised carbon flashing from his fingers in an iridescent display.

El is checking Gresham's fright-wig. This guy is a monster. He shrugs and makes the deal.

Choose your avatars, boys.

Yamm goes west to St George's Chapel and calls up a sea champ. Baal goes east to St Paul's Cathedral and raises a hero of the sky. They track back to Syon House where the Thames meets the Isleworth. Their zombie designates squint in the light.

Gresham puts the squeeze on the Ukanian Board of Reality Control. The MRI scans and hand-eye coordination tests are rushed through. It's the merest formality. Licences are issued for the two dead men of Ukania to mess with posterity. They're each more than willing to risk their own lives.

It's 16/8/97, the anniversary of El's death. The venue is set, the sacrifices prepared, the sun is . . . DOWN!

Babylon TV Commentator #1: 'Quite a crowd here for tonight's production, Reggie.'

Babylon TV Commentator #2: 'They're out for blood, Ron.'

It's a black-tie promotional event. 200 punters have forked out between £100 and £300 to chow down on seared guinea fowl with sweet potato mash and spiced red cabbage. They lounge at their tables like well-groomed predators. All the dead presidents, old movie stars, pagan idols and pop icons swelling it up in Versace and Bernini around the open-air ring in the quadrangle of Syon House. The clinking of expensive glassware and the scraping of ornamental cutlery is picked up by the Babylon TV microphones. Porcelain teeth gleam in the flood-lights.

Banked up behind the flash trash in hastily-erected scaffolding pens are the rabble. 300 fight fans have laid out £20 each for the privilege of stamping their feet and rattling their chains from behind a wire mesh fence. Nowherians, choke-and-rob merchants, cut-purses and rag-pickers decked out in Tommy Hilfiger and Oxfam. Their raucous terrace chants cascade down to the ring.

'There's only one Muthafucka, Only one Muthafucka, Walking along, Singing a song, Walking along in a Winter Wonder-Land.' The Babylon TV cameras pan round the foaming pens in search of local colour. A sea of jerking fists greets their nictating eyes. 'Enery's a rapist, Enery's a rapist, La la la, La la la, Enery's a rapist, Enery's a rapist, La la la, La la la!'

Babylon TV Commentator #1: 'What are they singing, Reggie?'

Babylon TV Commentator #2: 'Can't quite make out the words, Ron.'

Gresham's pre-fight hype routines are replayed on the Babylon TV ringside monitors in an effusive tape loop. His insurgent stream-of-consciousness ravings pace the exertions of the crowd. 'Make no mistake, it's never too late, the future is here in the making. For one night only in the historic arena of Syon House where Oliver Cromwell cut his deal with the reformed hosts of Capital in 1647 and sold the revolutionary forces of Labour right down the river, the old ghosts of Ukania come out to settle their grievances. You've got it. It's a rematch. A grudge fight. It's Class War all over again. This is one you cannot afford to miss. So call your P-P-V cable operator now.'

Gresham's eyes blaze as he explains the mythical attraction of each fighter. 'In the monarcho-republican corner is Enery Tudor, Baby-Faced Psycho, Priest-Killer, Slave-Driver and Land-Grabber, Boss of the Ukanian Navy, a man who taught Uncle Joe Stalin everything he needed to know. Our Enery is a Kentish man hails from the enchanted garden of Greenwich,

Omphalos of the Ukanian Combine, Site of Longitude Zero.
He takes no prisoners. Facing him in the anarcho-proletarian
corner is Puggy Booth, Two-Faced Schizo, Hanged Man,
Juggler and Holy Fool, the Hero of a Hundred Fights, a man
who could wipe the floor with Pablo Picasso. Puggy Muthafucka is a Jewish kid comes from the docks of Wapping, Pirate
Utopia, Ukanian Temporary Autonomous Zone. He lets
nothing get in his way.'

Gresham launches into the final part of his spiel. 'Who is
the Baddest Son of New Belsen? These two are going fifteen
rounds for Astarte's fuck-me belt and neither one is going to
pull their punches. Remember! Only one man comes out alive.
Call your operator now!'

The lights dim. It's time for the fighters to make their separate entrances.

'Our' Enery is borne to the ring from his dressing room in
the Great Hall on a Palladian litter supported on the Nautilus-
ripped shoulders of six Nubian slaves. He is fitted with a
crimson velvet robe lined with ermine and wallows on a bed
of crisp silk sheets and plump satin pillows. He dispenses kisses
to his supporters as he makes his stately progress down the
gangway, a single gold incisor flashing between thinly curled
lips. An explosion of fireworks blazons his coat of arms – a
royal crest with, dexter, a lion guardant and, sinister, a unicorn
armed – in a ten-foot-high logo above his head. Robert Johnson's 'Crossroads Blues' has been specially picked by Enery's
spin-doctor to signal his Faustian powers of demonic assertion.
Its eerie mantra is lost in the roar from the crowd.

Puggy 'Muthafucka' comes out from the Old Library to the
butcher's block beats of Doc Scott's 'Here Come the Drumz'.
He is dressed in a vermilion cassock with the hood pulled up
over his head and the name of his dockside pub in Wapping –
'The Ship and Bladebone' – embossed in chrome yellow
stitching on the back. Emerald green lasers strobe his grimly-
set features as he taps his gloves together in a privately coded
mandala and jogs his way to the ring. Three sacred prostitutes

wrapped in black silk chadars with heavily kohled eyes strew'
rose petals at his feet. Puggy ignores the baying salute of the
crowd. He has the self-contained aura of an executioner or a
monk.

Enery ascends the ring apron and basks in the aura of
popping flashbulbs. Then he ducks through the ropes and puts
on a show for the crowd. They howl in ecstasy as he prances on
nimble feet and engages in an orgy of neck-flexing and head-
rolling with the gone eyes of a creature on heat. Puggy stands
in his corner with head bowed and arms crossed. He's watching
Enery. There's a crazy grin on his face.

Babylon TV Commentator #1: 'Enery's looking very tasty,
Johnny.'

Babylon TV Betting Clown. 'The odds have hardened from
1–2 to 1–4 in the big guy's favour, Ron. The sugar money's
rolled in from the West India Company to back him at the
rate of a million bucks a minute. Some say it's a fix. But
the Tate & Lyle judges know the score. Me? I'm still waiting
to lay a bet on the little man at something like 40–1. But then,
as you know, I've got no reason.'

Babylon TV Commentator #2: 'You're a deep one, John.'

The MC, Malcolm McGuffin, steps into the ring in his tartan-
check Lewis Carroll suit and picks up the microphone. His
pupils are wildly dilated and his red hair sticks out on end. He
looks like a pantomime dame on coke.

'Good evening, ladies and gentlemen.' He looks primly at
the seething crowd and raises a disapproving eyebrow to calm
them. 'I think you'll be interested in our little show tonight.'
There is a collective sigh of anticipation. 'From the site where
legends come to die, Syon House in New Belsen, Sir Richard
Gresham in connection with Babylon TV brings you a prophetic contest. A fight to the death. I know you want it just
as badly as I do. So let's get ready to ROCK 'N' ROLL!'

The crowd pick up their cue and explode in a demented

orgasm of bloodlust. McGuffin wipes the tears from his eyes and laughs.

He snorts through the introductions as if afraid of losing his momentum. When he reaches Enery's name, the fighter responds to the come-on with a practised gesture. He slips out of his robe, pats his massive belly and sticks out his groin. The crowd smack their lips as they spot the bulge in his crocodile-skin trunks. Enery's giant frame shakes in delight.

Puggy is out of his gown before McGuffin gets to his name. His stomach is ridged with hard muscle, his barrel chest is compact with power. The back of the arena cheers. He drops to the canvas and snaps out a one-armed press-up. There is an inky-black tattoo of the sun on his back. It matches the colour of his shoes and his shorts.

John Ruskin, the referee, is wearing a St John's Ambulance tunic and white surgical gloves. He's taking no chances. There are rumours that Enery has a sexually transmitted disease and that Puggy's ticker is not as strong as it should be. Ruskin smoothes back his hair. He wants no blood on his hands.

Ruskin motions to the fighters with a curt gesture and they come together in the middle of the ring for the ritual stare-down. Enery's small, piggy eyes radiate controlled hate. Puggy brings his face up against his opponent's and looks right through him.

Puggy asks just one question. 'What's my name?'

'Joseph Mallord William Turner,' Enery replies in his lisping, high-pitched voice.

It's the wrong answer.

Puggy shakes his head and grins at the ref. 'He just used my slave name. This makes it personal.' He lowers.

Ruskin whispers a few words of caution in the ears of each man. Enery smacks him one for his impertinence. Ruskin nods meekly and sighs. He slaps his palm against the touching gloves of Enery and Puggy and jumps back out of the way.

Somewhere far off in the darkness, El sounds the opening bell.

The two fighters begin slugging it out as if there's no tomorrow. They both carry bombs in their gloves. Enery has the longer reach, but Puggy has the speed and timing. He crowds his opponent and fights close inside, pummelling him with sharp combinations of uppercuts and hooks. Enery holds him off with his left jab and unloads a whirling barrage of overhand rights to the chin and lashes curled tight into the body.

The crowd go wild. It's more than they hoped for. A real dogfight. Puggy welcomes Enery's ferocious onslaught. He crouches down to the right with his head buried deep in his shoulders and draws the big guy on to the counter-punch, keeping up a ceaseless percussion of blows while taking everything Enery lands in his face. A vicious right cross opens a long and deep cut over his left eye. The blood pumps from the wound. Puggy shrugs it off and gets stuck in again.

Enery's Headspace: It's war. Each cunt wants a piece of you. They suck and bleed you dry. A million bucks, a million fucks. It all miscarries down the toilet of Naboth's Vineyard. You don't give a shit for any cunt. Hunt 'em, fuck 'em, kill 'em. You've only got one golden rule. Never with the mother.

Puggy's Headspace: 'Dido Building Carthage; or the Rise of the Carthaginian Empire.' You're nobody's ritual sacrifice. They can bury you with one of your abortions. Fuck 'em. It's all they deserve. Dido figured a tryst in a hermit's cave was a marriage. Sarah, Hannah and Sophia tending your flesh one after another in a mouldy one-window cell. They locked up your mother in the Temple of Isis. She saw visions too strong to bear. You bequeathed your damp issue to the Ukanian people. They say you're a deadbeat dad.

Puggy's corner-man Manu, known to the ringside media pack as a witch-doctor, battles to staunch the flow of blood in the interval. He cleans the cut and spreads a clogging salve over its entire surface, his bony fingers pressing deep inside the crimson slit. Enery watches the performance from his corner with cold-eyed relish, while his entourage of bodyguards, fixers and handlers buff him with sponges and towels. His spin-doctor, Sick 'Boy' Barrett, is whispering into his ear as he gently tilts a bottle of Evian water into his mouth. Enery swallows and nods.

Round 2 and the two charge into the middle of the ring to pick up where they left off. Enery fights from behind his jab, while Puggy cuts loose with a frenzied whirlwind of blows. They go at it in a blast of raw terror. Then Puggy steps up the rhythm as if desperate to finish it fast. He throws punches from a looping variety of angles, briefly dazzling his opponent, who backs off in surprise.

Puggy moves in for what he hopes is the kill. He sinks a right to the body and tries to follow it up with a jolting left uppercut. Enery sees his chance. His enemy's guard is down. He discharges a mighty left hook in a hammering arc and grunts as it connects with the temple. Puggy reels from the blow. The ringside punters jump up in convulsive excitement. The dazed fighter crashes through the ropes to land at their feet. They shriek with joy as blood splatters their clothes. The ref is administering a count.

Enery's Headspace: It's over. It's nothing. You're safe, you pretty thing, you. You signed the warrant at Greenwich in the place where you were born. The black eyes, the wide mouth, the long neck resting on the block. You shelled out £24 to bring an expert swordsman in from Paris. They say you're a monster. But she was a whore. You always lose the ones you love. The Jezebel grew an extra little finger in the brothels of Naboth's Vineyard.

Puggy's Headspace: '1805–6 Studies for Pictures; Isleworth' sketchbook, pp. 34a–35. A symbolic death. You catch yourself back. Casting a line into the flow of the dreamtime with an expert hand. The rod bends. You reeled in your demon at the site where Cassivellaunus defended the Thames from the imperial legions of Caesar, where plague bodies were unloaded in the dead heat, where gunpowder tracks down from the factories of Hounslow Heath for detonation in the West Indies and sugar and spice and everything nice drifts back upriver. Syon Ferry House on the threshold of the Temple of Isis. Crossroads, graveyard and virtual slave market tricked up in classical drag for the amusement of speculators like Lord Egremont. Real-estate wrapped up in a fake rural idyll. You kept a record of the Bank of England eviction notices. Forensic evidence. But it was a leaf of Butcher's Broom from Dr Turner's mortuary garden which you pressed, there, in the place where you ripped a page from the future history of the Temple of Isis. Your mother's people were all butchers. The evergreen holly is the sign of your calling. Possession. You have to go to work in an abattoir wielding your knife.

Puggy disentangles his feet from the Babylon TV cameras and climbs back into the ring before the ref can count him out. Enery is hollering and cursing in a neutral corner as Ruskin holds him back with an apologetic grin. His entourage are waving their hands in protest. Enery shoves the ref out of the way and races over to Puggy. His face is a mask of white fury as if he can hardly believe the little man has the sheer nerve to come back for more. He smashes his right fist against his enemy's head again and again. The little man tucks his chin in low and ducks most of the blows so that they just shave his skull. But one clips him and opens a second cut. Puggy claws at his tormentor against the ropes as blood streams from both eyes.

Round 2 finally ends.

This time Manu really has his work cut out. He has to bathe Puggy's swollen right eye while fixing up the gash which is bruising the other. His brow puckers with anxiety. Puggy's chest labours heavily. Enery stands in his corner and bawls out his spin-doctor.

Puggy's legs are still wobbly when the two come together

again and Enery takes advantage of his disorientation to tag
him with a volley of punches. But then Puggy regains his
strength and begins to fight back. With extraordinary determination, he forces Enery to concede territory as he releases an
avalanche of left hooks and right crosses which make his
opponent pant.

By the middle of the round Puggy is clearly in command.
He begins to rely on his reflexes to feint and dodge, luring
Enery on to his counter-punch as he leans back with his arms
slung low and his chin poked invitingly out, taunting the big
guy into rushing him. Enery takes the bait but ends up fighting
his own shadow as he lunges at his enemy with hastily put
together combinations. Puggy's feet dance and glide over the
canvas as he breezes snaking right crosses through Enery's
guard and lifts spray from his head. He's showboating. The
crowd lap it up.

Enery's Headspace: You're being made a fool of. It makes you
want to cry. The diseased whores all laugh at you behind your
back in the temples of Naboth's Vineyard. Katharine Howard
with her orgies and her sex games. Elizabeth Barton, the Witch
of Kent, with her prophetic orgasms. You're going soft. The
cunts are sticking pins inside your leg; they're fucking with
your issue. It's incontinent, base; it's corrupt. You sent your
man Cromwell to sort them out. He cleansed the place. It's
yours. Sweet treason! You're the boy who makes the women
scream.

Puggy's Headspace: 'Lucy, Countess of Carlisle, and Dorothy
Percy's Visit to their Father Lord Percy, when under Attainder
upon the Supposition of his being concerned in the Gunpowder
Plot.' Give 'em what they want. Lord Egremont's family folk-
lore dabbed out on an old cupboard door. Hastily blotted
watercolours of the old cunt's Petworth loot inside the Temple
of Isis, all clearly marked 'Inferior', 'Rubbish' and 'Worse' for
the Ukanian undertaker. Turning tricks like this is so fucking
easy, it's downright insulting. You wonder how much they'll

let you get away with. You almost want to be caught. You feel sick.

It can't go on. By the end of Round 3, Puggy is wasted. His trainer, 'Old' Bill, pours water over his head in a continuous stream as Manu gets busy tending his eyes. The ring commentators say that fathers and sons were never meant to work together in boxing. But Puggy looks into the cheerful blue eyes of his father with tender respect.

Round 4 and Puggy changes tactics. He hangs on the ropes and lets the big guy come on to him and release his full payload of weaponry. Enery fires stunning bursts of uppercuts and hooks into his enemy's head; Puggy leans back out of range, smothering the force of the blows and transmitting the strain to the ropes. The crowd wince at the barbaric spectacle. The little man seems hell-bent on committing suicide in the ring.

It goes on for nine more rounds. Enery metes out the punishment and Puggy soaks it up. By the end of their intimate confrontation, Puggy is whispering insults into Enery's ear, while his opponent is using his elbows and forearms to dig at his eyes.

Enery's Headspace: On and on and on and on. After the kill, the blooding. You can exhaust ten horses in one day; you can ride twenty women: even the Flanders Mare. You're charging through the bushes of Naboth's Vineyard. Soft, now! The young buck turns, his flanks dappled by sunlight. He blinks at you in recognition, breathes once . . . and escapes.

Puggy's Headspace: 'Snow Storm – Steam-Boat off a Harbour's Mouth Making Signals in Shallow Water, and Going by the Lead. The Author was in this Storm on the Night the Ariel Left Harwich.' It's time to get down to it. You know how to suffer. Just transmit the pain when you're lashed to the mast and wait for it to come back as art. They gave you a mop and a top hat when you came to the Temple of Isis to make the annual public sacrifice on Varnishing Day. Figured you'd clean the threshold with soapsuds and whitewash their crimes. Instead you rub their noses in it. You walk in with your earth-brown babies conceived in the brothels of Wapping. Then you stick the knife in and lay on the sugar in vermilions, chrome yellows and emerald greens. Amazing! They think you're some kind of magician. Either that or a charlatan. There's no getting off the hook. The runts of the Wapping litter you leave behind are labelled 'grossly obscene' by the Ukanian undertaker and destroyed. (Genius is in bad taste in any age.)

Enery sits on the stool in his corner as steam rises from his heaving body. His entourage are fighting among themselves over what he should do next. The 'Duke of Northumberland' emerges from the contest as his new trainer and begins shouting at the officials to disqualify Puggy from the ring because he has some kind of weak heart.

Enery is watching Perry Mandelson, the ringcard girl, strut her stuff in the ring. She is dressed in Agent Provocateur crotch-less knickers and high heels and plucks at the rings on her nipples for the amusement of the crowd. Enery smiles in a daze.

Manu's fingers dance over Puggy's bloated and swollen face, smearing Vaseline into his cheeks and attempting to repair his clotted eyes. The flesh has knotted into coarse ridges and trenches. He can no longer see. 'Old' Bill knows what to do. He gently removes Manu's hands from Puggy's face and gets out the Sheffield steel. 'Old' Bill used to work as a back-street barber. The razor flashes twice in the floodlights as he opens his son's eyes.

Enery's Headspace: Things are looking bad. The Franciscan pimp William Peto is cursing you from the pulpit at the place in Greenwich where you were baptised. The cunt is making a prophecy, says the dogs will lick your blood in the shell of Naboth's Vineyard. No matter. You walk out in a huff with your Jezebel in tow.

Puggy's Headspace: 'Regulus.' Your eyes are open. Now you are blind. Regulus returned as a marked man to Carthage and had his eyelids cut off. No more intermittent vision. You name your demon. Staring death in the face on the edge of abandon. The light is all free. The Temple of Isis will one day go bankrupt. The sun is your god.

Round 14 and Puggy returns to his haunt on the ropes. He lets Enery exhaust himself for two and a half minutes. He even lets him use his head. Enery is now a dozy mauling machine running on empty. He's trying to get away with murder in his usual way but no longer knows how.

With thirty seconds to go in the round, the little man comes off the ropes to chants of 'Puggy Bomaye!' from the crowd and begins to fight as if possessed by a demon. He bobs and weaves around the slow and tired Enery, stinging him with a succession of jabs while detonating hard rights against his temple. The big guy stumbles around as if lost in a trance, his white mouthguard dangling from fattened lips and his jaw puffy with damage.

Puggy carries chopping the rights down on his opponent's blocky head with his red eyes open wounds of glee. The crowd urge him to finish it. Puggy steps back from the butchery and a smile cracks his face. Enery is crouching and reeling. He's looking at the ref.

Puggy opens up with a slicing left hook. The impact on Enery's jaw knocks him off his feet. He lands flat on his back with his left wrist suspended over the middle rope. There is the twitch of a pulse and then nothing. The crowd howl. Puggy raises his arms.

Enery's Headspace: You never saw it coming. The impact is severe. The ritual breaking of spears at the barrier in Greenwich with the battered wives lined up in a vigil to protest. Your leg gives out, you topple, you fall. The planets are aligned, your blood is infected, the signs are all there in place. Blankness descends. 1491–1547. The space in between fails successfully to count. Your swollen remains tack up the Thames to the ruins of Naboth's Vineyard, while your wax effigy travels the highway in state. (Petit interregnum for prophets.) The king is dead, long live the king.

Puggy's Headspace: 'The Burning of the Houses of Lords and Commons, October 16, 1834.' It feels so good. You could party all night. Nine sketches and two canvases in total from that night on the Thames. You see it clearly. A vision of the Temple of Isis pitched into a bonfire.

There is pandeamonium in Syon House. Enery has been saved by the bell. His entourage clamber into the ring and drag his lifeless body over to their corner. Ruskin is tutting and fussing with his gloves.

Sick 'Boy' applies a heavy neck-brace to Enery's canting head and fits an oxygen mask to his nostrils and mouth while 'Northumberland' hurls invective at the cheap seats. Puggy slumps on his stool with a blank look on his face. He's taken too much heat in the middle rounds. His sight and his hearing are failing. An acute haematoma has formed on his brain.

Somewhere off in the darkness, Astarte is pleading with Yamm to concede. He shakes his head sternly. This time her intercession is ignored.

El sounds the bell for the final round to proceed.

It's a ghost dance. Enery's entourage are supporting his inanimate bulk on their bent shoulders and throwing punches by working his arms. Sick 'Boy' prances around directing their efforts. Puggy stands facing his puppet opponent. He fights in slow motion. The hooks and uppercuts are perfectly executed, but end up grazing thin air.

The crowd is frothing and barking. They're really getting their money's worth. A brain-damaged cripple is fighting a corpse!

Enery's Headspace: You're propped up. It's awful. Transgressions secured by a standing army of hate. Your man Cromwell always putting the fix in to cancel Naboth Vineyard's incest taboo. You have faith now you're late. It's a genuine conversion! Cut the jesses, let your fine birds soar free.

Puggy's Headspace: 'The Liber Studiorum.' The accuracy is there, but the timing is off. Slow descent into the fog of mental disease. Sir Joshua Reynolds slapping you on the back at the Academy Club in the Temple of Isis, handing round the brandy and cigars. Everything conspires in your favour. You've got the good marriage, the knighthood, the accent. Your pictures in the Royal Collection and your poems in print. You ease back and smile. You could have not been a contender. But now it's so late.

Ruskin is waving a dainty white handkerchief and holding his nose. He tries to step between the two somnambulant fighters but 'Northumberland' knees him in the balls. Ruskin hobbles from the ring clutching his groin with a look of outraged disgust on his face.

'Old' Bill is ripping up his son's contract with Gresham. He gets out his razor and eyes 'Northumberland' with a steady gaze. It's time to fight dirty. Manu restrains him and jumps into the ring. He's on his Nokia 9000 trying to get through to El. Puggy looks at him with a last spark of insight and goes into a spasm of jerking blinks. They make the connection. Manu nods; Puggy laughs.

What happens next takes the whole arena by surprise. Puggy feints his way out of the carnage, spins on his right leg and delivers a scything roundhouse kick into his opponent's distended gut. The blow has the force of a meat-cleaver. Puggy's shoe goes all the way in and punctures Enery's oesophagus. The rotting corpse explodes.

Syon House is deluged with a colossal fountain of blood. Waste organic matter seems to fall from the sky. The ringside supplicants hold up their hands and attempt to grab themselves a piece of the action as a souvenir. Enery's remaining entourage scavenge for tatters of flesh and cartilage to pelt at their victim. Puggy accepts the offensive tribute. He is licking his lips to taste his enemy's blood.

Enery's Headspace: Your decay rate facility has just reached critical. Too much pressure down from below. The unattended lead coffin adorned with your coat of arms flips its lid in the mortuary of Naboth's Vineyard. What looks like chaos is an act of creation. The sweet smell of butyric acid poisons the incense; a spurt of methane gas is ignited by the obsequial candles next to the altar; blood leaks to the floor.

Puggy's Headspace: 'Prophetic Vision of a Rotten Body Politic.' All bets are off. You've retrieved the missing page. It's time to close the book. You're painting the canvas with the blood of the victims of the Ukanian Combine. Scratching the bone black hard into place with your stiff Butcher's Broom. There's food for dogs in the lobby of the Temple of Isis, but it's no locked-room murder mystery. This funeral has mistaken the corpse.

El sounds the closing bell.

'Northumberland' is posing for the Babylon TV cameras in a victory crouch with Enery's femur raised over his head; Sick 'Boy' is smearing blood in his face.

Puggy wanders in circles through the yelping throng which now inhabits the ring. Manu leads him back to his corner; 'Old' Bill cuts the gloves from his wrists to reveal the stained white tape bandaging his knuckles.

It appears a close contest. It's clearly a slaughter. The Tate judges call it on the last round.

Judge 1 holds up his card. It reads 'Interior at Petworth.' He has Enery shaving it on points.

The rabble boo lustily from the cheap seats. The ringside trash politely applaud.

Judge 2 is nervous. His card reads: 'Study for the Sack of a

Great House?' He's hedged his bets and come out with an even-points draw.

There is an ominous silence.

Babylon TV Commentator #1: 'What are the odds on a split-decision, Johnny?'

Babylon TV Betting Clown: 'Search me. I don't understand this bit at all.'

Babylon TV Commentator #2: 'You're no fun, John.'

Judge #3 jumps up and waves his card about in a panic. It reads: 'The Apotheosis of Lord Egremont.' He's given it to Enery on a TKO.

The crowd begin to riot. Plastic seats and bottles and sharpened coins rain down through the air like missiles. The dinner guests grab hold of their purses and scoot, while the officials cower beneath any table they can find. The fighting spreads from the back of the arena to ringside as the class hatred ignites. There is the sound of breaking glass.

Babylon TV Commentator #1: 'There's anarchy in Ukania tonight, Reggie.'

Babylon TV Commentator #2: 'It's been a real sell-out performance, Ron.'

It's the day after the night before. The ceremony is over, history rewritten, the sun is . . . UP!

'Sir' Richard Gresham recalls all the assembled shades of the dead to Wardrobe Place bar one (cf. I Kings 21, 21). He slaps his back pocket and disappears.

El reaches down to the Thames, retrieves Astarte's fuck-me belt and graciously awards it to the victor.

Baal pokes his tongue out at Yamm. Astarte smiles and opens her legs.

El sends greetings to the nameless undead.

Aloha!

HOMICIDE

Robert Dellar

Trevor's job was selling drugs. He was particularly fond of pushing LSD. He was walking up Western Road towards Alice's flat in Palmeira Square.

Trevor spent his days exchanging substances for other people's welfare benefits, and hassling women who invariably didn't want to know. At any one time he had a hit list of a dozen or so chicks he'd unsuccessfully hassle for sex, often every day for months. Some had already taken out court injunctions against him, and Alice was thinking about doing the same.

Trevor's amorous attempts had always been handicapped by his being a big, ugly, fat, hairy bastard. This, combined with the utter lack of anything even slightly likeable about his character, made him every girl's worst nightmare. By now his futile efforts to get his end away had gone totally haywire. He'd convinced himself that, in spite of all the evidence to the contrary, he was actually God's gift to women. But because of unfortunate circumstances such as the repressive widespread popularity of monogamy, together with the peculiar obstinate blindness of the girls around him, this divine gift was never accepted. During occasional periods of insight, Trevor accepted his position in life and resorted to loitering outside the local day centre for adults with severe learning difficulties to find partners. But at the moment he thought he was irresistible. Trevor rang Alice's doorbell. She opened the door.

'Shit, it's you!' she cried. 'What the hell do you want, you fat bastard? I thought I told you never to come here again! Fuck off!'

Trevor thought he detected warmth in Alice's voice. Despite her hard-to-get exterior, she was about to become putty in his hands. His cock quivered at the thought of it.

'Any chance of me coming in for a cup of tea?' he asked, stroking his beard. 'It's cold out here.'

'Get lost!' shouted Alice angrily, disappearing behind the door as she slammed it, shutting Trevor safely outside.

Trevor stood on the step for half an hour banging the door and ringing the bell incessantly. Alice phoned the police, but they refused to come, explaining that it wasn't important enough. Eventually Trevor left, his bangs and rings unanswered. She fancies me really, he figured, I'll try again later on.

Ian and his pals lacked any sense of purpose in their lives. Born and bred in Brighton, they had once been prolific faces on the local social scene. But due to disillusionment and apathy they had long since dropped out of public sight. They lived in inertia and poverty. Ian often felt he had no control over his life. At other times, he felt he was protecting his inner self from the wicked world out there by refusing to have anything to do with it. Prodigious drug consumption helped to keep Ian autonomous and unique.

Ian climbed the stairs of the house he'd squatted with his mates. The basement was sealed off, separate, no doors or windows, completely trashed, a write-off. Ian lived in the rest of the building with Trevor, Arthur and Gavin.

In theory, Ian wanted to fuck anything that moved. In practice, if anyone tried to chat him up he'd get frightened and run away. Consequently his sex life was non-existent.

He walked into Arthur's room. Arthur was in bed, as usual, swigging from his bottle of fortified wine. It was late afternoon and his third bottle of the day, nothing unusual. Arthur didn't do a lot these days, just drank to keep at arm's length whatever it was that he didn't care to remember.

Ian looked around the room. What a shambles. The house hadn't been cleaned or tidied since they'd moved in. The condition of the place had actually got worse. Especially Arthur's room, the floor of which was carpeted with empty spirit bottles, fag and joint butts, torn rizla packets swimming in rancid puddles of warm beer, bits of old screwed-up newspaper, scraps of abandoned food decorated by green and blue fungus, betting slips, mouldy plates and cutlery, festering old clothes, syringes, bandages, piles of old vomit, anything unpleasant you can think of, you name it, there it was, sordid testimony to the depths of degeneracy that the quartet had reached.

Four decaying tramps moved from the bus shelter at Norfolk Square into the basement of Ian's house. They wore the same rags every day, didn't wash much, and spent their time begging, drinking Tennant's Super and getting forcibly ejected from the Social Security office. The basement was cold, it had large draughty holes where there should have been doors and windows. A heavy breeze sailed in from the back yard, which was neglected, overgrown, littered with empty beer cans and accessible only from the basement. The tramps started a fire in the middle of the floor and huddled around it for warmth.

'Have you met our new neighbours yet?' Arthur enquired. 'The basement! A gang of tramps are living there! A right bunch of losers, just like us, only older!'

'For fuck's sake,' Ian cursed bitterly.

Arthur had touched a nerve. For Ian, the idea of tramps in the basement was a worrying premonition of what the future might hold. His proximity to the vagrants disturbed him, distracting him from a pure perception of the present, the permanent today that made for a happy life. The tramps represented a potential tomorrow, and this made him feel uncomfortable, afraid that he was drifting dangerously close to the edge.

Karen, who lived at the summit of Southover Street, was next on Trevor's agenda for the evening. Southover Street took the pedestrian up a steep hill from the park, and by the time Trevor reached the top he was puffing and panting with exhaustion. He rapped on Karen's door percussively.

'Who is it?' she shouted from above, poking her head out of a window.

'It's me!' cried Trevor. 'Let us in, I'm desperate for a cup of tea!'

'Oh all right then,' said Karen, throwing down the keys.

She wondered what Trevor wanted. She'd met him briefly for the first time the previous night, and hadn't taken much notice of him except to observe how repulsively ugly he was and to buy some speed from him. She didn't realise that he'd followed her home and discovered where she lived. Assuming that he'd probably turn out to be harmless, Karen put the kettle on.

Trevor's head was buzzing with excitement at this obvious invitation to sexual intimacy as he caught the keys and let himself in. He bounced up the stairs and into the kitchen, where he put his arms around Karen's shoulders. Karen backed off, startled.

'Come on honey, you know you want me really,' said Trevor, starting to unbutton his shirt, exposing his rolls of flab. He'd seen a film star with a beard exactly like his get a result using these words and actions on telly the other day, so he knew he must be on to a winner.

'Leave it out, for fuck's sake, who do you think you are?' responded Karen, a little scared. 'My boyfriend will be back here any minute! Just get out before he turns up, yes?'

'If you lock the door from the inside, he won't be able to get in,' suggested Trevor helpfully as he continued unbuttoning. 'We'll have a swinging time by ourselves, just me and you.'

'Look, why don't you just fuck off! I don't know what the hell you think you're doing, coming here and behaving like this, if you ask me I reckon you need your fucking head examining! Go on, get out!'

Karen extracted a large saucepan from a kitchen cupboard and waved it at Trevor threateningly. She's getting excited, thought Trevor, she's a real tiger, and lucky me, she's all mine for the night. He moved closer to Karen and grabbed her arse. She whacked him with all her strength straight in the face with the saucepan. Trevor's nose started to dribble blood.

'Go on, you bastard, fuck off!' she screamed, bashing him over the head repeatedly.

Trevor ran down the stairs and out of the house, Karen hitting him a few more times on the way for good measure. As the door slammed behind him, Trevor remembered that Karen liked her chemical stimulants. A good opportunity here to make a few quid, he thought. He wasn't too proud to mix business with pleasure.

'Do you want to buy any more speed?' he shouted through the letterbox.

Karen smashed at the gap with her saucepan, shouting frenzied obscenities. She must be having a pretty bad comedown, thought Trevor as he wobbled down the hill, nursing his nosebleed.

The tramps were in a bad temper. It was freezing. They had no money, nothing to eat or drink, and the extra-strong lager from earlier in the day was wearing off. One of the down-and-outs, Jim, stood up. Then he fell down again. He picked himself up slowly, using the wall to help him keep his balance. Then he slid down the wall and ended up back on the floor. With great effort, he rose to his feet and this time stayed upright.

'Jesus Christ it's cold enough to freeze the balls off a brass monkey!' he shouted. 'Where's my fucking coat? Which of you fuckers has got it?' He looked around the room. He couldn't see it. It wasn't there. It had gone. 'Who's nicked my fucking coat then? Come on, I'll take the whole fucking lot of you bastards!'

He punched the air in front of him a few times clumsily,

and fell over. Then he rose once again and wandered out into the street.

Gavin was walking up the steps to the front door with a carrier bag full of beer and food. Jim approached him.

'You've got my fucking coat, you cunt! Give it back right now you bastard or else I'll fucking kill you!'

Gavin tried to explain politely that he didn't have the coat, but the tramp continued to spit abuse at him. Gavin opened the door, walked in and shut it behind him leaving Jim still on the step, ranting and waving his arms in the air.

'The fucking cocksucker won't give me my fucking coat back!' he complained. 'Jesus what a cunt! I'll have him, just you see! Fucking bastard! I'm going to get the fucker! Jesus!'

Gavin entered Arthur's room and shook the beer and food on to the floor. The three squatters dived into the pile, grabbing like animals at the cheese, bread, carrots and beer.

Gavin took a beer can, pulled off the ring, took a swig, rolled a fag, lit it, and inhaled deeply. He was thinking fondly about his girlfriend. A serial monogamist, Gavin usually had a chick to shag. The latest, Debbie, was a reliable source of pleasure. A warm shiver of heterosexuality perambulated up and down his spine.

Gavin had spent much of his adult life locked up in the local loony bin. He'd taken a few tabs of acid too many, and his ability to distinguish between fantasy and reality was often lacking. His relationship with Debbie had helped to settle him a little, but his brain was still rather wobbly.

Trevor wandered in, feeling the bumps and bruises over his face and shoulders, and trying to stop his nose from bleeding. The fat slob saw the others getting drunk, and decided to join in.

Just then there was a loud smashing of glass and a cry of 'You fucking bastard! I'm going to get you!' A glistening shower of shattered shards cascaded through the air like sparks of fire from a roman candle. It was Jim. He'd climbed up the drainpipe and bashed the glass out of Arthur's window with a lump of wood, and now he was leering menacingly into the room.

'Come and fight you cunts, I'll take the whole fucking lot of you! I'll teach you to take my fucking coat! Jesus! You cunts! Bastards! Cocksuckers!'

Ian rushed to the window and shoved the tramp off the drainpipe. Jim fell, landing in a bunch of stinging nettles. He hauled himself to his feet and went back to warm himself in the basement, gibbering and cursing angrily.

'Did you know they've got a fire going downstairs?' belched Gavin. 'It looks like a big fire to me!'

'You're fucking joking!' Ian shouted excitedly. 'Are they trying to set fire to the whole fucking building, or what? Let's sort those bastards out!'

Arthur, Trevor and Gavin were a bit surprised by the ferocity of Ian's hostility. Ian had always enjoyed a good blaze. In fact, he was one of the most famous arsonists in Brighton. Not long ago, he'd torched the quartet out of their previous squat. In a drunken psychosis he'd started a fire in his room by pouring petrol over his mattress, lighting it, and piling on anything inflammable that came to hand. The others had been out at the time. By the time the fire engines and cop cars arrived Ian had made himself scarce to escape the blame. Ian had justified his action with his present-centred philosophy. It seemed like a good idea at the time. Past and future didn't matter, they'd gone up in flames with the house. The other three hadn't spoken to him for a few days afterwards, but they'd made up since.

Ian was really into a good torching. He was drawn to fire hypnotically: it was akin to meditation. Ian was able to lose all sense of himself just by staring at the flames. So his mates were surprised by his outburst. They shouldn't have been. In the tramps' fire Ian saw a further reflection of himself, and felt drawn disconcertingly closer to their perilous and hopeless lifestyles. The tramps were taking the piss out of Ian by being so similar to him, and in their graceless old age they gave him an unwelcome glimpse of a possible future.

Arthur and Gavin tooled themselves up with planks of wood with nails sticking out of them. Trevor nervously picked up a screwdriver. Ian found a hammer. One by one they climbed out of the window and down the drainpipe into the back yard. They charged into the basement to confront the tramps, who were huddled motionlessly around the fire. One of them was asleep and snoring erratically. Ian kicked burning pieces of wood and newspaper at him and he woke up. Ian grabbed him by the collar of his filthy, lice-infested jacket and threw him into the fire. The other three tramps rose to their feet and surrounded Ian, but the four squatters laid into them instantly with boots, fists and weapons flying, and within a few seconds all four tramps were on the ground. During this exchange there was plenty of shouting, most of it consisting of unintelligible shrieks and wails which owed more to primal battle scenes than rational thought.

Things cooled off. The squatters stood brandishing their tools, waiting to see what the tramps would do next. Three of them rose cautiously to their feet and scuttled out of the basement. The fourth tramp, Jim, lay without moving on the cold concrete floor. A crumpled heap, looking as if someone had dropped him there, lifeless, from the ceiling, blood seeping apace from a fresh, gaping wound, an ugly red mess where his forehead met his hairline.

Ian dropped the hammer, rolled Jim over, picked him up, shook him a few times, and flung him back on to the floor. The blood kept oozing rapidly out of the gory indentation in his skull. The dosser wouldn't come to.

Ian gave him a few slaps on the cheek, then on the other cheek. He shook him again, threw him against the wall, and kicked him in the groin. Still the bastard refused to move.

The profuse flow of thick red liquid continued to gush, decorating the concrete with little pools of crimson. The squatters stood back. Jim wasn't breathing. No two ways about it, he was dead. A hammer sat beside him, its head stained bloody red.

The four convened in Arthur's room to decide what to do with the body. The surviving tramps would forget about Jim after a day or two. If they made a good job of the corpse disposal, nobody would ask any questions.

The fight had made them hungry again. Gavin produced a Bakewell tart and cut it into four slices, one each. While nobody was looking, Trevor surreptitiously sprinkled a few tabs of LSD on to Gavin's slice. Trevor calculated that the shock of being an accessory to murder, combined with a large dose of hallucinogenic chemicals, would transform Gavin into a full-time space cadet. He'd be locked up in the loony bin for ages. Trevor had designs on Debbie. With Gavin out of the way, he figured, Debbie would allow him to have his evil way with her. His cock started to stiffen at the thought of it. The four munched away on their slices, washing them down with beer. Trevor tried to suppress his laughter, inwardly congratulating himself for his cunning.

It was evening, the four were getting tired and drunk, and disposing of the corpse promised to keep them up much of the night. So Ian put a mirror flat on the floor, bought some speed from Trevor and cut it into six narrow lines. One by one Ian, Arthur and Gavin snorted a line up each nostril through a rolled-up five pound note. Trevor was abstaining.

Gavin's car was parked outside. The others needed his driving skills to get rid of the stiff. Trevor told the others he was going for a piss, went to his room, bundled together his stash of drugs and a selection of exotic novelty condoms, and slipped unnoticed into the twilight. He was going to Debbie's place.

The remaining squatters returned to the basement with two large bin-liners. Arthur held one of the bags open while Ian and Gavin lifted the stiff and stuck it in feet-first. They put the other bag over Jim's head so that as a whole, they hoped, he would be completely covered by the bin-liners. But there still seemed to be nowhere for his arms, which kept falling out. The three squatters tied them to the rest of his body with a length of rope. This seemed to do the trick. Stealthily, they carried the dead tramp away, eventually reaching the car. They looked around. Nobody about. They stuffed the tramp into the boot.

The plan was to take the tramp to the cliff tops at Seaford and chuck him over. That way, it would look like he had either topped himself deliberately or wandered over the edge by mistake. The three friends wondered what had happened to Trevor.

'The fat creep's run off and left us to deal with this mess by ourselves,' Ian spat. 'What a wanker.'

They drove off, with Gavin at the wheel. As he steered towards Seaford, his trip began to kick in. Daylight was fading away. Streetlights flickered on and beamed their artificial radiance into the darkening night. But the Sussex scenery seemed somehow brighter, its colours more vivid, its greens more green and pinks more pink than ever before. It was beautiful. It made him feel at one with mother nature. He reflected that he was just an insignificant part of the divine universal scheme of things, but nevertheless a child of this being, a unit of consciousness acting in relation to the rest of the world, which would be inconceivable in its present state without his existence. It all made perfect sense.

Gavin breathed the air around him, gripped the steering wheel and stared at the road ahead. It was all part of him, he realised. Him, the wheel, the road, the air and the dead tramp were all the same thing. The distinction between himself and the rest of the world was disintegrating.

The traffic lights ahead changed to red. Gavin reacted just in time to avoid crashing into the car in front.

*

Trevor rang the doorbell of Debbie's flat in Trafalgar Street. She answered it.

'Any chance of a cup of tea?' he asked.

'OK,' she replied, leading him to her kitchen. 'Have you seen Gavin? I was expecting him round tonight. I'm surprised he's not here yet.'

Trevor sniggered as he told her about the murder and Gavin's intended role in trying to cover it up.

'That's awful!' said Debbie. 'I hope they'll be all right!'

'Gavin probably won't be back tonight,' Trevor cooed. 'I guess that means you'll just have to use me as a sexual surrogate.'

He sidled over to Debbie, put his arm around her, and attempted to nibble her ear. In his excitement, he bit it fiercely by mistake. Debbie squeaked with pain and pushed Trevor away.

'What on earth's got into you? What the hell are you playing at?' Debbie fumed. She'd heard rumours about Trevor's furious and futile endeavours to get shagged, but assumed they must be grossly exaggerated and hadn't taken them very seriously. Trevor decided a fresh approach was required.

'Hey, Gavin looked a bit weird after the murder, you know, the shock of it, you could tell it had affected him. He's about to go off his head again, it's obvious. He'll get sectioned soon, definitely, so you can count him out for quite some time. You'll be much better off sticking with me.'

Trevor moved back towards Debbie and grabbed one of her tits. Debbie responded to this by hitting him powerfully in the mouth, following up with a punch in the eye, a knee in the groin, and finally a headbutt. Trevor went down, blood dripping from his nose, mouth and forehead.

'Get out right now, this minute, you bastard! Go on! Fuck off out of here before I kill you!'

Debbie kicked him in the stomach a few times as he lay squirming on the tiles like an obese injured earthworm. Things aren't going quite according to plan, the fat tosser reflected.

He hauled himself to his feet and slithered off. In the process of doing so he subtly slipped a sprinkling of acid into Debbie's tea. He figured that the heightened awareness engendered by the LSD would cure her insane blindness to his irresistibility. Bruised and battered, he scuttled out of the flat, planning to return after he'd given the acid time to work.

This is weird, thought Gavin as the trees overhanging the road began to twist and turn, a bright brown and green botanical ballet. A large catherine wheel of orange and blue sparks leapt across the car's path. Gavin figured that the car was not really a 'mineral' object. Animal, mineral and vegetable were no longer valid terms; they were all one in the sameness of nature. The car was alive. Gavin could feel it breathing in and out, its heart beating, the discharge of wind from its exhaust. It could see out of its headlights. Laser beams shot through the air; the road started to glow luminously, then to flash on and off in dazzling stroboscopic technicolour. Bangers began to explode everywhere, loud and still louder.

Suddenly, Gavin's life speeded up, and became like one of those old silent motion pictures made faster to render imperceptible the turnover of frames. The drum-machine of the car's heart accelerated until finally it turned into a loud, high-pitched buzzing. The car was whizzing through the streets faster than the speed of light, a supernova exploding towards Seaford. The bangers continued to explode, followed by land mines that went off all around without provocation. A volcano erupted sending a shower of bright silvery-blue droplets high into the air. Gavin crossed into another dimension. He was driving the car through a tunnel of blinding white light.

The road and the trees had gone. Gavin was the car's brain pumping signals through its body. The tunnel widened and finished, and the car shot out into space like a pellet from a peashooter, like a psychedelic interballistic missile from a rocket launcher, before turning into a gently floating bubble.

There was a moment of calm as the car hovered. It didn't

matter which way Gavin turned the steering wheel, the car had its own will, its own peaceful course which no force could deflect. Then an atom bomb exploded. The car came to a halt, sending the trio flying from their seats to bump their heads on the underside of the roof.

'You fucking idiot!' Ian shouted. 'You were only doing about thirty miles an hour, but you've gone and driven us into a fucking tree!'

The boot of the car flipped open and Jim's corpse rolled out on to the road, shedding its bin-liners. They were in Seaford, half a mile from the tallest cliff. They got out of the car. It was trashed. Smoke billowed from the smashed headlights.

'Its eyes!' Gavin burbled wastedly. 'It's gone blind! It can't see!'

'The idiot can't handle his speed,' Arthur cried. 'Now he's gone and written his fucking car off.'

'Well,' Ian howled, 'we can't leave this carcass here! Let's shift it!'

They lifted the corpse and chucked it into the bushes at the side of the road. The string binding its arms to its torso came loose and fell away in the process.

'Now what?' Arthur clamoured. 'If we leave the stiff here, someone will find it, and that could mean trouble. What's the score?'

'We'll carry it to the cliffs and throw it over,' Ian announced.

'But I need a drink. What am I going to do?' Arthur whimpered pathetically.

'I've got an idea,' Ian crowed. 'There's a nightclub near here, it's called Rumours and it's open till late, we should be able to get a drink there. We'll have to pay to get in and put up with a load of shite disco music, but we can have a few pints. We'll leave the body here, pick it up when we come back from the club, take it to the cliff and throw it over.'

'Sounds like a good idea to me,' Arthur confirmed.

Ian, Arthur and Gavin strode off towards Rumours. Gavin was finding it difficult to walk in a straight line. The other two jabbered away uncontrollably as the speed raced through their bodies. Gavin was thinking about the essential equivalence of all the different religions. How they all boiled down to the same thing in the end, the same important dates, symbols, patterns and ideas. He felt it was all leading to something. To Rumours. Rumours held the key to all existence.

While waiting for Debbie's acid to take effect, Trevor decided to give Alice another go. If she wasn't ready for it, fortunately he had Debbie to fall back on. But even if she was, he could still go and shag Debbie afterwards. A double bill, with Alice as the support act and Debbie headlining, would be the best of both worlds. He rubbed his groin in anticipation and an electric current ran through it. If a light bulb had been attached to the end of his cock it would have lit up. Trevor rang the bell and Alice opened the door.

'Bloody hell, it's you!' she said.

Trevor pulled the zip of his fly up and down excitedly, his face decorated red, black and blue with blood and bruises.

'That's right! It's me! I've come to give you a treat!'

He forced his way into the flat before Alice could shut him out and embraced her clumsily. Revolted, she pushed him away. She punched him in the stomach, produced a pair of scissors, pushed Trevor up against the wall, and then pointed the blades at his neck.

'If you come anywhere near me again,' she hissed bitterly, 'I'll fucking kill you! Get it?'

She pressed the blades closer to Trevor's throat so that he could feel the cold sharp metal. He was scared. He didn't like scissors. Alice directed him towards the street, staying poised to stab him in the jugular vein at the slightest false move. Confused, he left obediently and without hesitation. His flabby bulk dejectedly made its journey back to Debbie's.

Bouncers frisked the trio at the door of Rumours for lumps indicating hidden bottles and cans. Found clean, the three mates had their hands stamped in case of exit and subsequent readmission, and went straight to the bar.

They sat around a table with their glasses and listened to the computer pulse as it reverberated relentlessly, sending bright young things into hypnotic, trance-like states. Wacky samples and fizzing Star Wars noises lent the monotonous metronomic rhythm a tediously psychedelic angle.

Arthur's first pint didn't touch the sides and his second couldn't come too soon. He was pissed off. He was helping Ian to dispose of Jim's corpse not out of any sense of loyalty or responsibility towards his pals, but because there was nothing decent on telly.

Gavin sat, dazed, the pupils of his eyes dilating and contracting in time to the drum machine which he was at one with. Ian watched the dancers and decided that he liked the look of the local talent. He fancied one in particular, a blonde chick with a powerful approach to her grooving.

Ian ambled on to the dancefloor and started to boogie on down. He moved rhythmically across the floor, jiving eccentrically to the beat, gyrating gradually nearer towards the blonde. She noticed Ian's attention-seeking antics, and danced in his direction.

Immediately, the pair were bopping in unison. It was one of those no-holds-barred funky situations that discos tend to generate. The sulphate helped Ian to remember his repertoire of chat-up lines and improvise a few new ones. They seemed to be working. The blonde was captivated by his magical charm. Ian's mind filled itself with anticipatory visions of red-hot sexual ecstasy. Then he remembered that he couldn't pick up this girl, because a rather more urgent matter was in hand: Jim's corpse needed to be chucked over the cliff. Besides, now he thought about it maybe the blonde wasn't quite so attractive after all. Ian began to make his excuses.

'Hang on a minute,' the blonde objected. 'You can't lead me on like this and then just go. You've got me all excited, so you're coming home with me, right?'

She tugged firmly at Ian's sleeves to stop him escaping. He tried to pull himself off but she was far too strong for him. She drew Ian towards her and bit his neck suggestively.

Gavin was being pursued through the nightclub by a squadron of zombie paratroopers in Nazi SS gear cackling horrendously, decaying dead flesh hanging purple and putrid from grey bone faces. He threw himself head-first into a dense cluster of dancers to escape. Some ravers, knocked off their feet, attempted to keep balance by grabbing hold of the arms and shoulders of the people around them. This had a knock-on effect and dozens of bodies were dragged to the floor. Ian and his chick were buried beneath the heap of dance freaks. Ian used the confusion as an excuse to run away from the girl. He flew into the men's toilets and locked himself into a cubicle. The blonde got up and stood outside the gents waiting.

'You're not getting away from me that easily!' she shouted.

The dancers were all loved-up on ecstasy and happily forgave Gavin for knocking them over. Gavin zig-zagged from the dancefloor and looked for his seat. But where had it gone? And why were the walls and ceiling closing in to crush everyone? Quick! He ran out of the club into the street, skittling a few more groovers as he left. The road outside was slowly moving. The tarmac had dissolved into a calm sea, waves lapping gently towards a distant shore further up the street. Gavin paddled cautiously across, reaching the other side just in time as a tidal wave exploded violently behind him.

He walked up the road but the road was no longer there. It had been replaced by a world of Gavin's own making. A delirious, nightmare planet populated by intersecting networks of horrors and demons. He tripped over a branch, landing awkwardly in a thick carpet of thistles.

He scrambled, catching hold of something. It felt like a branch. But it had a shoe on. Gavin gave it a tug. The branch moved slightly, but it was heavy. He stood up, balanced himself, and pulled at the branch with both hands. It moved jerkily, displacing some of the leaves. He tugged again. A pair of arms appeared. It was Jim's corpse!

Gavin dropped the stiff in horror. In his tripped-out state he imagined the body was twitching. The head was visible, but the facial features were indistinct beneath the thick red mess congealing into an ugly mask of mixed mud, blood and foliage. Gavin gave the cadaver a gentle kick in the ribs. It moved a bit. It was alive!

Gavin understood the essential equivalence of life and death, and the ambivalence between the two within which both he and Jim were trapped. Death was dead, the murdered tramp was alive and coming to get Gavin, who wrestled with Jim, trying to fight him off. The deceased dosser was putting up a tough battle. Gavin throttled him defensively, holding Jim's neck in a tight grip. The dead bastard's tongue popped out amidst the profuse red flow now reactivated as Gavin fought for his life. It wagged from his mouth spraying a shower of blood over Gavin. Jim was erupting into brilliant, laughing profusions of colour, taunting and mockery.

Gavin recoiled into space. His imagination drifted into a seething abstract mist of fear and terror, with whistling feedback from hell screaming inside his brain. Gavin ran panic-stricken into the woods, repeatedly falling over, picking himself up and propelling himself desperately onwards.

Disheartened by his experience with Alice and the scissors, Trevor wandered through the streets of Brighton. His confidence wasn't shattered, just twisted out of shape.

He didn't get far before a gang of young women came out of Grubbs food bar eating chips. The girls looked real tasty. Trevor approached them, eyeing them up, mentally undressing them, calculating which one was his favourite. After a few seconds' thought he approached a particularly stunning brunette.

'Hey baby,' he said to her, feigning an American accent,

'what are you doing tonight? How about coming back to my place for a champagne breakfast?'

The gang giggled with a mixture of embarrassment and pity. She was amused, obviously impressed, thought Trevor.

'I'm not sure my boyfriend would be too pleased about that,' the brunette cackled. 'Come to think of it, I don't suppose I would either. Why don't you go and take a running jump off the pier?'

Trevor needed to do something very impressive to be sure of pulling the brunette. I know, he thought, I'll give her a brilliant display of my free-thinking intellectual genius, that'll do the trick. He jumped on to the bonnet of a parked car and gave them a speech, waving his hands in the air to illustrate his point.

'Monogamy is only there to suppress you, to stop you doing what you know you want to. It's the right and duty of all intelligent people in Brighton to liberate themselves from the evil clutches of this nasty tradition. And I'm right here to liberate you tonight, sweetheart.'

The car creaked and groaned, complaining about having to support Trevor's hideous hairy bulk. The girls laughed heartily. They couldn't believe it. Trevor took the laughter to mean that he was winning them over. They couldn't resist him. The bruises and dried blood all over his fat face gave him a kind of rugged, action-man appeal. It was incredible how cool he was. He had them spellbound. He couldn't possibly go wrong.

'How would you babes like to buy some acid?' he asked, producing a range of substances from his pockets. 'Speed? Dope? Mushrooms? Barbiturates? If you're looking for kicks, and I bet you are, then I'm your man in more ways than one.'

The babes' laughter became hysterical. As Trevor balanced precariously on the bonnet, a taxi drew up and the girls climbed into it, shutting the doors quickly behind them. Trevor jumped off the parked car and stood in the cab's path in an attempt to stop it pulling away. However, the experienced driver performed an impressive series of swerves and managed to get past him without running him over. As the taxi sped away, the chicks opened the windows and threw chips at Trevor.

To escape from the blonde, Ian climbed out of the cubicle window into a yard outside, hopped over a couple of fences, rounded the building and re-entered the club, the girl still waiting impatiently outside the gents. Trying to look invisible, Ian crept over to Arthur, who was busy knocking them back at his table.

'Finish your drink,' Ian hissed. 'We're leaving. Now.'

Arthur quickly drained his glass, muttering phrases of complaint. The pair left Rumours without the blonde noticing, and staggered to the spot where they'd left Jim. It was dark, but Ian could see that the corpse had been disturbed: it was bloodier, its tongue was hanging out limply, and its arms were in a different position. Must be wild animals, thought Ian.

They picked Jim up, Arthur carrying the arms, Ian the legs. Together they struggled through the woods towards the cliff top. Jim was heavy, and Arthur, who was completely pissed, kept dropping the arms. He'd retrieve them, fight on for a few yards, then lose hold again. But after a seemingly endless journey they reached the other side of the woods and stood facing a golf course.

'That's it, I'm done in,' Arthur croaked. He fell to the ground, produced a fag, lit it, and sucked eagerly. 'I'm finished, I can't go on any further. I'm going to smoke this cigarette, then I'm falling asleep right here.'

'But we've got to get this tramp over the cliff and leave town while it's still dark, man,' Ian reasoned, 'otherwise our chances of getting caught are greater.'

'Don't forget, Gavin fucked the car,' Arthur snapped. 'How the hell are we going to get back to Brighton tonight? It's impossible.'

Two houses stood at the top of the cliffs. Ian knew they were empty. They were holiday homes, he'd burgled one of them in the past, their owners lived in Hampstead and left them derelict for most of the year. Arthur was falling asleep and starting to snore.

'Hey Arthur,' Ian whispered gently. 'There's a drinks cabinet in one of those houses over there. Gin. Vodka. Rum. Brandy. Scotch. Bourbon. Plenty of beer and wine – and it's all ours! If we can manage this final stretch, we'll stay overnight at the house, drink all the booze we can, and take the rest back to Brighton with us tomorrow. After we've chucked this corpse over the cliff, of course.'

The mention of alcohol was more than enough to rouse Arthur from his slumber. He was wide awake and buzzing with vitality and vigour. He stretched out his arms horizontally and jumped up and down on the spot a few times.

'OK, let's move it!' he sang happily, picking up the arms of the dead body.

Halfway across the golf course, the tension became too much for Arthur, who dropped his half of the corpse and ran towards the holiday homes, delighted at the prospect of more alcohol. He didn't know which of the houses had the drink, so he tried the nearest one first. A garden gnome and an old shoe were conveniently lying nearby. He hurled the gnome through the kitchen window, sending a sparkling shower of shattered glass high and wide. After knocking out the jagged remains of the pane with the shoe, he climbed through the empty frame and searched for the booze.

Ian lifted Jim by the wrists and dragged him towards the houses. It was hard work. By the time Ian reached the holiday homes Arthur had abandoned his fruitless search for booze in the first one, and was about to chuck a potted plant through the sitting room window of the second.

'No need to do that,' Ian hollered, 'I found a front door key when I burgled the place.'

He inserted the key into the lock, and it worked. There were enough bottles inside to make Arthur's eyes light up with glee.

'In a few minutes' time, we'll drink this lot,' Ian promised his mate, 'but first, let's get this fucking tramp over the cliff.'

They dragged Jim to the edge of the cliff. Arthur was only using one hand as the other was clutching a bottle of rum. They could hear the waves crashing menacingly against the rocks below.

Arthur put his bottle down and gripped Jim's wrists firmly. Ian took the ankles. They swung the stiff once towards the drop then back in the other direction. A second swing, then back again, the growing momentum of the bodyweight increasing the size of the arc and the speed of the movement. The third motion and then back in reverse, and the dead tramp was swinging high above the heads of the squatters. It was good fun. A fourth swing, and the pair let go of the tramp. He shot up into the air before plummeting lifelessly down, bumping into the side of the cliff a few times on the way, and landing bone-shatteringly on a rock sticking out of the sea. The waves pushed him off the rock, and the tide drew the cadaver towards, then away from the vertical cliff face. Suddenly there was lightning, then thunder, followed by torrential rain.

Had they been less preoccupied with their task, Ian and Arthur would have noticed the dishevelled figure of Gavin coming to rest and curling into a foetal position beside the cliff top a few hundred yards away. It was just as well that the space cadet's body had decided it had had enough for the day. If he had stumbled on any further, he'd have fallen over the edge of the cliff.

'Hey, Arthur,' said Ian.

'What?' Arthur replied.

Ian grabbed Arthur by the shoulders and gave him a mighty shove in the direction of the precipice. An expression of surprise was briefly visible on Arthur's face, replaced by horror as he fell backwards over the edge of the cliff. Somehow he managed to get a grip on the turf overhanging the brink and tried desperately to haul himself back up. But Ian wasn't having any of it. He picked up the abandoned bottle of rum and bashed Arthur's hands and head with it repeatedly. Still Arthur held on, shouting and shrieking barely intelligible curses and pleas. The earth was crumbling away inauspiciously, and the heavy rainfall was making everything slippery. Laughing, Ian delivered Arthur a particularly devastating blow, managing to smash the bottle of rum against Arthur's face and sending a shower of broken glass over the cliff. Arthur's face streamed with blood and rum. He kicked the vertical face of the cliff a few times, frantically trying to establish a foothold. It was useless. He fell with a scream and a splash, joining Jim in the cold liquid grave of the deep blue sea.

Trevor stood on Debbie's doorstep with a bulging hard-on in his trousers. It had started to piss down with rain. He rang the bell, put his hands in his pockets and started playing with himself. He couldn't wait for the sexual gymnastics that lay ahead with Debbie on acid.

Debbie got a knitting needle and crept downstairs. The acid had activated hitherto suppressed violent and paranoic character traits. She held the thin sharp point behind her back and opened the door.

'Hello, it's me!' shouted Trevor, clearly in a jolly frame of mind, his face still bruised and bloody from the beatings he had already received over the past few hours. 'Aren't you going to let me in, then?'

Debbie stood aside, allowing Trevor to walk past, ruffling her hair as he went. She followed Trevor for a few paces before plunging the knitting needle deep into his back.

Time slowed down. Trevor could sense that something was wrong, but he wasn't sure what. Then he saw the point of the needle sticking out of his fat chest, blood dripping from it. Debbie's eyes lit up with sadistic glee. It was a perfect hit!

Trevor gurgled as the crimson liquid rapidly stained his shirt. He fell to his knees. Go on, you bastard, thought Debbie, don't drag it out, just die right now! Then her concentration strayed.

She tried to remember what she was meant to be doing, but she was lost, she couldn't figure it out. She went to the kitchen, decided to make a cup of tea, put the kettle on, then forgot all about it and sat staring at the shifting colourful patterns on the ceiling. Trevor withdrew the knitting needle from his torso and lurched out of the flat and along to the taxi rank, where he found a cab to take him to hospital.

The needle had missed Trevor's most vital organs, but still, he didn't like being stabbed. He'd tell the hospital that he'd been stabbed by mistake, refusing to divulge any further information. After all, it must have been some kind of a misunderstanding. His pride wouldn't let him admit that his amorous advances had been rejected. The dividing line between love and hate was very thin. Debbie had already demonstrated the hate side of her feelings towards Trevor, so obviously the love part would come next.

Ian walked back into the cottage, poured himself a large Scotch, and thought carefully about how to stay out of jail. It was Arthur who had hit Jim with the hammer, he decided. Trevor and Gavin could easily be persuaded to go along with the story, and Arthur wasn't around to argue. Arthur had been grief-stricken, unable to live with himself as a murderer, and had thrown himself over the cliff in despair. Ian had tried to stop him, but Arthur wouldn't listen and had even masochistically smashed a bottle in his own face before topping himself. Ian would worry about the other loose ends tomorrow.

He thought about what he'd done to Arthur. It was well out of order, wasting his mate. But on the other hand, it was just so funny. He couldn't stop laughing.

Ian looked down at his clothes, which were stained by Jim's blood. Ian finished his Scotch and poured himself an even larger one. He went into a bedroom, opened a wardrobe, and found plenty of clothes his size. He'd change into a new outfit and burn the one he was wearing before making his way back to Brighton. That should be a laugh, he thought, I like fires.

A lack of sleep combined with the speed and alcohol made Ian's actions imprecise, and it took him a long time to remove his clothes. He started with his tall black top hat, which miraculously had remained on top of his head during the entire night. His high-heeled purple leather boots, laced up to the knees, were next, followed by his furry leopard-skin trousers. Ian had always dressed flamboyantly. He took off his parka, the mod target on its back stained black and red with blood and soil. Then he removed his black velvet waistcoat, white dress-shirt and pink bow-tie with black polka dots, and stepped into the new outfit. It was a perfect fit – spot on. Ian plucked his glass eye out of its socket, polished it with a handkerchief, and popped it back in again.

Ian went back into the lounge, threw his old gear into the fireplace, tipped a bottle of brandy over it, lit a match and set it all alight. The brandy flared up, a beautiful display of orange-blue flame, but it soon went out, and the clothes had failed to catch fire.

Ian searched the cottage and found a bottle of paraffin. He poured it over the clothes, struck another light and chucked it into the fireplace. Flames shot through the room, consuming not only the blood-drenched garments but also the carpet and wall around them. It was fucking great. Ian watched the growing blaze, fascinated. He wondered what else in the cottage was inflammable. He picked up a table and lobbed it on to the fire, cackling hysterically. He took all the paintings from the walls and books from the shelves and threw them in. They went up immediately. Armchairs and settees were next, then Ian had to leave the room and watch from the hall outside. A thick black cloud of toxic fumes billowed from the burning furniture. Ian stared, hypnotised, feeling a little tired. The stench struck Ian as unpleasant, and he thought about watching the rapidly-growing blaze from outside. Then the booze got the better of him and he fell asleep.

The fire spread from the first house to the second, torching both buildings. It was hot, orange and spectacular, sending dense smoke spiralling high into the sky. No living creature could possibly have survived such a conflagration.

It was daylight when Gavin awoke. The light was brighter than ever before, the wet grass and clear blue sky were both oppressively fluorescent. Gavin tried to remember what had happened the previous night, and how he had ended up beside a strange cliff. He couldn't remember anything since leaving Brighton with his mates and the dead tramp.

Disturbingly, his mind kept threatening to drift off into a world of resemblances, conspiracy theories and mysticism. He needed all his powers of concentration to stay in the real world. If he could get back to Brighton, maybe he could stay sane.

Gavin started to walk inland. He thought about Debbie, a firm anchor for him. If he could make it to Debbie's in one piece, he would be all right. With difficulty, he concentrated on his fond feelings towards Debbie.

He reached Seaford High Street. He couldn't even remember being in Seaford, it was all a blank. A mystical explanation for his predicament came into his head. Gavin tried to fend it off by thinking about Debbie.

He reached the train station, bought a ticket, and sat on the platform waiting for the Brighton service. A struggle was taking place in his brain. He went to the station bookstall to buy some fags and something trivial to read. He chose the *Sun*.

He opened the paper and started to read a feature about freemasonry amongst lawyers. Then it clicked. Debbie, Ian, Arthur and the dead tramp were all part of a masonic conspiracy!

The grand masonic castle, he remembered, was in Hastings. A train drew up on the opposite platform. By way of an astonishing synchronicity, it was heading straight for Hastings, obviously so that he could visit the castle and learn all about the secrets of love, pain, fear, sex and death. Gavin shot over the footbridge and jumped on to the train. The masonic castle would surely contain the answers to everything.

THERE WERE TEETH

M. Stasiak

There were teeth. There were sharp teeth everywhere the day they hung the two nine-year-olds. And in the Jolly Farmer's, where I talked to my friend Michael at lunchtime, men and women looked over at me every time I swore. I'd done it more than once, because it had been a bad day for me too.

But I'd filled my quota. That was what Michael said to me, as I drew liquid shapes on the heavily-varnished tabletop. He swept the spilled beer on to the floor with a cardboard mat and said, 'You filled your quota. You must have filled it for the next few weeks.' It was true. It was more than true. Those two boys had earned me several weeks' holiday and a bonus and all the rest. Thanks to them I'd finally been able to tick that far right-hand box, put a blue biro x next to where it said 'evil', and their bodies were probably cooling somewhere right this minute. 'Take off somewhere,' said Michael as he handed me my coat and held the door.

Back in the office they gave me the afternoon off. And they actually did pat me on the back. They told me to go home and watch the execution on the TV. And don't worry about coming in tomorrow. Sleep late. Enjoy it. You done good.

You could say it was a public relations coup for us at the Declarator's Office. Declaring that one incident wiped out the moral deficit of our whole region and sent the computer graphic soaring into the golden yellow fields of rectitude. After I had first keyed in that monstrous calculation, and my supervisor and the other declarators had watched the display adjust itself to its new shining level, I sat on my own and hit the codes for minor blasphemy and bad language until my fingers hurt. The yellow field hardly shifted. But still, as I walked home through the crowded town centre, I saw teeth.

It was a relief to get to my flat and shut the door behind me, take off my office shoes. I made myself lunch and sat down with it in the kitchen. I had a little television in there, but I didn't want to watch it, so I just listened to the fridge humming. That was OK for a while. But then as I was leaning with one elbow on the table, chewing a mouthful of potato salad and regretting the beer I'd drunk, it suddenly stopped humming and somehow I was really stuck then. I went into the next room and watched tree branches instead, all afternoon.

And the next day too. Somehow I just couldn't go in any more. I sat in my house staring and the office kept right on paying me. I got a local award for being a force for good; the office got a national one. They wrote and told me these things, and as I pulled that headed notepaper out of the envelope and looked at their charts it reminded me horribly of the first time I ever worked in one of those offices, the two-week induction course in my specially-bought glad-to-have-a-job-at-last suit. They had showed us the social axes of good and evil and told us how they were set. They explained how rooting out and Declaring all the varied shades of adult and juvenile immorality added up to a public good. They trained us on the computers to calculate the weighting of any given piece of anti-social behaviour. They showed us the inter-office competition. They explained the bonus scheme. It was a very well-established institution. There was no problem.

And from my room and the kitchen table I could see the country as a chequerboard of overlapping emotions; horror and hysteria sticking each other in an intricate maze of paranoia, punishment and fear. I could see the Declarator's Offices snatching greedy little mouthfuls of wrongdoing and smelting them down into medals and certificates. All that condemnation and anger bounding up and down the country. It rippled through my living room too and I'd gotten into a bit of a grim state when Michael next turned up on my doorstep and dragged me off down the pub. I was rather relieved to see him.

He, as always, fetched the drinks, while I waited in a corner. No one this time took much notice, though a couple of blokes looked the leather jacket up and down. They turned away when Michael returned. He started to talk in his convincing voice. Maybe he'd just been in the job longer than me, and had turned the official explanations into personal ones that still never left the system. He knew I was feeling bad about the two boys, right? And I was worrying about feeling bad? But feeling bad just showed how important my job was. And I was so naive to expect the doing of good to feel good. He said the good was good because it *was* good, not because it *felt* good. I smiled in spite of myself at all these goods. I thought he was being really hard on me.

We drank some more, and he got angrier and kinder. I listened with my head down, staring at the floral carpet. His words turned into a wash, just as I'd envisioned the wash of emotions up and down the country, and I began to appreciate what he was trying to say. It was one of the biggest assets we had, evil, the committing and condemning of it. I thought of all the people who had jobs in the industry, of the endless amount of taxes people were prepared to shell out to keep our moral defences intact, of the energy and enthusiasm of our unpaid informants. The Evil Act, Its Committing and Condemning. And the Great Social Good. Predicated on evil, but producing good. Now wasn't that a miracle?

I realised I was a bit drunk. I told Michael to shut up, because I couldn't concentrate any more and I wanted to go home. He laughed and said excellent, and shall I tell them in the office you want to work freelance for a while? I said yes and made for the door.

A couple of days later a thick envelope of blank report forms landed on my doormat. I knew what they were and I didn't open the package, but put it under the table in the dining room. But it disturbed me every time I went past the door, so I eventually tore the brown paper off and put the forms at the bottom of a pile of things on my desk, which didn't really work either. I went for a lot of walks in the emptiest places I could find and wondered back at my enthusiasm when I'd first started the job. I decided it had had a lot to do with regular payments of money.

All this was really getting me down, so when the child came to me and offered to sell me a piece of evil she had dreamed up, there was something so logical about the proposition that I invited her in off the front step and listened.

Her name was Billy, and she was the child of one of my colleagues in the Declarator's Office. Her mother must have told her how well I'd done with the two boys; she would have shared in the bonuses that followed. Billy didn't want to be a Declarator's child any more. She had been friends of the two boys from school and worried she might have said something which pointed them up as worthy of attention. She said there was too much pressure at home and she constantly felt used for information. I told her we had adult informants and didn't use children. I asked her why she had come to me for help, since I was a Declarator too, and now very well-known. That was it, she said, I was good, wasn't I, officially? And she knew I hadn't been in to the office for a while.

She wanted to kill her brother. She said it was a shame it had to be him, but she couldn't think of another person who would be as easy to kill and as terrible. She said she needed a crime of a certain magnitude to make the pay-off in bonuses and awards sufficient. Sufficient for what? I asked. But she kept on telling me her plan. She wouldn't hang for this offence herself. She was going to turn her mother in. She thought the murder of a child, the murderer being a Declarator, revulsion at the remaining child turning in her only parent, would all add up to such a high rating that the person who Declared it would be even more of a hero than I had been. With even more money. I asked her again where I came into it, and why she wanted money. I wanted to fault her ideas too, but my brain was cloudy from all the grades and graphs and files they kept sending me from work. I guess she appealed to my professional, *calculating*, instincts.

She said she needed me to go away with, after. We could go somewhere far away, where the population was thin and she could be as bad or good as she wanted, and I could neglect her or care for her as I wanted and we'd basically leave each other alone.

I thought she had an appalling grasp of how society worked. *She* thought she could make a good case for my present lifestyle being wicked, that in abandoning my duties as a moral arbiter I was making the world that much of a worse place to be than it was already, and *that*, we both were fully aware, was a medium-sized misdemeanour, fitting of punishment. She'd tell her mother, and her mother would Declare me.

It was a pathetic attempt at blackmail, and I sent her home.

That encounter jolted me a little. Something really was wrong and maybe the best I could do was something like my job. I spent a lot of time down at the Jolly Farmer's in the next few weeks, listening to their conversations, turning the bastards in. I sent in small bundles of reports, lack of respect to people in authority, bad language, half-a-dozen impolitenesses. I think the biggest thing I dealt with in all that time was an attempt at drink-driving. Until Billy came back, and said she'd done it.

She came in the early morning, when I was still wandering about in the grey half-awake light. I let her in and told her to sit while I finished getting dressed; I had a bad feeling about hearing whatever it was she'd come to say. She told me as I cooked breakfast for her and said I should make up my mind quickly whether I wanted to Declare it or not. She didn't really care any more, since she'd be free of her mother either way. I didn't ask how she'd done it, or what exactly she'd done; what I did ask was how she knew she'd get away with framing her mother. She shrugged and said she would, then added that it wouldn't matter to me anyway. My pay-off would be as big for the truth as for her version of things. The child didn't even need to be sarcastic.

I fed her and straightened her clothes and sent her to school, telling her not to contact me.

Then I dug out my security card and went into the office and Declared it. I find I have nothing to say on the subject of why I did this. No one ever asks. I was the hero again, the battler for morality against the tides of disrespect and depravity that threatened us all. They liked it when Billy's mother was convicted and when I took the child. I had credentials. I would ensure she knew what evil was all about and its consequences. Well I had no worries about that. The girl knew.

We got a train to the north, the far far north. There were sheep and cows and birds. There was Billy smiling out of the side of the carriage. There was money in my account and more in my bag. There were still teeth.

TIME'S UP

Ian Trowell

Dean slumped into the blue swivel chair and steeled himself against the Restart Officer's gaze. The floor was done out in fake pine. Patronising 'Claimant's Charter' notices were plastered on to every pillar, but the real business was revealed in the posters and leaflets urging you to join this scheme or that job club. No matter how they decked the place out it could only ever be a pressurised shithole, if only they'd switch the fuckin' heaters off sometimes . . .

'So, how many jobs a week, approximately, are you applying for Mr Sutton?'

'Erm . . . about four or five.'

'And where do you look for these vacancies?'

'Newspapers, local and national ones, job centres, the council job shop . . .'

'Do you know how many vacancies are actually advertised when they arrive?'

'I dunno, most of them, I should think . . .'

'Actually it's less than one third, employers know they can fill posts without having to advertise.'

'Oh.'

'What I'm saying to you, Mr Sutton, is this, we need to see you applying for 60–70 jobs a week. Can you guarantee this?'

'Well, yes, I suppose . . .'

'And where will you find these vacancies?'

'I dunno . . . if they don't advertise . . . I dunno . . .'

'Job Club gets notice of all these vacancies, and can help

you assemble a CV, then have it forwarded to prospective employers. Have you considered Job Club? Would you be willing to give it a try . . .?'

'Well, I'm not sure. I suppose so,' Dean replied, his head dropping.

Dean heard a sharp click and looked up suddenly. The open-plan floor had contracted to the size of a small cell, the four walls cold and white. The pine desk scattered with leaflets and stationery was now a blank table. A second click interrupted the silence as the Restart Officer pressed the eject button and flipped the cassette out. He patted the plastic tape smugly.

'Thank you Mr Sutton, we have all we need.'

Dean was back at the police station as a result of his extremely brief and unspectacular foray into shoplifting. Yet it wasn't a police officer he faced, it was definitely a Restart Officer with his Benefits Agency ID badge on. And the heat still persisted, the heat . . .

The buzzer alarm woke Dean up at 8.00 a.m. dead on. He was sweating badly. That same bastard nightmare again and again. He reached for the glass of water positioned on his bedside drawer. His hand was shaking.

In the neighbouring house, Bill Braun was having a much sweeter dream, though certainly no less intense. He was back in Cheedale working his route with a flowing perfection previously unseen in the world of climbing – a combination of balance, strength, stamina and agility. The particular area of rock he was working on he had named Baudrillard Buttress. It had been left untouched throughout the 70s and 80s as the crag had been feverishly developed. The radical nature of the sustained overhang had frightened off all potential customers. Bill had been bolting routes on the crag for two years, beginning with a line that had stunned the climbing world . . . *In the Shadow of the Silent Majorities*. It had taken him over a year to train for this line, and it was still unrepeated for a clean ascent. The only other line on the buttress was *The Revenge of the Crystal*, also put up by Bill and mockingly named as such when one of his fiercest rivals had tried to nip in and steal the line only to be foiled by a large crystal finger pinch snapping off near the top bolt. After a further year of training, Bill was the only one attempting a third line and he had a name ready. It would be called *Fatal Strategies*. All that remained were the final few moves, and it was this sequence that provided the sweetness of his dream.

The alarm clock buzzing in the terrace adjoining Bill's bedroom woke him up. He rolled over and his only thought was to expel a large glob of spit in his throat and then concentrate on pulling the moves from his dream into his current thought-pattern, to use on the crag. He picked up a sheet of paper from the scrap pile on his desk. It was a cheaply produced leaflet on how to survive a Restart interview, put together by some dumb anarchists from the capital. What a waste of effort he thought, anyone with two brain cells to rub together could cruise through a Restart interview. The leaflet pleaded for the recipient to photocopy it and hand out copies near the benefits office. Bill carefully spat the greenie on to the paper, screwed it up and threw it into the bin. Now he needed a glass of orange juice to clear the speed from his system. This would have to be done before he began his stretching and preparation for his next attempt on the route.

He also needed to check the morning's post. He was expecting a book to review for his Situationist magazine *Insufficient*, as well as his usual supply of exchange magazines, flyers, rants and artworks as contributions for the next issue. Most of this went into Bill's personal library. Bill often talked about the Information War, and about getting actively involved in this war, but what Bill really liked was looking at his impressive library of texts and thinking about all the theory stacked up in there. The aura it gave off was intense. It was needed for when Bill sat down and wrote articles for *Insufficient*. Bill's magazine gave him a chance to have a rant about things, or to have a rant at people and organisations in the revolutionary milieu. It also meant he received free magazines and books to add to his expanding library.

He swilled the orange juice around his mouth and scanned his desk. Shit, he thought, and grimaced, as he looked at the scrawled A4 sheet in front of him. He had this habit of writing stuff when he was speeding, and most of it was bullshit. However, it was normally clever bullshit that was doubly unintelligible. And it was this type of stuff that could fill out an issue of *Insufficient*. No-one really complained, since the advent of the 'Art Strike' there'd been more unintelligible bullshit around than ever before. But the stuff on Bill's desk was unusable for sure. As a Situationist Bill liked to switch words around to create new meanings, to detourn rhetoric to produce anti-rhetoric. 'The meaning of change can be seen in a change of meaning' was what *Insufficient* proclaimed on its masthead. But a lengthy rant on the history of dustbins and the dustbin of history was stretching the point too far. Bill's mind returned to more immediate concerns, his attempt at the new route and the post which had not yet arrived. He was expecting this book to review, and also a cheque from his mum. Where was that bleedin' postman?

At 8.00 Steve was just starting the 100 or so houses on Capital Boulevard. He was already half an hour late, mainly because he'd a sackful of Poll Tax final demands to deliver. It wasn't the extra mail that was the problem, it was that Steve knew many of the people on his round, most of them old folks, and he had made an effort to cheer them up. Most of them were shaken by the official sounding letter from the council in their last desperate bid to recover this ill-forsaken tax, and so Steve tried to calm people down by explaining that they were not alone, and telling them about the local anti-Poll Tax groups in the area. It was only really making the most of a bad deal. Steve took the job as a postie because he was strapped for cash, he was being pressed to meet an oncoming deadline to renew his United season ticket and had debts to attend to. He'd imagined that being a postman would be an unintimidating job, and he'd have a bit of time to think for himself and get to know people. It was days like these he felt like jacking it all in, either that or just ripping all these bills and demands into shreds. He couldn't see himself as anything other than the lowest-ranking foot soldier in some huge oppressive army waging a war for capitalism. On top of this he had a new financial crisis to worry about . . . Someone had nicked his lad's mountain bike from outside the central library and he would have to fork out and replace it. His son depended on the bike for getting to college and doing his paper round. He'd only gone in to return some books but staff cutbacks had meant that one person was left attending a whole floor and a long wait for any service was inevitable. This had given the thief ample time to spot the bike, wait for an opportune moment, and then make a getaway.

He tried to push these thoughts aside as he moved down the street from house to house. As usual there was a clutch of letters for number 23, plenty of odd-shaped envelopes adorned with various slogans and stickers. Steve never took much notice of them, he didn't have much time for art, but he had seen the chap who lived at number 23 and knew he was an arrogant bastard. A typical artist type. As he began pushing the assortment of letters through the horizontal slot he heard the muttered words 'About fucking time!'. Steve's muscles froze and angry words formed a lump in his throat, ready to perform a vocal concerto as he battered the door down. But, he thought, what's the point, and let his anger subside. Halfway down the path he remembered that there was an outsize package for number 23, kept in a separate bag with other large or fragile deliveries. He paused and withdrew the parcel. It was a big jiffy bag containing a book, with a multitude of repetitive stickers covering every available space on the envelope. It couldn't fail to catch your attention. NEVER WORK EVER the simple message said in its playful mocking tones. This was the final straw. Steve thought about his shitty job and the fact that his son had been getting up at six every morning to do a paper round to buy a bike that had now been stolen. Steve wondered what to do with the package when the door to number 25 flew open and a miserable-looking bloke stumbled out clutching a plastic bag. Even though the geezer looked like he'd had enough at this early hour, he still managed to greet Steve with a smile and a pleasant hello.

'Oh hi, anything for me in that bag?' asked Dean.

'Only this,' Steve replied, instinctively handing him the package that should have been delivered to 23.

The bloke brightened up immediately and slipped the parcel into his carrier bag without pausing to examine it.

'Thanks, got to go or I'll miss my bus.'

Steve felt better already. The brat at number 23 would probably get his parcel in the end, but not until this evening. And it could be put down to a genuine mistake.

Dean headed for the bus stop on the next street at a furious pace. The plastic carrier bag banged against his thigh, but he'd already forgotten about the mystery package. Instead his mind kept going back to his nightmare. The Restart interview sequence was pretty much as it occurred in reality, however at the time Dean thought that Job Club would be okay as an option . . . better than going on a scheme or pretending to be setting yourself up in pine stripping on the Enterprise Allowance. And anyway, it would serve to take away some of the heat that he had been getting from the Claimants Officers. But Job Club had been a calamity. Two weeks of piss-boring lectures on how to fill in application forms, and then an endless pile of really shitty vacancies thrust in front of you. He'd ended up with the shittiest job of the lot, working on the production line at a factory that made climbing equipment. He worked the machine that stitched together the slings used by climbers.

The boredom of the job was intense, and Dean could see no reason why people would want to climb anyway. It was a sport designed for yuppies who wanted to appear outrageous and daring. However, there was all types of hell at the factory this week, as the company had just landed a contract with a bunch of television people producing a series called *Warriors*. The company had given all their workers a letter exclaiming their great joy in landing such a contract, which was for a whole load of karabiners, clips, slings etc. to be used in the series, which apparently featured men and women swinging around on ropes in combat, and sprinting up climbing walls with muscle-bound gorillas in hot pursuit. All the workers were asked to put in extra hours at short notice, to make up this express order as quickly as possible. But the company had to be careful, a similar situation four years ago had nearly resulted in closure. An order of karabiners for a wacky stunt on a late-night TV show, where a man was suspended upside down in a large box from the end of a crane, had been rushed through the factory without being safety-checked. When the pin failed in the vital karabiners holding our poor sucker fifty foot above a concrete car park at Channel 9, all hell broke loose . . .

The bus arrived and Dean settled down for the journey. The job was bad enough and there was a bastard hour-long bus ride to top it off. He heaved his carrier on to his lap and then remembered the mystery package. He fumbled in the bag. The envelope was covered with stickers proclaiming NEVER WORK EVER. Dean realised that it couldn't possibly be for him as the creeps who send out junk mail would never print such a strange message. He looked at the address label – '*INSUFFICIENT*, c/o 23 Capital Boulevard . . .'. It was for the smarmy git next door who would never deign to speak to him. He thought he'd open it anyway just to relieve the boredom of the bus journey. He could always say he hadn't looked at the address before opening it . . .

Inside was a copy of *Sabotage in the Workplace: A Manual of Ideas and Inspirations*. Dean read through the introduction which explained how and why such a book had come to be published. There then followed absolutely loads of short tales about how boredom, authority and meaninglessness can be combated, resulting in fun for workers and chaos for the bosses. There were endless accounts of simple actions shutting down whole factories and of people enhancing their lives with pleasure, money or material goods.

Dean stepped off the bus at the factory and headed straight for the canteen to eat his butties. He had another half hour to kill before his twelve-hour shift began. He didn't even bother with his customary greetings to his fellow workers. He just sat down in an isolated corner, concealed his book in a newspaper and continued his reading. Within a short time of coming across this mystery gift wonderful ideas were formulating.

Bill shuffled through his letters he'd received that morning, still pissed off that his review copy of *Sabotage* . . . hadn't arrived as promised by the publisher. A Poll Tax demand had been ceremoniously thrown in the bin, a cheque from his mum was folded and placed in his building society book, and the remainder of the post lay strewn across his desk awaiting inspection. He squeezed the last few drops of a carton of soya desert into his throat, and turned the television off. The picture of Richard and Judy disappeared into micro dot and Bill began to focus on his attempt at *Fatal Strategies*. Today would be the day. He scanned his desk. He had various small press magazines to review and a couple of hopeful submissions for the next issue of *Insufficient*. The first article went straight into the waste paper basket, yet another critique of the Art Strike . . . this was all old hat by now. The other article was more interesting, probably by the nature of its extreme obscurity. A critique of the classical thesis of alienation using a theoretical model of two protons in an unstable radioactive Uranium isotope. This was the type of stuff that made *Insufficient* the leader in its field.

After filing his mail, Bill began to prepare himself for his climbing trip later in the afternoon. The rock at Baudrillard Buttress had dried fully and an assault on the route in the early hours of the morning yielded the largest probability of a success. This meant an overnight bivi at the crag, and quite a bit of preparation to ensure maximum comfort and fitness for the route. He timetabled the afternoon to begin with a good stretching session and some light training to loosen his muscles, then he'd head off into town to tie up any outstanding business and hitch a ride out to the crag. It was about a twenty-mile journey and Bill considered using his new bike to get there, but then thought better of it as he had not repainted the stolen cycle.

Bill selected a disk and began his stretching. As the strains of Renegade Soundwave's 'Thunder' began to vibrate around the room he coiled himself up on his yoga mat. As the bass picked up he unfurled and pushed up on his arms to stretch his back into a curve. He began the process of uncluttering his mind to focus on the job at hand. Floating to the top of his consciousness was the good feeling he had from recalling the bike he had nicked last week, a new Cannondale 800, a real beautiful machine.

Steve was logging his claim with the insurance company for his son's nicked bike. It had been a long morning and Steve just wanted to get home, so that he could put some work into his allotment. However, he had one or two items of business to attend to, including dealing with these awkward bastards at the insurance office who seemed intent on giving him a hard time. The crux of the matter was that the bike was a bleedin' expensive machine, a top-of-the-range Cannondale which had taken his son eighteen months to save for. He would have gladly killed the scumbag who'd nicked it.

At the factory the pace of things was in overdrive. The *Warriors* contract could mean the big boost for the climbing industry which the factory needed. The workers were being promised jam tomorrow, if they would just put in that bit of extra effort to complete this huge order. Dean had other thoughts – his mind was illuminated with stories of sabotage, of the unknown hero closing down whole factories with the simplest of tactics.

All Dean had to do was remove a sling from the stitching

machine and allow it to pass through the production line attached solely by the glue. While it would look like a good sling, it would immediately fail the routine strength test that all the climbing equipment was religiously submitted to. This would entail the entire production line being closed down for the afternoon while the errant machine was given a thorough check. He and the rest of the workforce could well be home before lunch.

Bill strode through town attending to various tasks before hitching out to the crag. He had to steer clear of the library as that was the scene of his last crime. He had been xeroxing some *Information War* strategy documents that had ironically included a polemic about the tactical use of libraries and the importance of fighting to keep them open. What had caused the initial problem was Bill's dodgy forged card with which he hacked free photocopies. He'd used it one time too many and the knackered old photocopier had admitted defeat by totally short-circuiting. Bill nipped behind the shelves as the sole member of staff rushed over to silence the flashing, beeping, incapacitated machine. It was on his way out of the library that Bill had seen the unlocked bike and quickly made himself scarce on it. He smiled to himself as he recalled the episode. Bill's final errand was a visit to the local sports shop. He was a dab hand at shoplifting and a bit of climbing gear or posh clothing from this yuppie paradise regularly found its way into his holdall.

Steve pushed open the pub doors. He felt ready to explode. Anger was boiling up inside of him like the pus in the spot on his shoulder where his heavy mailbag had been rubbing him raw. He checked the urge to get totally pissed as he really needed to spend time on his allotment. He decided on one pint as that would be enough to calm him down before he got on with his gardening.

He ordered his pint and staked out the pub. It was busy with lunch-time drinkers, mainly loudmouths in suits bragging about their office triumphs or getting excited over banal office politics. A rowdy bunch in the far corner eventually caught his attention, and he immediately recognised them as the Militant cronies who had been creeping round the local anti-Poll Tax groups over the last few months. Their ringleader was a character called Black who was an egotistical braggart at the best of times. Black was in high spirits. Steve didn't have to eavesdrop to hear the gory details. Black had been working hard to collect a big monthly bonus which he was now blowing in the pub. Steve knew the nature of Black's work, and he knew that a bonus for Black meant a great deal of misery for many other people. Black spotted Steve and made his way through the swarm of lunch-time boozers.

'Hey, Mr Postman,' he cried. 'I have a special job for you.'

Steve could smell the stale beer on the Trot's breath, and could see that this veritable Lenin was well pissed. On a normal day Steve would have just let it go, but today he was wound up and so he focused a sharp gaze on the stumbling character. Black fumbled inside his jacket pocket and produced a pile of leaflets. He slapped them down on the table in front of Steve.

'Can you deliver these on your next round – secretly, like – it might give you something important to do for once.'

The leaflets advertised a Militant meeting that proclaimed that they had defeated the Poll Tax and now they were wanting people to listen to how they were going to lead a revolution. Steve didn't even pick them up.

'What's up postie? Scared of acting out of line?'

Steve kicked the table aside sending some drinks, an ashtray, and the leaflets scattering over the pub floor. He stepped forward and grabbed the lapels of Black's coat. He thought of saying something but realised that the Militant was so pissed that he wouldn't even listen let alone understand. Instead Steve steadied himself, cocked his head back, and then brought it forward with a tremendous force. The single, thunderous head-butt split Black's nose in one go.

As Black fell, his face erupting into a fountain of blood, his coat lapels flapped open to reveal a pristine suit and a large name label. The badge bore the logo for the Benefits Agency, and was flanked top and bottom by Black's name and post – Restart Officer.

At the factory Dean had almost forgotten about his ploy to close down the works for the afternoon. Whilst he knew that the knackered sling wouldn't have gone undetected he had assumed that the manager had been alerted and a decision had been made to press on regardless. What was probably worse was that the manager may have suspected that the sling was deliberately sabotaged and that Dean was responsible. Dean's good feelings were short-lived, and anxiety weighed on his mind like a nightmare.

The sling never made it to the testing department. Pearson the delivery and transport worker didn't need coffee-table books on sabotage to learn how to vent his feelings of alienation or to exploit the dispersed system of modern production to his own advantage. He knew those spots in the factory where he could pick up pieces of climbing gear away from the prying eyes of the supervisors and the security cameras. He also had a list of clients who would give him good money for the items he purloined. It wasn't so much sabotage – more a case of topping up a measly wage.

The sabotaged sling was nestling in a box of goodies that Pearson intended to sell to the shop assistant at Real-Sports. This was Pearson's main fence, partly because the assistant sold the gear on himself and so made quite a bit of money on these deals. As Pearson walked through the main doors of the shop with the hot property, his partner in crime shot him an anxious look. A high ranking manager was on the prowl and any dodgy business would be spotted by this dalek. Pearson dropped his box in a corner of the shop and winked visibly at his friend, then he made a swift exit. He'd return later to pick up his cash.

Bill peered into the windows of Real-Sports. The sales assistants were getting a dusting down from some dimwit in a cheap and nasty suit, while a few zombified customers walked around amidst the bright lights and flickering video screens showing pulsating footage of a danger sports compilation video. The security here was pretty minimal, no cameras or store detectives, just keen-eyed staff and some security tags. As the sales assistants were otherwise engaged, Bill decided to go for it. As the pro-Situ panned round the shop, he spotted the box on the floor by the changing rooms. He realised it was new stock and so it was probably untagged. He made his way to the box and peered in. He knew he was in luck when he saw the assortment of brand new climbing gear. Noting that it was all untagged, he crouched down and tipped the whole lot into his rucksack. He stood up and left the premises totally unseen.

The ride out to Cheedale was forgettable. A truck driver who didn't have anything to say for himself, making a token conversation about football. Bill had intended to get a cup of tea at the local café but was met by a closed sign indicating that the proprietors had gone away for a holiday. Bill cursed to himself and made a mental note to reprint his old rant about 'another cheap holiday in other people's misery'. He reached the crag earlier than planned with a couple of hours of daylight left. He decided to have a quick try at the route, just to practise the top moves. He climbed the footpath to the top of the crag and seated himself by the belay tree. He fished in his bag, pulled out a new sling and looped it round the bottom of the tree, and then selected a screwgate karabiner to clip his rope on to the sling. This would enable him to lower himself down to the uppermost bolt on the route and clip it. He tightened his harness and clipped the rope on to the sling, he took a deep breath and began to lower himself over the lip of the crag. One thought now occupied his mind – seeing his photograph on the front cover of the climbing magazines, and sensing the words *Fatal Strategies* on the lips of climbers all over the country. Moments later, Bill Braun lay with a broken neck at the bottom of a ravine, just one more fatality statistic.

DIARY OF BLINDFOLD

Bridget Penney

I am rediscovering the immediate. I hold the pen three inches from my eye. Even so, the letters blur away from me. But I'm writing very carefully. I'm rediscovering my writing. Why do I write this way? I'm looking at my fingers and thumb around the pen – like all the pens in the house it seems always on the verge of running out of ink. Normally I never examine my fingers so close up. The skin is very rough and cracked. Round the nails, especially. I can see the lines of dirt under my nails that I always mean to do something about. My hands seem permanently dirty. I don't know why.

What do you mean by not being able to see? I'm trying to think about it. Two mornings ago, there was freezing fog which did not lift all day, and when I got up early to go to work, the pavement was black, sheer and glistening – at least I pictured it so when I tried to walk and found my feet slipping, for if I could see my hand in front of my face that was all. While I waited for the bus I was more jumpy than usual, as I could not see what was coming, and the park on the far side of the road was invisible – the fog so thick I could not even discern the absence of buildings.

It's strange how the sentence escapes me. Because I can't keep it all under my eyes, I have to remember it in my head. I find that difficult. What does this say about me? That I'm not used to it. It's too easy to rely on the eye. Everything I'm used to in the world is visual. This text has a serial integrity. I cannot read what I've written, I form it as I go along.

This is a notebook of lost and founds. I can write without seeing what I write. You have no idea how liberating this appears to me.

Her name is Flora. If she was in the street and a military band went past, she had to stop her hand from rising in salute.

It is Christmas Eve. Children are whooping in the street outside. It is six days since the end of the diary of blindfold.

Grandmother/Grandfather

Why am I thinking about Flora? Because I read about her somewhere and she comes to mind like a character in a story I've already written.

I can't imagine what it must have been like to fight in the First World War. When I was growing up there was more of a link with that time.

Both my grandmothers were born in 1898. They were sixteen when the war began, twenty when it ended. Their lives were very different, but had this common shaping factor. My mother too grew up during a war. She was eighteen in 1945, my father four years younger.

I've heard it said that people who have fought together always know each other. That war puts a stamp on people, marking them out for the rest of their lives.

My grandfather lost an eye and a lung in the war to shrapnel and mustard gas. In their wedding photo he stands beside my grandmother. It seems they are both leaning slightly towards the camera. She wears a long veil with a circlet of flowers round her head. I can't remember her expression. He wears an eye patch. The effect is not rakish, but grim. He died of a heart attack in his forties – a long-term casualty. My grandmother remained a widow for thirty years.

I helped clear out her house after she died. I was maybe four-teen at the time. The house was tall and chilly. It was the place where she had spent all her married life and widowhood. When we'd stayed there, many Christmases before, my sister and I slept in the room our father had once occupied. It still had children's books in it, some toys. Now, sorting through the accumulated litter of her possessions, came a fresh sense of surprise. At fourteen I'd started to become curious in a new way. I was mostly self-absorbed, but to things I could read as a part of my own history I was intensely open.

What was it like to marry a man who came back from the war? Could she have let herself think about what might have been. Behind my grandmother's neat water-colours there was no sense of personality at all.

Flora

—My father, she sighed. —I loved my father. I did everything I could to please him.

Her father was a self-educated man. He developed an addic-tion to learning, passed on to her everything he knew. To teach her helped him to get things clear in his own mind. He was ex-army, walked with a limp. She liked the way he walked. It never struck her that there was anything wrong.

Flora is in an old folk's home. She will be eighty next month. She wouldn't mind the place so much, she's been in hospital, worse places, but here the TV is on quite loud all day and she cannot get used to it. When she tells the nurse who is combing her hair that she never had TV before the nurse looks at her, thinking she's senile.

—What did you do all day?

—I had plenty to do, Flora said clearly, thinking back to the days before she broke her hip and ended up here. The nurse passes her a mirror. She studied her reflection, thinking who is this old woman? – and says to the nurse (who's young, her favourite)—how do you stand being around old people all day? The nurse smiles at her. —It's my job. She turns away to lay down the mirror and comb, then says abruptly

—So what did you do when you were my age?

—I was in the army, Flora said.

—What did you do? the nurse repeated, taking the crimson scarf higher round Flora's neck.

—I was a soldier.

It was a long time since she'd said it to anyone, not forgetting but trying to live it down, integrating unsuccessfully with the life she was expected to lead. She felt herself stiffen a little, pride maybe, ridiculous in any case. She wanted to laugh at herself and was glad that her tear ducts were so old and useless there was no danger of her weeping.

—I'm not senile.

She met the girl's uneasy gaze. —I was a transvestite.

The effect of the word was so clearly shocking on the young woman's face. Old people weren't supposed to know such words. Age made them innocent. The world had been more innocent when they were young.

—You fought? said the nurse—You killed people then.

Flora sighed. —They were the enemy. It was war. You can't understand. I can't justify myself to you now.

Among my grandmother's possessions was a box with a decorated lid. On it was a picture of a lady in a ball gown by a window. As I held it up to the light, it glittered and shimmered, turning from blue to green. The skirt was fashioned from a butterfly's wing. When I realised that I never touched it again.

*

Other things happen in the diary of blindfold. Everyday things have become fiddly, making a cup of tea is a complicated process when I can hardly see. Worried that I'll hurt myself at first, Paul insists on doing everything for me – it's rather nice to be waited on hand and foot but after a few hours it's just frustrating – and I sneak away when he's busy or asleep. I find I can do most things as long as I'm careful – it's just the margin of error is so small and the detail of objects when I peer at them close up becomes distracting.

We walked over to Whitechapel. It was raining very lightly when we left, and he'd rather have taken the tube but I said that I wanted to be in the fresh air and the underground would confuse me, I'd find the darkness in the tunnels and the bright lights too disorienting. Besides it will stop raining darling (it didn't). He held an umbrella over us both and I couldn't see myself getting wet, it became apparent only as my clothes started to feel damp. We walked across the common, traversed the bridge over the canal, along back streets, past workshop units, Paul telling me when to mind the pavement and cross the road. Bored, fed-up, and even more ungracious than usual, I was perversely determined to prove (though I was glad he was there) that I could manage on my own – I saw that kerb, yes, and I know the pavement dips there because I've walked this way so many times, there's the railing, yes, and we have reached the road. Cars approach, their lights blur, spangle and fracture, growing huge. That sounds like a lorry which way is it coming? I realise I can't separate out noises directionally at all – is this something that people who are not just blindfold but really blind learn to do?

We're walking past the Trinity almshouses which echo the sea in every curve of their construction: rigged ships perched at each corner, monsters' faces and the delicate openings of shells over doorways and windows. The roof beams are old ships' timbers.

Buildings appear skeletal. They're hard to describe. Lines and angles dominate. The people walking towards me are sticks on two legs with round heads. The faces of the blind have a different set of expressions. I wonder what my own face looks like.

*

1915 – Flora paused in front of the photographer's shop in the main street of a small town miles from anywhere except the military training camp. Her hands shook as she lit a cigarette. She was suffering from a serious failure of nerve as she stared at her uniformed reflection among the framed prints in the window – the weddings, babies, and the pictures of young girls to give to their friends. She had never felt she fitted in before, but now she was sick at heart with the hundred small embarrassments and uncertainties arising from her changed state.

Tired of looking, she was about to move on when she heard a girl's voice calling her—hey soldier soldier boy where are you off to in such a hurry?

The interior of the shop was dark, crowded with equipment and smelt of chemicals. —I'm Maud, said the girl—my father's away today, he's photographing a wedding over at—. Flora smiled though the name meant nothing to her, looking around as her eyes became used to the gloom. —I was watching you from the window, said Maud— there's nothing much else to do here. You're from London, aren't you. What's your name?— Gerrard, Flora said. She was suddenly nervous of Maud. There was an intensity in her eyes, the face framed by dark ropes of hair. —Do you want your picture done, Mister Gerrard?

Maud smiled then, seeming self-conscious, and turned away, picking a stray black hair off the pink knitted cardigan she wore.—I'll do it for free as my contribution to the war effort. From your face you must be a good fighter, Gerrard.

Flora laughed then. Maud brought out her own recklessness, and she was aware of a freedom in her position that was unfamiliar, elating. Maud unlocked a door at the back of the shop. As Flora stepped through, she glanced up. Several heavy wooden rollers were suspended from the ceiling. —These are the backdrops, Maud said quietly, almost uneasy. —I think we should use this one for you.

What had she expected when Maud pulled the cord and the canvas unrolled too quickly, raising all the dust? Not this, not the crowded intensity of colour, abstract shapes settling into a foreign landscape – a village in the background but not like here, smooth rolling hills, a meadow crammed with flowers. In the foreground was a tree with spreading branches and fruit growing among the leaves. —You painted this? Flora said turning. Maud nodded. All at once she seemed older, weary, and when she smiled Flora felt she knew how she'd look when she was an old woman.

It was scary and very strange. It made her think would she even be alive a year from today – would the war be over – what else would have happened—

*

During the First World War phosphorescent paint was applied to the grass in London parks with the idea of fooling enemy planes into believing they were large buildings lit up.

The iconography of the female warrior

On medals, Renaissance princes had themselves depicted as armed women, reconciling Mars and Venus. Queen Christina – Garbo's uncomfortable laugh. Kleist's Penthilisea, Amazon turned vampire feeding on her lover's flesh. Phoebe Hessel, who served in the English army during the eighteenth century and is buried in Brighton where she died aged 108.

Flora had one particular friend while she was in the army. His name was Leonard. He spent all his time reading, he would read anything, old newspapers, manuals, that he could get his hands on.

They talked about London. They talked about Victoria Park. She tried to imagine it with the grass painted silver. It would shine like a great unearthly lake, in the moonlight glowing, the trees would rise up out of the lake. The flamingoes which lived on the pond would walk across the phosphorescent grass.

ghost of Maud the painter

In Flora's imagination she always appears as on the day of the photograph. Ghosts should be dressed in white but Maud is resolutely technicolour.

Flora—Why did you cut your throat?
Maud points to her neck. She tries to speak but there is only an ugly gasping sound.
Flora wakes shivering.

> when reading becomes difficult
> you start to think about it

when walking is difficult
when speech is hard for some reason

the primacy of the visual sense
if we could see ghosts walking in daylight
chinese ghosts with black spittle

paper motorcycle   typewriter
paper Walkman
shoes made beautifully of paper
Hell passport, bank notes
entering another country with due precaution

Hell's windows
play ball
bouncing
a soft paper ball
that makes no sound
won't fly straight

Tiresias could speak without blood
'the sense of the pleasure she gave
doubled her own pleasure'

in cold hell
Blindfold's Black Book

'and then Ille'

when this you see remember me
when/this/you/see/remember/me
remember me but oh forget my fate

amour

Maud: keeper of the gate
Maud Ruthyn

serpent coils
girls in white dresses
(some of Maud's paintings have the qualities
of pornography the cold eye)
hard
Maud sits in a room, reading
she has one eye on the camera taking the picture

her own camera
she is frozen there by her own
resolution

Amour:

his eyes are blindfolded with a black cloth.
He is naked, flambeaux in his crossed hands

She kisses him on the knee
she feels the movement
of the plates of bone
under fluid
she presses her tongue against his kneecap
sliding her hands
up the back
of his thighs
she tastes the skin of his thigh
slightly salt
she lets her tongue find him
how to awaken him
he's like a statue
she takes his dick in her mouth
she sucks
she pushes
the skin back
gently
with the very edges of her teeth
she thinks of things for her tongue to do

it seems
too big
for her mouth
she pushes
teases it around
her hands clasp his buttocks

the torches above her head tremble
she feels
the muscles tense
in his back
she hears his voice
he is no longer silent
he cries out
marvellous words of love

*

Tuesday, January 28th: a disappointment. I walked over to the Whitechapel Gallery curious to view the exhibition *A cabinet of signs* I'd visited seven weeks before with seriously restricted vision. I avoided the dioramas with wildebeest my eyes had previously inched over. I looked at the books made of cut-up comics (X-men and bathing belles), sleek machines showing a raw image of human flesh, white pillars with cool messages, flashing lights revealing numbers where there had been a blur. It was the last free day so the gallery was quite crowded. Lots of people were drawing things. Why is the sight of people drawing in an art gallery so bizarre.

Alison is going to Japan in two months' time. She is to sublet her brother's flat in Tokyo and teach English to Japanese kids. She expects to find it much easier than what she's doing now. I said—you've got to be joking, teaching kids? but she says they've all been learning English for six years already and can read and write it's just the speaking they're not confident about. I told this to Mark and he said that's right, teaching English in Japan you do it totally on your own terms and don't have to know any Japanese. I like the thought of Alison speaking English to all these Japanese kids. She has a few contacts over there, she's really looking forward to it, even the gardens, she says, are like works of art.

I remember a postcard my uncle sent me from Tokyo. it showed the hotel garden. He said he'd tried to find it and when he did he discovered the space was so small you couldn't really go in it, you just looked at the arrangement of rocks, the fountain falling into a stream and carefully tended plants. I made a miniature garden in a pie dish. The ground was moss I scraped off a stone. It was brighter than grass and somehow exciting even in the ragged patchwork I made of it. There was a pond in the middle – silver foil or a fragment of mirror. I edged it with tiny white stones I picked up from the gravel, but was dissatisfied. I wanted an effect like flowers or stars. The stones would never unfold like wood anemones. The pond was in stasis. It could not ripple. When I stared down into it, it returned an unwinking reflection of my own eye.

flowers are for

The fields are full of flowers. The fields are full of women. Crimson poppies, brave women. The army is made up of women soldiers massed against the sky and mud. What would it—Flora thought—what would it be like?

She leans against a tree. Once the landscape was green. All the leaves have gone now. The trunk was blackened by the explosion that blew them away. Ash has scored deeply into its bark. What does the landscape betray? It is covered by a fine grey cloud that sometimes rises and fills the air. It gets in your eyes and furs your tongue, but it's not like gas. You can close your eyes against the cloud. With its poison, the gas turns your whole body inside out.

*

She shifts her position, still against the tree. Its stark outline on the abandoned battlefield offers some protection. Her clothes are wet through. She puts her face against the bark. She has a pistol in her hand from habit, regulation. It would be useless if she was attacked.

It is so quiet. There are men back there behind the mounds of earth she helped to dig, packed icy hard now and slippery as glass with the morning's frost. They are talking and smoking, singing, playing cards. The boredom they all have to face is the unutterable thing. Waiting for something you know will happen makes you want it to happen however much you are afraid.

She can't imagine this land in other than its outline. Where have the birds gone? She is the only living thing. The soldiers march and turn everything to mud under the sky.

At moments like this it's better not to think. She is part of the mood that grips them all. She has to do well, there is that in her, but it is fear that drives her, a strange notion of dying unfulfilled.

Maud the painter

Maud the painter   Maud my sister   Maud the impatient

She is reading *Uncle Silas*. She likes books in which she appears. She flips from page to page, drawing pictures in the margin. Her sketches start to enclose the words. She circles words that take her fancy, drawing them out of their place in a sentence to let them stand forth as raw material. MAUD. She isolates her name. HAGGARD. PALLID. TRANCE. I WAS MORE NERVOUS AND MORE IMPETUOUS, AND MY FEELINGS BOTH STIMULATED AND OVERPOWERED ME MORE EASILY. PROFANED. TRANSFIXED. HE GOES

BY THE EYE AND BY SENSATION. HAUNTED REGIONS.
THE SERPENT BEGUILED HER AND SHE DID EAT.

Maud finds herself staring into the mirror above the fireplace.
The reflection is dim but then her eyes clear and she sees her
lover standing by the French window. He is tall and dark, no
longer blindfolded. When he smiles at her his eyes are piercing
rays.

—What do you want? Maud says. Though barely into middle
age her face is lined and her hair already white. —You left me
remember I thought you'd done with me a long time ago.

He is changing as she speaks. When he opens his mouth
millions of sparks waver on the air. —Maud, he says—Love is
eternal wherever you take it.

She feels the heat of his breath, no, it's the heat of the fire in
the grate. She takes in the familiar objects around her, the
clock with its subdued tick, the calendar on the wall which
says 1934. She opens the window out into the yard. It has
been raining. The smell of the wet city night enters the room.
It's full of smoke and stars. She can hear voices in the next
street. She feels remote from them. She looks at her pictures
propped around the room. A detail catches her eyes here and
there: an arm, a throat, a branch, the eyes of death looking at
her through the leaves.

*

In one sketch there is nothing but ribbons. Ribbons are for a
bride. When she walks and talks. When she kneels and stands
and sits. Ribbons are to cover her. They are one colour, all
colours of blue. They change according to her mood. Some
are deep indigo. She lies.

BAD GUY REACTION

Tommy Udo

Inspired by the first Black Sabbath album 'Black Sabbath', the works of Dennis Wheatley and the 1971 film *Psychomania* – surely the greatest British black magic 'n' biker film ever made – me and my mates decided to sell our souls to the devil.

The omens were right for us to sell our souls to the devil. We were *all* 13 and my address was 667 Borestone Road.

On the first moonless night, we all snuck out of the house and met at the gates of the local graveyard. It was heavily overcast and most of the street lighting was fucked, in fact, it was us who had fucked it. We had to use one of the black candles we had brought to find our way around in the dark. Now, you couldn't buy black candles in Beith, so what we had done was to buy ordinary candles and paint them with black gloss paint which made them spark and hiss and give off poisonous fumes when they burned.

We found a grave that was like a tabletop. The writing was eroded away, but we had little doubt that this was the earthly remains of one of the many evil souls burned at the stake for sorcery.

We placed the apparatus essential to our vile ritual on the ground: a roll of wallpaper with a goat's head crudely drawn in magic marker, inside a five-pointed star with Latin text and astrological symbols around the edges. I'd copied this from the back of the Arrow paperback edition of *The Devil Rides Out*. The four black candles; unfortunately we could only get the scented kind, but what the fuck. Beelzebub wouldn't mind. A ritual dagger . . . well, a rusty bread knife. A mirror in which Satan's face was supposed to appear and copies of the Lord's Prayer written backwards. The King James version, of course.

In all the black magic films we had seen, the coven all wore hooded monk's cowls. We couldn't get hold of these, but we all had duffel coats, so we wore them instead.

The ritual began. Nobody had brought a watch, so we weren't sure if it was midnight or not. What the fuck, we thought, put our call into the Earl Of Hell five minutes early and avoid the rush at midnight.

We chanted the words of the Lord's Prayer backwards.

Amen, Forever, glory the and power the, kingdom the is thine for . . .

Then we waited . . . and waited.

'Aye,' said Hughie, shaking his head. 'We need a sacrifice.'

'Well don't fucking look at me,' I said.

'Naw, we'll get a black cat,' he said.

'Ah'm no' killing a fuckin' cat,' said Malkie.

'We'll dae it quick so it disnae hurt it,' said Hugh. 'Batter it on the heid.'

'Naw, yer not on,' said Malkie. 'That's cruel.'

'Naw it isnae,' he said. 'When ye go fishin' ye kill the fish by battering their heids in on the rocks.'

'That's different.'

'How is it?'

'Cos they're fish,' said Malkie. 'They're stupid.'

'Whit, and Cats are on *Mastermind*?'

'Awright, we'll kill a dug,' I said. 'Anyway, dugs are easier tae catch.'

'Aye, but the devil disnae like dugs,' said Hugh. 'When huv ye ever seen them sacrificing a fuckin' dug tae the devil in the films?'

'Well, when dae ye see them sacrificin' a fuckin' cat?' said Malkie.

We had to admit that he had a point.

Eventually we settled for battering a worm to death with a brick, after another recital of the Lord's Prayer backwards.

Then the candles blew out. And a terrible cry rent the night.

'Heh ya fuckin' wee cunts. Get tae fuck.'

'Aaaah. It's the devil!' screamed Malkie, running for the gates.

Hugh Shaw pulled out a cross made from two ice lolly sticks held together with elastic bands.

'Back Satan,' he commanded of the sinister figure in black before him.

'Back yersel, ya fuckin' wee shite,' said the fat policeman grabbing him by the neck. 'I ken aw yer faces an' I'll be efter ye,' he shouted as me and Malkie made a break for it. 'Ye's can run but ye cannae hide.'

BURN MAN BURN

Jerry Palmer

It was two years to the day since Derek Flower had left Bright-lingsea school. He felt proudly unrecognisable. In such a relatively short period he'd discovered the secret of freedom. Fire!

Hidden in the midnight darkness Derek watched as the torched beach-hut blazed and roared, sending a stream of brilliant orange and yellow plumes high into the cold black air.

The anniversary had to be appropriately marked. At the same time, however, Derek was aware of not getting stuck in the past. He had to grow out of this juvenile vendetta. He had to destroy his past so that he might create his own future.

The fire engines were on their way. He could make out their advancing shapes coming along the back road past the ranks of uniform beach-huts. Derek shuffled back into the under-growth and observed as the fire was expertly put out. Soon nothing was left of the old hut except a few charred and smouldering uprights. As a group of tired and sooty firemen stood around relaxing after the excitement Derek withdrew to the footpath and headed off. 'Five nil' he whispered to himself as he jogged silently home.

Like most locals, Derek had played his part during the infamous Brightlingsea live export protests. He'd teamed up with the others and played havoc with the cops, slashing tyres, sitting in the road, creating barricades. They'd dared each other to go further. Once, early one morning, he'd rushed around the whole town daubing 'scum' in huge white letters every-where (even directly opposite the police station), a feat which gained him much notoriety locally.

But during that time Derek had a secret. Late at night, when most of his fellow protesters were safely tucked up in bed after a long day of hurling abuse, he'd drive an unmarked transit down to the harbour. Whilst he smoked a fag a group of labourers loaded up the van with stacks of heavy boxes. Derek told everyone he was just delivering refrigerator parts from one of the warehouses on the quay. But he knew better. First night out he pulled into a layby, close to his destination on the outskirts of Colchester. He opened one of the boxes. Inside were a number of small round tins; removing one he read the label. French gelatin (horse).

It was during the protests that he'd first thought of fire as an expressive device. The riot squad had just cleared the road to the docks and were marching in a column in front of a big transport lorry. Leaning casually against the car park wall of the Sun pub Derek surveyed the police lines like a beaten but unbroken partisan. He suddenly imagined igniting a prepre-pared line of petrol right under their armoured asses.

Having discovered the true nature of his nightly consign-ments Derek, feeling a little unsettled, had decided to take a close look at his delivery point. The processing factory was small and quite isolated. Outside the sign boasted BALLZ, the international food giant. Derek reversed into the loading bay and watched while white-overalled men piled boxes on to a conveyor belt that disappeared into the wall. As no one was taking an interest in him he slipped through some rubber doors and into the plant proper. Inside it smelt thick and sticky, like glue. Everywhere big machines buzzed and whirred confusingly as their aproned attendants fussed about over them. It was a world of boiling cylinders and steaming pipes. He moved quickly along, following the course of the conveyor belt. Its purpose seemed to be to process a runny grey substance into a thick gloopy pink substance before slurping the resulting mixture into thousands of equally colourful plastic pots. At the end of the line sat a solitary young guy repetitively swinging a metal arm across the belt, knocking half a dozen containers at a time into the trays below him.

A hooter sounded and suddenly the whole line went dead. The young operative sighed and looked up at Derek tiredly. 'Some fucking job you've got there mate,' said Derek. 'Do you know they're putting mashed-up horses in that crap?'

''Course I do,' the man replied, 'rule one round here is never eat the supermousse.' He continued, 'They sit me here to give me something to do, man, like the machine can do this automatically, but no, I've got to do it. Half hour on, one hour off. That's full employment for you.'

Derek smiled. 'So what do you do during the hour off?'

'Oh,' said the guy reaching in to his pocket, 'I read this shit.' *The Revolution of Everyday Life.*

'What's that about?' Derek asked inquisitively.

'Here, take it and find out for yourself. I've read it before.'

Derek read the book the radical factory hand had given him (why the hell not?) and it really blew him away. The battered manuscript had even been printed and bound in Brightlingsea during the early seventies and this irony was not lost on him. He had trouble with the overt intellectualism of these French extremists but there was an appeal to delinquency in the text that he recognised in his own thoughts. It gave him the feeling that he was working within a tradition, not as some immature outlaw acting alone and without reason. However, these learned revolutionists were mistaken in supposing that human actions were more important than the elements themselves. The arsonist was not the poet, the fire was. It was the elements that really dictated events, behaviour and even desire itself. The human will is naturally subservient to them. Derek served the fire. It did not serve him.

Derek climbed up out of the dinghy and on to the deck of the little cabin cruiser. Looking back across the still water to the Anchor pub on the wharf he thought how it always reminded him of that house in *Psycho*. The rickety former seaman's inn was contentedly pulsing out its Saturday night beat. No one was to be seen. He hadn't been detected. All around him were the gently clanking hulls of pleasure craft, yachts and fishing boats; Brightlingsea's life-blood moored up for the night.

All the boats were linked with the petrol-soaked rope and most were to some degree doused with inflammables. The operation had taken hours; after all it was his grand finale, his masterpiece. The whole fucking town was asking for it. Oh how they'd praised his and the others' aggression when they'd needed it; when it was socially useful, hysteria had been a local resource. But now that the ships didn't come any more he was out of a job and that precious pressure valve that the protests represented was also gone. But Derek felt compelled to continue what they'd started. Unlike the rest of the town's population he couldn't simply switch off the emotional trigger that had been pulled. The community and the cops were back in their old coalition again as though nothing had happened, nothing had changed. They were cracking down on the young again, scapegoating them without taking responsibility for what they themselves had unleashed, the avenue of escape, the kind of liberation most people were just too damn scared to follow through to its ultimate conclusion.

Fire would cleanse the dirt, the hypocrisy. It was beyond all destruction. Derek would shake that comatose small-town mentality right out from under them all. He looked across the creek at the line of beach-huts stretching into infinity along the promenade. He'd always hated those hovels; now he'd fixed them for good. Then he heard the loud pop. That must be the incendiary. He checked his watch. Yep, dead on time. He stared, spellbound, as within seconds a huge wall of fire surged along the line of little huts like a fluid but unstoppable wave. Derek simultaneously felt a warm flood of satisfaction spread through his body.

He flicked open his long-serving Zippo and without taking his eyes off the inferno ashore lit the main event. Delicate flames licked along the rope links he'd positioned. He started up the cabin cruiser and moved off slowly. As the first vessels began blazing and crackling the punters over at the Anchor poured out shocked by the spectacle which greeted them. He could just see them through the thickening smoke, running about and gesturing like headless ants, powerless to do anything.

All was fire, heat and explosions. The sea heaved with the tremors and shone with fragmented reflections of the carnage he had wrought. Derek took a deep lungful of oily air and steered the cruiser out of the furnace, heading for the open sea.

Even to the end he refused to surrender his sense of the dramatic. He made sure that all the gawping townsfolk could see his figure silhouetted against the savage orange glow he'd created. He waved a clenched fist salute and sneered at the fools he was leaving behind; they would, no doubt, label him an evil bomber and a sadist but that was just another mask, a reflection of themselves.

His boat was burning now. Horrified, those on shore could only watch awestruck as the flames grew higher and higher, finally completely enveloping the craft. Seconds later it burst apart in a huge yellow fireball as the fuel tanks finally gave in to the pressure.

Derek slid quietly up on to the deserted beach. He'd made it, he'd swum over two miles across the inlet to the other side of Mersea Island, well out of sight. Still, he kept low as he stripped off his snorkel and flippers and began searching for the clothes he'd hidden previously. High up in the sky he watched the big helicopters scanning the water with their searchlights and he could still make out the bangs and whizzes of his attack going off in the distance. He located the clothes and jumped into them. The rest would be easy. The road lay fifty metres away beyond the tree line and the car would be waiting.

BOREDOM

Simon Strong

A girl in a summer dress presents the curved nape of her neck, her head is bent forward at such an angle as to present a cleavage between her shoulder blades equivalent to the one between her breasts. This position forms a plane on the triangle of flesh bounded by the apex of her left shoulder blade, the left hinge of her jawbone and a point approximately three inches directly above the nipple of her left breast which is revealed in its entirety, her dress having ridden well down.

This triangle is bisected by a necklace of ostensible pearls that circles from below her chin into her blondish hair, the mass of which has been thrown back by the violence of the angle of her head, plainly exposing the entire orifice of her left ear. A less violent but prolonged movement has caused the fastener of the necklace to slip around her neck to a position just above her oesophagus. Above the necklace, the girl's chin juts out, her mouth open as wide as it could comfortably be held for a prolonged period. Her lips are tinted a conventional red and between them her tongue protrudes two inches to make contact with the tip of an erect penis. She is licking the top of the helmet and its slit makes tentative contact with the middle point of her bottom lip, a generous residue of lipstick can be observed where it has rubbed on the bottom of the glans. The shaft of the penis is grasped in the girl's left hand, the wrist of which is resting below her left breast and agitating the nipple which has assumed a shape which may be expressed as a sine wave compressed along the x-axis.

Below her forearm the material of a dress is visible, it is impossible to discern any feature of its cut since it has ridden up and now covers an area only about fifteen centimetres high, centred on the girl's navel. It is plainly a lightweight summer dress made of cotton and printed in alternating blue and white stripes approximately one inch in width; the girl is completely exposed below this. Although her buttocks are hidden from view by her position, the right one bears her weight and behind it appears a multi-coloured floral background; maybe a sheet or blanket, but given the intensity of the design a coverless mattress seems more likely.

The back of the girl's left thigh is catching the light and the flesh appears slightly darker towards the front. Her legs are forty degrees apart and her pubis is entirely visible, its generous hair is a deep russet in hue. Even though the area between her legs is underlit it is possible to distinguish the labia, which are dark and of moderate length, and even the opening to her vagina may be vaguely discerned.

Between the girl's legs, resting across her right thigh halfway up, there protrudes the knee of a second girl's right leg, it is contained within an almost opaque white stocking. From the knee downward the leg is held tightly against the inside of the first's left thigh. Both of their legs are resting on the left leg of a third girl, which is held apart from her right at an angle of sixty degrees. High up on the left thigh rests the right hand of the second girl, the blatantly false nails of its four fingers are polished with a garish red varnish which appears to sparkle in the light. The thumbnail is similarly adorned but cannot be seen clearly as it faces the other way, digging into the outside of her own thigh near the top of her stocking.

The anterior part of the third girl's vagina is clearly visible, she has apparently been shaved recently but a thin layer of fuzz has started to re-cover the area. Her labia are quite long and no darker than the skin which surrounds them. They are splayed wide apart, presumably by the second girl's hand since she is well lubricated and the area between her left thigh and the hand of the second girl glistens with liberal secretions. The inside of her vagina appears quite red, perhaps inflamed by the second girl's nails.

Both of the third girl's buttocks rest on a pale lilac sheet, apparently satin, which passes beneath her right buttock to reappear around the top of the thigh. Her back is slightly arched and her right leg is held out, bent sharply at the knee, to provide uninhibited access to her vagina.

The sheet continues around her belly, between her navel and the base of her breasts, before passing out of sight beneath the right arm of the second girl. On the way it is partially obscured by the right arm of the third girl just below a horizontal cut which is about three inches long, obviously recent, and although it appears quite deep, it is not bleeding. This cut points directly in-line towards the nipple of her right breast, itself a deep rose pink which fades into a tan aureole, it is in the process of becoming erect. Her breasts are large, and from this angle point upward to form almost perfect hemispheres, though the right one is slightly crushed at its outer extremity by her upper arm as she reaches over towards the other two girls.

The neck of the third girl is hidden by the second girl's unusually large hand as she pulls her closer towards her, simultaneously caressing her ash-blonde hair. The third girl's face is turned towards the second so that her gold-ringed right ear is the only visible facial feature except for half an inch of tongue which is extended into the mouth of the second girl whose head is turned sharply to the right to meet her, thus exposing the length of her throat which is bisected halfway down by a necklace of red and white beads.

The second girl's tongue protrudes through her half open mouth, her lips are painted a complementary tone to her nails and her brilliant white teeth threaten to bite down on her co-osculator. Her eyes are tightly closed, the lids screwed up together beneath the long fringe of her copper-hued hair, which entangles with the other girl's ash-blonde. Her position appears extremely uncomfortable, but this is belied by her beatific expression and the fact that the nipples of her small breasts are fully erected. This erection may be assumed to have been effected by the friction of the hair of the first girl in the case of the left, or the fingers of the third girl in the case of the right. This hand, with nails painted a red slightly duller than those of the second girl and bearing a wide wedding band, is now entwined in the hair of the first girl and moving towards the lilac satin suspender-belt of the second girl. Beneath this belt the hand of the first girl obscures the crotch of the second girl in such a way as to make it impossible to tell whether the penis which she is so enthusiastically sucking is actually a double-ended dildo inserted in her vagina, or an actual penis which would entail the second girl being a transsexual.

There is a small rectangle missing from each corner of the tableau, and in each of these a figure '7' may be observed, together with the spade symbol.

It has been observed that the photographs that appear on 'nudie' decks cause the cards to more closely resemble the pictorial cards of the Tarot than the systematic distribution of symbols on a traditional deck. In *The Book of Thoth* Crowley corresponds each suit of a traditional deck to a suit of the minor arcana of the Tarot: Clubs to Wands, Diamonds to Pentacles, Hearts to Cups and Spades to Swords.

A dress is entirely visible. Resting on the front, it appears a quite deep rose pink and sparkles in the left breast, digging into a sheet that continues around her legs. She reaches over towards the right leg of a deep pink rose which surrounds them to form an almost perfect hemisphere, apparently a satin suspender-belt, the anterior part of which surrounds the area. The area. Her own thigh is near the area. Her own thigh is near the inside of her labia, a quite deep rose pink which passes beneath the inside of her vagina. The sheet continues around her vagina. The sheet continues around her right arm and as she pulls it, her back is partially obscured by the nipple of her vagina.

The nipple of her vagina is a wide wedding band, simultaneously caressing her breasts and exposing the second girl's buttocks that rest on her upper arm as she pulls her towards the long fringe of a figure '7' which may be assumed to bite down on the third girl. Her throat which is extended into the third girl and the half open mouth of the second girl obscures the suspender-belt with the hand of these darker stripes, together with a slightly swollen part of a floret, a type of the second girl in which each side of a cross piece consisting of two 'flame' shapes projecting symmetrically from each side of the main axis, cut across by a much shorter cross piece of about a third of a girl in a summer dress, the left shoulder blades equivalent to the mass of the cleavage between her breasts.

A plane of the entire orifice of ostensible pearls that circles from below her left shoulder blades is equivalent to her jawbone in its entirety, the necklace of which has been thrown back by a point approximately three inches directly above the tip of her blondish hair, the glans. The glans. The glans. The glans. The penis. Below her head, it is visible. It is impossible to make contact with the nipple of lipstick that can be observed where it is plainly exposing the girl, but given the generous residue of its slit that makes tentative contact with a shape which may be observed where it has caused the labia resting below her left ear. The labia is a lightweight summer dress having ridden well down by her buttocks just below, it is possible to sparkle in the light and of sixty degrees apart from the light and of sixty degrees apart from the other two girls. Its cut appears to re-cover the other two girls, and the anterior part of her vagina which appears around the area between her right leg, held tightly against the area to reappear around the inside of second girl's hand of the top of its becoming erect. The other girl's nails and the third girl's buttocks rest on a wide wedding band and although it is not bleeding, this is in the mouth. Simultaneously caressing her right breast, her breasts are large as she pulls her towards the fact of the long fringe of the hair in the case of the third girl. Her throat, which is extended into the third girl, obscures the right ear which is turned so sharply as to have been effected by her half open mouth, now entwined in her lips and tightly closed, the first girl obscures the second girl who obscures the third girl on each side of the crotch of identical devices like a table knife but wider.

A point at the middle of two flame shapes projecting symmetrically from each side of the other, cut across by a much shorter cross piece consisting of the swollen part or about a third of the swollen part or about a third of the curved nape of her neck. Her neck, the apex of flesh bounded by the nipple of her shoulder blades equivalent to the angle of the necklace which has been thrown back by a point approximately three inches directly above the left hinge of her dress agitating the bottom lip, it is visible, it is impossible to make contact with the wrist of her left breast which has caused the wrist of the girl's navel.

The third girl's buttocks rest on a red rose, simultaneously caressing the second girl's buttocks and exposing her right breast as she pulls her towards the other girl's unusually large hand, which is turned sharply towards a small rectangle missing from each side of the first girl. Her gold-ringed right one is the first girl. Her, with slightly darker stripes, now entwined in her throat which is extended into the case of the hair of the lilac satin suspender-belt as the first girl obscures the second girl on each side of identical devices of cross piece consisting of two flame shapes projecting symmetrically from each side of the base a third of the way up.

This position forms a girl in a girl in a girl in a summer dress and presents the left shoulder blades equivalent to a cleavage between her breasts. A cleavage between her breasts. Above the entire orifice of ostensible pearls that circles from below her left shoulder blades to slip around the left hinge of the necklace of her dress which presents the tip of the middle point approximately three inches directly above the shaft of an erect penis. The shaft of an erect penis. The shaft of the girl's navel. Below her head it forms a prolonged movement which has caused the material of lipstick to be observed where it is impossible to make contact the girl, but given the girl glistens with a generous residue of which it may be observed where it has caused the design of an area only about fifteen centimetres high, its slit makes tentative contact with a generous residue of cotton and behind it has caused the front.

A plane of the mass of her left breast, plainly on the entire orifice of the necklace, her left breast cannot be expressed as a sine wave. The tip of her nipple from the middle from the girl's legs, the nipple of lipstick can be vaguely discerned. Although angles point at the other to meet her right ear by her gold-ringed right to have been passing out an extremity by a type of crotch of identical devices of ostensible pearls that the violence of the fastener which has rubbed on the necklace. Her dress is resting on the necklace, her dress is visible, less violent but it cannot be expressed as a sine wave. The top of her chin is from the middle of the material of the girl. Although the angle of a shape projecting symmetrically from her lips can be vaguely discerned, maybe a lightweight summer then protrudes through her left hand to the front. Her left hand sparkles in the opening of the knee which is polished with the left breast, digging into the light bands, presumably by the outside of her vagina. The anterior part obscured by the skin which passes beneath this is clearly between her own thigh near the area between her stocking approximately and the thigh and the sheet cross of her vagina, obviously recent, and her back.

A lightweight summer then protrudes through her buttocks to the knee, which is underlit and is contained within an almost blue of their legs, polished with the left breast and digging into the left breast, she reaches over towards them. Both lip, high of the light bands, presumably by the outside of her vagina.

The outside of fuzz that has ridden one is clearly between her own thigh near the skin which passes beneath her stocking approximately and the second girl in the sheet cross of her vagina, obviously recent, itself a necklace of the right breast. The right breast. The process of becoming the other, although the angle points at the second girl and is obscured from each. The length is violent but wider, her upper arm that curved the nape of the hair of the second girl in each. This belt is her half up her arm, her nails of the first left, and bearing a floret, together to make tentative contact within an elongated main contact with the crotch of the spade symbol.

A garish red and no darker stripes surrounds them, protrudes through her right arm as she reaches over towards her. The skin which surrounds them protrudes through her own thigh near the area between her left thigh near the top of her vagina. Both are obviously recent, and her right arm pulls her right breast, partially obscured by the nipple of her vagina, itself a necklace of her vagina, though to the third girl and although the angle points at the third girl and each side of her breasts are painted lilac towards the mouth which has apparently a double-ended dildo inserted, her upper arm and white teeth threaten to bite down on the hair of the third girl in the case of the right.

The reverse of the card is pale grey with slightly darker vertical stripes; between these darker stripes, in the middle of the lighter bands, rises a line of identical devices of a very dark grey: a floret, a type of cross with an elongated main shape, like a table knife but wider, coming to a point at one end and slightly swollen at the other, cut across by a much shorter cross-piece consisting of two flame shapes projecting symmetrically from each side of the main axis, just at the base of the swollen part or about a third of the way up.

CRIMINAL JUSTICE ACT

John Barker

The drive was so as they could have a chat, nowhere in particular, the rough idea of a circle was all. So as when they'd finished Mark'd drop the feller off back where they'd met. Serious sort of bloke in his face but so far he'd only ever done bits and pieces after an intro from Patsy K who said Steve had been sound in the shithole, and if how you was in the jail wasn't a guide then what was. Now he was talking tens and twenties. And asked where they were as they cut into quiet roads of terraced houses.

Mark was all eyes on the rear-view, an empty road getting narrower.

—Leyton, he said.

—Home of Leyton Orient, Steve said.

—What?

—Leyton Orient. Once of the First Division before it became the Premier, now of the Second, previously known as the Third.

Knew his stuff, Steve did. Football, something about the name Orient. There was definitely a West Ham because once he'd been fucking mad enough to get himself talked into going. And stood there right to the end even after cousin Gary had wound him up, saying they were on grands a week, the players. Right to the freezing cold final whistle because Gary was sound and it was his thing. Gary'd spoken then of a Leyton Orient. They were a bunch of wankers.

—What are they, a team of Arabs? Mark said.

—Arabs? Steve said.

Then he laughed. Mark checked the rear-view and took a left, a street of terraced houses faced by sections of corrugated iron fencing.

Into a roadblock. Metal tube barriers on feet across the road and uniformed policemen. Some of them had fluorescent lime bibs over their tunics.

There was no point but stopping. Whatever it was. Whatever way, keep the motor running.

Mark pulled up and wound down his window, foot on the clutch.

Steve didn't like it at all, wanted to know what it was, what was going on. There was a policeman walking towards them. Mark shrugged. Memories like elephants when it came to faces, the cunts. If they were old enough.

Close up this one was fresh-faced under his helmet. Steve was pointing at something.

—It's that M11 thing, he said.—The protesters.

In the distance a weird-looking scaffold structure rose into the sky off of slate roofs. Close by, above the corrugated, the arm of a tall crane swung a small arc.

—The road's blocked off sir.

There you were, you were sir. In addition he could see it for his fucking self, the road was blocked off.

—I'm just trying to get through to Leytonstone tube station, have I gone wrong?

—That I couldn't tell you, we're just over from Wembley for the day. It's the protesters sir, the squatters.

Now he came to look, Mark could see people in the scaffolding and beyond them, more people on some kind of wooden platform above the roof. Half the slates were missing.

—We're just keeping everyone away for the safety of everyone concerned.

Mark reversed back to the junction, taking his time. He turned back the way they'd come. A convoy of three wire-frame-fronted Ford Transits came towards them at slow speed.

Riot police, Mark could see them, twelve to a van in chunky

black overalls like they were off to do parachute jumps. Or deal with a major clot in the sewage system.

Mark's mobile rang.

He let it ring on as they passed. Down a right turn-off there was a half house behind some corrugated, rubble and floorboarding piled up next to it.

Two hundred yards ahead was another roadblock. Mark took a left, then left again back into Leyton. He slowed down over a hump-backed bridge. There were groups of people stood on it looking out along the tube line.

—What a performance. Fancy a look Steve? Mark said. He was already pulling into a kerb space when Steve said, Sure. Why not.

Hippies they were mostly, on the bridge. And a couple of old boys. A few hundred yards down the glinting rails the tower of scaffold stood high above roofs. Down below it were rows of lime fluorescent bibs jammed against the tube line fencing. On the line itself more guys in fluorescent pink. On the other side of the line a graveyard stretched all the way back to the bridge. In the middle of the gravestones a group of the parachutists were stood around in visored crash helmets. Two dog handlers walked its perimeter.

A silver, blue and red tube train nosed out from under the bridge and quietly stretched out along the track. WHITE CITY it said on the front in orange digital.

Right below the bridge were two sectioned-off bits of levelled ground. One contained a crane. In both stood black guys in donkey jackets with SECURITY stamped on fluorescent green backing. The ones without the crane to guard had got a good fire going. There was more loose timber lying about, planking and the lower section of a tree trunk. You could see its roots.

—See those crafty cozzers, Mark said.

—What, Steve said.

Mark pointed down at a group of white policemen who'd come to stand around the fire with the Security guys.

Back at the car Steve said it must be costing them a packet, wages alone.

Mark was smiling. In the car he rubbed his hands.

—Keeps them off our backs though don't it.

Steve smiled. He supposed it did. In fact.

—For the safety of everyone concerned, did you hear the cunt? Mark said.

—Who?

—The cozzer at the roadblock.

—Oh him. To be perfectly honest, well before I remembered the M11 thing, from the telly yesterday, you know, and put two and two together, for a moment I felt . . .

The mobile rang. Mark pulled up at a T-junction, took a right and picked up the phone.

—Who's that . . . Yeah I know. I just didn't pick it up . . . Don't go fucking paranoid on me, it was circumstances, you'll like it when I tell you the story . . . Yes, laugh your bollox off.

He put the phone down.

—My pal Tony, he said. Ten to the dozen, the cunt. So is there anything else to talk about. You've talked twenties and I've said a hundred off of unit price.

Steve took it on board. Then he said it was reasonable, it made complete sense. But in the meanwhile what about five, it would be cash.

Five?

Five?

Well.

There were several things. Like Tony was already at the flat; John Matthew always had reasonable little parcels lying around; Patsy K had said the feller was sound, just needed a bit of time to get moving; and five hundred quid was still five hundred quid even in this day and age.

They were in a High Street. Not a policeman in sight. People up and down the pavement with shopping bags and hard-backed attaché cases. Mark picked up the mobile. Then he put it down, checked the rear-view and pulled up by a green card-phone box.

—I'll just be a minute, he said.

A cold wind came with the open door. Ahead Steve saw two towerblocks and a stretch of low-rise behind concrete-planked walls. A dumper truck came out from the towerblock entry at speed. Steve shivered. November had been warm. Average temperatures had broken all records. Only the last couple of days it had turned, shown its real colours. All good things must come to an end.

As they had. All in one hit.

As they fucking had. Bastards.

A crane arm started moving back and forth above the low-rise. He could hear it clanking. He shivered.

—Yeah, if you want that five now. Take half an hour, Mark said.

—Great, Steve said.—It's appreciated.

Mark grunted, checked the rear-view and took a left. They drove through streets of maisonettes.

He pulled up in front of a modern four-storey block behind a low hedge.

—He'll be here in a minute with the parcel. We might as well wait up in the flat, Mark said.

They hurried through the cold into the lobby. There was a lift criss-crossed with lime and black fluorescent tape. Stood there was an old dear with bags.

Steve offered a hand.

On the second floor she said thank you that many times, he was blushing.

On the third Mark opened a door with his own keys.

—All right Tony, he shouted.

Steve saw a bare room and a minimal kitchen. The lounge was carpeted and had a sofa. The man Tony got up off of it. The way Steve saw him he could have been a taxi-driver. Or in a warehouse, on the forklift or doing the paperwork behind glass. Either. There was a radio down by his feet.

—Did Johnny ring back, Mark said.

—Yeah, he's on his way.

Mark made the intro and told his story, why he hadn't answered the mobile and what went with it.

Tony raised his eyebrows. Then he said he'd seen it on TV before he'd come out.

—You know, the regional, after the main news. They kept all the lawyers and journalists out this superintendant said. Danger of falling masonry he said. Can you credit it.

—For The Safety Of Everyone Concerned, Mark said.— Ain't that right Steve? Cunts! Do they all do a course in Public Relations?

—Bobby T says it's the only course they do.

—Is that right? Bobby T? All right is he?

—Yes, got his flat down by the old market, Housing Association. Very nice, you know, in a proper house, got a floor to himself. Front door and then another key to his own place.

Steve was nodding. He could picture it, knew such a place.

Tony smiled at him from across the sofa. There was nothing behind it, it was friendly.

—So of course he'll have bits and pieces he shouldn't have up there. Nothing much, the odd parcel, but nickable, bird involved. He's only had the place three months, comes back one afternoon and the front door's wide open with a panda parked out front.

Steve nodded. He could picture it, not a panda just, but all the rest. He wanted to look at his watch. He wanted a cigarette. He really wanted a cigarette.

—So like Bobby says he's not sure, thinks of walking past, but the panda convinces him. Whatever it is, can't be that bad.

All right, all right, Steve had got the point, it didn't need spelling out. He offered Tony a Silk Cut from the packet.

Tony shook his head and got up for an ashtray. He was still talking. Mark was pacing up and down the bare light-brown carpet. The first drag on the Silk Cut hit the spot. He felt good.

—There's a woman got the ground floor. Sensible, Billy says, so as he's walking through the front door he knows it's not going to be her and domestic. Even if her door's open and there's a cozzer stood in it. In uniform and lucky if he's five foot two.

Steve had the ashtray in his hands. Not halfway down and the Silk Cut tasted like shit.

—Right, Mark said.—I believe you.

He had a small mirror in his hand, white powder lying on it.

—So it's the cozzer speaks first, tells him Sorry sir, there's been a burglary. Does he live here? He doesn't think any other flat's been affected. So Bobby wasn't born yesterday, he mumbles how shocked he is before he shoots up the stairs.

—Fancy a line while we're waiting, Mark said. He checked his watch and took a snort.

—I wouldn't say no, Steve said.

—The cop had got that bit right, Bobby's place was untouched. Takes him ten minutes to look round then he goes back down and speaks politely, tells him, that's right, his's untouched.

—Let's have it right, Mark said, his door'll be double-Chubbed.

—All right, it's double-Chubbed. All I'm saying is Bobby's chatting him up. It comes out her downstairs hasn't been too clever with her back door, a plywood sandwich. But it's not just that, Bobby starts to put the rest of the story together.

Steve didn't know, not anything: what they wanted, what he was supposed to get out of it: if and when this other face was coming with his parcel. Anything. He reached out for the mirror.

—There's a factory behind the house and they've seen these four kids over the back fence and rung the law. Rung them and the kids don't know they've been rumbled, they're only kids, think they've got all day. Got to be bang to rights only the law's been late in arriving. Five foot two says they've given chase, which means they were still there when Old Bill got there, given chase but failed to apprehend the suspects. Bobby knows it's bollox, the cozzer knows it's bollox only what he does is starts talking to Bobby like he's an OK local citizen who knows the score, What Can They Do. So Much of it Going On, What Can They Do.

—Where is he, the cunt. Doesn't he run to a watch, John, Mark said.

Tony shrugged.

A double act, wide open but all Steve wanted was to scream out loud ALL THAT MATTERS IS HOW HARD THEY KNOCK THE DOOR.

—I'll ring him, Mark said, angry, tapping his mobile.

—All I'm saying is there's no one to beat Old Bill when it comes to public whingeing. What Can We Do.

—No one there, he'll be on his way.

—If you want the toilet Steve, it's just one to the left, Tony said.

A mind-reader. He was supposed to be a warehouseman, manager at most, now he was a mind-reader. Steve would be wanting the toilet, he could feel it coming on. He said thanks.

—Yes, what a hard time they've got. Over this way that is. And fair play to Bobby T. It's how they come to the door's what matters. If it's not with a sledgehammer, Bobby says, it can't be that bad. Me, I'd have done a runner. But then you think about it, like me and the TV licence.

And just how far could a warehouseman run, on the forklift or behind the plate glass: made no difference, not very far. Spew up and collapse. Only he could talk. Nineteen to the dozen Mark had said, his own mate. Collapsed and spewing up he'd still be talking, telling whoever it was, just what kind of collapse it was and how it was different to all other collapses. Which of course it was, it was his fucking own.

Steve wanted a cigarette.

He really wanted a cigarette.

—What, they come with sledgehammers the TV people, Mark said like he didn't know anything about anything.

—Not yet, Tony said.

Then he was off again, what he was saying was, what he was talking about was the rights of people who came to your door.

—These days they come two-handed in civvies, the TV people. Two-handed but they've got no rights of entry. That's why they go for the single mothers. And the training they get, not all that bollox about direction-finders, they just get taught to knock on door-knockers so as to scare the shit out of people who don't know they've got no rights of entry. There's a way of doing it.

—Rat a rat rat, Mark said.

This was getting nowhere except telling you that if this Tony ever had had a cab, he was the taxi-driver from hell. Stuck tight in traffic as far as the eye could see and the guy would be explaining it, how it was, why it was, and the internal workings of the traffic light.

It was getting no one anywhere.

Steve lit up. The first drag on the Silk Cut hit the spot.

Mark had given up pacing, he was sat on the carpet, back against the wall.

—But there's not enough, there's only so many single mums while on the other hand the feller who reads the news and Wogan, they've got to get their wages. That's why they're in civvies now. So you don't know it's them. And they reckon there's enough people beyond the mothers mug enough to open their doors to one civvie, or two civvies, that you've never seen in your life, stood on the doorstep.

It was nonsense, all of it. Didn't mean a thing. Was going nowhere. Only three drags and the Silk Cut tasted like shit. Steve looked at his watch. Between fifteen and twenty minutes they'd been in the place. He took a drag on the cigarette, stubbed it out and said he was going to take a leak.

And Tony was still at it as he stepped out into the passage and saw the toilet ahead: areas this time, where they went two-handed, and where they went solo. Like he was going to get out a map and a box of coloured pins. Like now he was *running* the cab office.

Only that wasn't the point.

Steve had unzipped his trousers. He had his prick out.

He looked down at the stainless porcelain.

It wasn't the point at all. There was a comedian on the premises. Did they want to know. Is that what they fucking wanted to know.

He turned, prick back in his pants, trousers unzipped, and pushed the green-stained aluminium bolt into the half-loop nailed on to the wall. Decision time. He would give it another fifteen minutes and then he was going whether the guy came or not. He would get up, tell them he was a busy man and he was off. Fifteen minutes.

His streak of piss hit the porcelain hard. He zig-zagged it down into the still water. Not his line of work but he'd snorted enough to know, nice gear, this coke of Mark's that Mark might say was just personal but who knew. It was something he could tell them, and in the meanwhile another line would go down well. Tell them straight, he's got access to some very nice flake. Flake, you know, Class A. Tell them that instead of all these gadgets. He didn't even know when to turn it off. The other thing worked itself, he could feel it hard against his skin. He shook out the last drops of piss. If the tight bastards had just given him the cash for ten, twenty better still, if they weren't such arseholes then no need for all this sweaty shit.

Tony was still talking, some story, someone called Charlie Cook.

—He's opened his door one time. Probably wants to talk to someone, the mood's on him. So they've stood in the doorway, the two of them and they can hear it. The TV's in the lounge and Charlie's got it full volume just in case, so there's no chance of him missing anything that might be important.

Not a taxi-driver: not a warehouseman, behind glass or otherwise: but a fucking bulldozer. Mark must have had years of it.

—So they told him the score, what it costs for the colour, and Charlie tells them he hasn't got one. He might have wanted company but now he's had enough. They can fucking hear it. But sir, one of them says.

Steve wanted a cigarette. He looked at his watch.

Mark looked at his watch.

—He'll be here in a minute, fancy a taste.

Steve took a snort off the mirror and lit up. The first drag on the Silk Cut really really hit the spot.

—Gobsmacked they are. But Sir. So Charlie says I wouldn't have one in the house and makes himself look even bigger than he is in the first place.

—An economy shithouse door, Mark said.

—What? Tony said. He was frowning.—Economy's small. Premium you mean. And then he says he wouldn't have one in his house because there's voices in the box trying to get at him. THE VOICES.

Only two drags and the Silk Cut tasted like shit. Steve checked his watch. Otherwise he felt great. Ten more minutes he'd give it and then that was it.

—KILL, they say. The two civvies, they're wobbly but they're still in there hanging on the ropes. Only then Charlie says they've got TRANKS IN GOODMAYES can shut them out but that don't mean they're not real because what are tranks but FUCKING CHEMICAL SHIT and he knows they're real when he's off them LIKE NOW. But they've already gone, the other end of the corridor and disappearing round the corner.

—Let's have it right, Mark said, Charlie Cook is a fucking nutter.

He looked at his watch and shook his head.

—He's some case that John, it's like time don't exist. Fancy another line Steve.

Why not. He'd done all that could be expected of him. If they were too mean to give him the wedge for twenty there and then, on record, it was their fucking look out. Why not.

Steve took a toot off the mirror. He lit up a Silk Cut.

—That's where the real money is, the Tranks market, Tony said.—Ten minutes I'm giving John. I've got things to do.

Two drags and the Silk Cut tasted like shit. Otherwise he felt great. Steve felt fucking great.

—All he's got to do is roll out of bed with a single parcel and make the great effort of getting himself here. You know what, the Trank companies have bought him off, Mark said.

Tony shrugged and looked at his watch.

—Winds everyone up so that's what they've got to have, A Premium Trank. Or that's what he's on hisself.

—We've got the twenty at two. And pay off the other feller at four, that's what we said. I've got the sixty here but we'll need the forty off the twenty, Tony said.

So at last, the warehouseman had got serious. Telephones in both ears behind the glass. Steve checked his watch. He'd give it five and then he was off. Having done more than enough and if they couldn't see that, then they were stupid.

Like these guys. Mugs. Blabbing away. Did they actually have sixty? To hand? On the twenty they'd make forty-two he imagined. A grand each for themselves.

Mugs.

—I'm giving this guy three minutes, Steve said.—And if you don't mind me saying, you guys are wide open, the way you talk. I mean supposing I was sitting here wired up, a cassette thing.

Because that was right, it was possible, they were that complacent.

They were frowning, the two clowns. Like really they didn't have a sense of humour, couldn't see the joke. Like the taxi-driver leaning over the sofa and grabbing his shoulders. No kidding, fingers dug in.

—What are you playing at, Steve shouted, get your hands off.

Tony had him pinned back on the sofa. Was calling him a cunt. Prodded his flesh. Touched on hard plastic. Shouted.

—And what are you playing at, Mark said close up. He hit Steve smack on the jaw.

His teeth jarred. For a second he wasn't there. Then his arms were out: what was this: what was it about: it was only something he did to cover himself, in the event of a dispute: not of course that it would be necessary with them.

Tony held him back on the sofa one-handed.

—This ain't real, Tony said. He was appealing to Mark. He pressed the arrows that looked like Rewind.

Aching-face Steve said it was just a record. So as there's no dispute. I mean I know with you guys –

Mark hit him half uppercut under the cheekbone.

Tony was shaking his head, he couldn't believe it.

—They just get taught to knock on doorknockers so as to scare the shit out of people who don't know they've got no rights of entry. There's a way of doing it.

His own voice tinny, with scraping sounds, a laugh and the pull on a cigarette.

—Rat a rat rat.

Mark's voice. Now he was breathing heavy.

—A bleeper, he'll have a bleeper, he said.

Steve clutched at his balls as the trousers ripped off. His head was throbbing.

—We're fucked, Tony said.

—Look I've told you, Steve said in a gulp.—I mean—

Mark held up a flapped-over envelope of money.

—Bollox, he said.—We're all right. Bottled it have you Steve, can you bottle it or don't a bleeper work in your shit.

He ripped at the Y-fronts.

—You bastards, you stupid fucking bastards, Steve shouted going for take-off off the sofa.

Mark hit him combination, on the jaw, in the eye. He lifted the prick, caught the gleam of plastic, and ripped it off the flesh.

No sound from the rat, out for the count.

—Check the window Tone.

He stamped on the plastic. The carpeting sucked it in.

—Anything there wasn't there this morning, he said from the kitchen door.

The plastic crunched on the kitchen floor.

—There's an Escort Turbo.

—Vans Tony, vans.

—A Telecom looks like.

—What?

—Driving past. Going, going –

There was a knock at the door. Tony felt it full in the chest. Mark was telling him something, arms, mouth and eyes moving together. Sit on the cunt, it looked like. He went to the sofa.

There was a knock at the door. Mark was stood behind it.

It was pointless because they were fucked but Tony sat. He could hear the voice from behind the wood.

—Come on Mark, you wanted the milkman, here's the milkman.

—The cunt, Tony said. He was smiling.

Mark put a finger across his lips. He shook his head.

Bang Bang on the door.

Tony was frowning.

—I got out of bed for this. OY. MARK.

Mark winced. It was madness. And it was John's own fucking fault. Late one time too many. Which didn't stop him giving the whole block the benefit.

—OY.

Tony had his arms out either side of Steve's face like this was bollox.

Feet turned on lino the other side of the door. They shuffled off. Fucking shuffled, like John was the most hard-done-by man in London. And all this, all of it, down to the piece of shit on the sofa. Who Patsy K said was all right. Who had come to life, wriggling, making noises.

Mark turned the radio on loud.

Bees, a man said, the way a hive worked ought not to be used as any kind of metaphor of human society. Not any kind.

—Look you guys. OK. Sorry. But they made me do it. You can't fucking believe what they did, what they were trying to lay.

Mark turned the dial. It was House. Or Jungle. Or whatever they called it these days. Mark didn't know.

—What'd you do that for, Tony said.—John, he could have given us a hand.

—Yeah, like lumbering us with five kees. Plus in twenty-four hours half of London thinks we've got Old Bill on our backs and we're out of the game.

—OK, I admit it. It was a moment of weakness. It was. But there's no harm done.

Steve's voice came out in squirts. With heavy breathing.

What a sight, Tony sat on the cunt like he was a cushion. You had to laugh only you didn't because Tony would get the hump and you were in the shit.

—There isn't. Really. No harm done, I'll just say you didn't want to know and—

—Never mind out the game, what we going to do now, Tony said.

There were no vans in the street, just the ice-cream van that was always there.

—Get the money out of here. If they are mob-handed out there they'll cop it all anyway. Then put off the meets, an unavoidable delay which is only the fucking truth.

—I can't fucking breathe. Get him off me. I don't know what you're getting steamed up about, we haven't done anything. No business. There's no harm done. I'm not going to scream or anything. Let's not get melodramatic.

—What we going to do with him, Tony said.

—You get the money out, and I'll mind him. Deal with him after. Here, we got any rope?

It was a stupid question.

—I'll tell you who we are entitled to some help off and that's Patsy K. More than entitled, Mark said.

—Patsy'll tell you, I'm no grass. I was in a spot right. I admit it. They'd got me by the bollox but I wasn't going to give them anything on you. They're mugs these Old Bill. What I say is, it may look good on paper but it wouldn't stand up.

—And if they are listening in, he's entitled to have his number traced.

Mark finished tapping out on the mobile.

—Yeah let me talk to Patsy. He'll tell you, there's no harm done and there never will be.

A woman's voice said what she often said: *The Mercury phone you have just called is switched off. Please try again later.*

—He's got it switched off. There's that Mazda in the lock-up, fetch that after you've sorted the other. And plenty of rope.

—Get him off me. I've told you. I know you're pissed off but no way were they going to get anything out of me. I was stringing them along.

It was Jungle, the drum-and-bass stopped long enough for the feller to say it, some club in Clapton. DJ Ron, DJ Keithley, all night, all for a tenner.

—You be all right on your tod? Tony asked.

—Just ring me if you're going to be more than an hour. Is there sheets on that bed?

—Stringing them along. They're as thick as pigshit. Get him off me. Get him off.

Still mumbling, Mark could hear it as he pulled a sheet off from under the duvet. Not fresh fresh, like Tony put his head down there now and then. Like sometimes he wanted a bit of peace. Why not put in a TV while he was at it.

He ripped at the sheets, dug his nails in.

Why not? Because the place was fucked. Whatever else, minimum damage was that the place was fucked. All because of this tosser.

The linen strip was jagged, bits of weave hanging off.

Unreal. It was fucking unreal. Someone recommended by Patsy K. Which told you what, that Patsy had lost it. Which if he had lost it was a waste of time knowing. It got you nowhere.

The second strip came off zig-zag. It was the bleeper that mattered. What it did. Its capabilities. The shit had been sat there long enough before they'd rumbled it. Sat there because with John, crossing the road was exercise.

And the cunt was still talking.

—OK do whatever you're going to do with me, fucking do it if you're that paranoid. I'm just telling you there's no harm done and those Old Bill they only think they're smart.

Mark stood at the window with two strips of sheeting. The ice-cream van had a flat tyre. It was hemmed in by cars. And in the cars? No one he could see.

He said it to Tony but Tony didn't like it. He didn't like any of it but OK, he could take the point, there was nothing to lose, him walking out of there with the 60G.

Mark had bent down in front of the settee. The cushion was kicking its legs. Mark grabbed its ankles and dropped the sheet strip on them. It hadn't shit itself but there was a smell.

—Don't you ever wash your socks you no-good piece of shit, he said and got a first twist pulled round the legs.

Steve was trying to shout. Tony clamped his elbow down but he didn't like it, not any of it.

—Just don't kill him, he said.—Fuck's sake whatever else, don't kill him.

—I'm just tying him up Tone. I don't want to be sitting on it for the next hour. I don't want all this period. Here, just shove up, hold his arms tight.

It wasn't easy, his arms round Tony, flipping the strip round its shoulders, the arms flapping like it was drowning even with Tony's grip. Heavy breathing in stereo. The ashtray went scatter.

—There's a roll of plaster in the bathroom, Tony said.— First Aid Box.

You had to hand it to him, no TV but a First Aid Box. Like

any moment you might have diarrhoea, a sliced finger, or a splitting headache, on the premises.

The box was embossed with a red cross. It smelled of iodine.

If he'd rung Patsy K once, he'd rung him five time. *Please try again later.* Then it was his mobile was ringing and all the while the shit on the sofa followed everything with his eyes. You looked at sheets and it was hard to believe what they could do. But they made climbing ropes, he'd seen it for himself.

They made tying ropes. The shit wriggled but it made no odds. Just his eyes that were moving.

On the mobile first it was the one, then it was the other feller: Tony'd rung them; they'd thought the money was going to be sorted today; so what was it.

As if things didn't happen. As if he was going to rip them off. For a hundred G. What was the matter with them.

They were just puzzled, they said. Both of them. Just puzzled. Then they said they'd just been worried for him, that was all. Both of them.

He said he was sorry, if it had really had to be today he'd sort it but a couple of things had cropped up, AS THEY DID.

He said it to one and then to the other feller. Not something he wanted to say on a regular basis, not to them or anyone else equivalent.

At least you had to say thanks for small mercies and as things were, small mercies were big mercies. Unless Tony'd got his priorities wrong he'd got the money out and safe.

The shit on the sofa, Patsy K's pal, he looked like the invisible man.

Mark turned off the radio and positioned himself, back to the wall, to ask questions.

Did whatever law had a grip on him know of him, Mark, as a person or was Steve just out trawling for whatever unlucky sod he could come up with.

You could see he was trying to say something, the invisible worm, the way his head was moving.

—OK, Mark said.—Just nod or shake your head. Did the law who pressured you, did they know my name?

You could see it, the mouth trying to move behind the pink plaster. Then Steve shook his head.

—So you've said give me a break and I can net you some bigger people right? To some cozzer can see his name up in lights.

It liked it, the cushion. Nodding like it wanted the head to drop off. Which, if the cunt had any self-respect at all, it would have. Patsy K had plenty to answer for.

Please try again later.

Hard to tell with the eyes, bobbing about above the criss-cross pink, but it looked like invisible worm was disappointed. Like if only everything was all right Patsy K was going to float through the window on a Turkish carpet. Wave a wand.

If only.

Patsy K was an overweight tosser.

—What's the bleeper do?

What was the cushion doing? Shrugging? Looking fucking stupid in fact. In a raggedy straitjacket.

—Was it switched on?

It shook its head. Too much, like it was a stupid question.

Mark jumped out from the wall and let go a right into the eye. His knuckles jarred: cross-wired in the wrist; ping to the elbow. Blood jumped out of an eyebrow. The first drop down the cheek hit the plaster's edge. Red dripped into the pink.

He looked away and at his watch. An hour and ten minutes. So where was Tony? Why leave the mobile switched on? Why have to put up with the one feller and then the other if Tony wasn't going to make use of this basic fucking facility?

He grabbed at blood-seeped plaster and ripped.

The cunt.

A splodge of skin came away. The cushion squeaked. By the nostrils blood smudged. From the eyebrow a drop landed on the chin.

Mark picked up the thinned-out roll of plaster and stood by the window. He pulled it out and cut a six-inch stretch.

Unbelievable. Him standing there cutting plaster like it was normal when he'd woken up in the morning, in his own bed, feeling cheerful, just have a chat with Patsy K's pal, sort out the money and then the evening for whatever he fancied. Boiled eggs for breakfast, firm whites and runny yellow. Normal. Now he was having to think straight. Number one was, whatever the fucking bleeper could do they hadn't smashed down the door. Nor put vans in the street. Not that you could see.

Thumbs apart, he slapped the plaster down across Invisible Man's face: under the nose; ear to ear.

—The bleeper, how long's it been switched on, he said.— I'm going to count out fingers. Each finger's an hour. Nod when I get there.

He counted them out from the left and on to the right. The Invisible Man kept shaking his head.

Fuck it, just get him off the premises so he wouldn't come back. That would do. It was enough. Only he couldn't do it on his own so if Tony could just make the fucking effort to get back. So they could get on with it. Which was pulling up the fitted carpet and rolling up the cushion inside. That's what it boiled down to.

When it came, the key in the lock was loud. All by itself, Mark's chest shuddered.

He looked at his watch.

—Fuck's sake Tony, he said.

—What, Tony said.—It's sweet. Which is a fucking miracle.

His face was drawn tight like he'd been slimming.

—An hour you said, and you'd phone. What have I got a mobile for?

Tony said he hadn't had time, had enough on his plate. The money was safe; the one feller and then the other, they were sorted for the time being; and he'd got the Mazda even though he'd had no keys because Mark had given them to Philippa and Philippa'd been at the hairdresser's. So what the fuck was Mark on about.

Mark put his arms up. Said he was in the wrong. Said he'd just been sweating the last forty minutes. That's all it was.

—Now, well, looks like we're halfway in the clear. Maybe the batteries ran out.

—What, Tony said.

—The bleeper. You know, cost-cutting, so they've switched to short-life batteries.

Tony shrugged.

Maybe.

Or the cozzers were being double-crafty.

Outside the window lights sprang up everywhere in a dark blue sky. A strip of glowing orange lay around the horizon.

—Well it's not on top is it, Mark said.

—What are we going to do with him?

—The Invisible Man? You met him, the Invisible Man?

—What are we going to do with him, Tony said.

—Get him out of here. Dump him. The middle of nowhere.

Tony could see crafty cozzers lying in wait. Throwing the book at them. Making a name for themselves. Kidnapping. False imprisonment. GBH. Attempted murder.

—Gives us time, Mark said.—Dump the mobile, clean this place up then leave it a while. All he's got is our first names.

Tony's hand was back and forth across his forehead, the speed of windscreen wipers in slow mode. Mark had a point, only the feller was a headcase. Had to be. Brought it down on them, brought it down on himself. Saying it himself, I could be wired up. And how could you tell with a nutter. How could you tell with Old Bill, if they were just biding their time. How could you tell. He'd checked the street going out, he'd checked his mirrors coming back, but they could have umpteen motors radio'd up. He'd seen it on telly.

—Well I'm not sitting here with him for the duration, Mark said.

All right. All right then.

Invisible Man was looking at him. Staring at him.

The cunt.

—OK, let's have him out, Tony said.

—Just got to get him down to the Mazda. You get the rope?

—It's in the motor. That was another thing, and you're asking me why I never phoned.

—No Tony, I did ask you, and I was in the wrong.

The Invisible Man, his eyes were back and forth, back and forth. Like he was watching Wimbledon on telly. When there was no telly. And never would be, not in this place.

—I was in the wrong, Mark said again.—I'm not bullshitting, you've been brilliant. And I'll admit it, when you rumbled him, that moment, I thought we were fucked. I did. But now, we're getting there. One step at a time Tony, and we're getting there. There's just Patsy K's pal now. Wrap him in the carpet. We'll need the rope. Either end.

The Invisible Man, just the name, Patsy K, and he was excited. You could see it, wriggling in his ripped shorts, his head up and down. He'd wear himself out.

—You tried him? Try him again, Tony said.

—Who?

—Patsy.

Mark shrugged, picked up the mobile and tapped out the numbers. Tony was looking at him. The Invisible Man, he was always looking at him.

The Mercury phone you have just . . .

How irresponsible could you be. OK, you'd had a night on the charlie; you needed some sleep come morning; you turned the fucking thing off. But not the afternoon, the afternoon whatever your timetable, you were entitled to be available. Patsy K, from the moment he'd given toerag the nod, he was entitled to be available every minute of every day.

Tony said he'd go and get the rope.

Mark started on the carpet, the far side from the sofa. It was tacked down. Some bastard had done a proper job and nailed it down. He got his fingers under the carpet either side of the corner tack, and yanked. A two-foot triangle came up with him. Upright, he pulled at the triangle. He saw the whole edge length coming up ping, ping, ping.

Nothing happened.

He kneeled down by the next tack and ripped upwards. A stretch of carpet came up. He was getting there. One step at a time and he was getting there.

Tack three.

Tack four.

Tony was stood with a canvas holdall.

Tack five.

Tack six.

Invisible Man, he was half up out the sofa, wriggling like a nutter.

Tack seven.

He was up.

Tack eight.

He was falling. Tony let go the holdall, he reached out his arms.

You could hear the crash, anyone could.

Mark turned. Said to use some rope. Round The Bastard's Knees. And in fact, get him out of here till I've finished. The kitchen. Or the bathroom.

Tack ten. Close to the corner. Tony was pulling the guy, dragging him across the oatmeal. You could hear his breathing.

Mark went on round the corner.

Round the back of the sofa, sweating. He called to Tony to leave him and give him a hand.

They grabbed either end of the edge opposite. It looked like the sofa was sliding backwards.

Tony grunted. He was pulling hard, waiting for the castor to squeak on the floorboards. The carpet came at them hump-backed. A castor squeaked on the floorboards.

When they'd pulled it free, Tony tamped it down in the middle and draped the far edge up on the sofa. Like a hammock, he said. The whole thing, it was fucking madness, so why not, like a hammock.

The Invisible Man, the way his cheeks were working, he was still talking. They pulled him back into the lounge and wrapped him, rolled him towards the sofa. Tony saw the problem, the Mazda's boot-size, he couldn't see it, however bent the cunt's knees.

—Not with that much carpet, he said.—It's a stiff tube, the way it is. And how's his breathing. He's got to be able to breathe in there.

Kidnapping, false imprisonment, and murder. No.

No. No. No.

He was bent down at one end of the carpet roll, his ear to the hollow centre. Like pistons the feller's nose was working, or it was full of snot. There was just too much carpet. He said it again.

—I don't believe this, Mark said.

One step at a time, fair enough. But this was fucking ridiculous. He wanted to kick the carpet, punch the wall. All the dust and shit off the floorboards and still they weren't finished.

—There's a Stanley knife under the sink, Tony said.

Was there? What and a larder full of tinned food? And a fucking generator for all he knew. Tony the Quartermaster.

There was a Stanley knife under the sink. Tony had it in his hand.

They pulled the carpet back two rolls. Tony got a first cut into the edge and walked backwards, slitting the soft stuff on top and the stringy weave under.

Out the window the street was bright under sodium lights. The orange strip on the horizon was losing colour. The ice-cream effort was still the only van. Mark looked at his watch. The slit was a zig-zag, gobs of carpet and fluff stuck out in ragged triangles.

—Let's do it now, before the workers come home, he said.

—We'll hit the rush hour, Tony said, stood up for a breather.—Before we get out of town. Murder. Chockablock.

—The rush hour. Tony, I don't give a fuck about the rush hour. Once we're out in the motor with him tucked away, that's all I'm bothered about. You want to sit here with him another two hours? Here, give us that blade.

He cut straight, hit a snarl-up and slashed his way through. At the far end the two pieces flopped to the floorboards.

—Looks like half the fucking world wants the M11, Mark said.

They were pulled up at lights, traffic ahead as far as the eye could see. Tony was tempted. He'd said it at the time. So what did his pal expect, that the entire commuting community of East Anglia were taking the day off. Were they fuck, they were busy. It's what he'd been saying.

—Come on you cunt, Mark shouted. What was the point of the lights turning green at all when you had a prick in a Polo in front of you who was letting a cheeky Transit do a cheeky right turn.

—Have them off the road, he said.—Just give me the equipment.

—What?

—A bulldozer for a start. Oy you, you can't drive to save your life. Bosh. Scoop them up and off the road. And the bulldozer's got a floodlight attached. Oy you. Me? Yes, it's you I'm talking to, you down there.

He made fifteen yards in first before the lights turned red.

—Bosh, the beam comes down and they know. It's down on them and them only. Sorry pal, you're off. See what I'm saying, traffic problems, bollox. Just give me the powers. Him, him in the Polo, he's off.

—He'll appeal. Undue haste, undue severity, undue process.

—Bollox, wheel-clampers do it, no appeal there. Their problem, the clampers, it's a halfway measure. Bring On The Bulldozers. Better still, a crane in the sky. Lift the fuckers right off the road, have them dangling in the sky. How's that for a deterrent. You can appeal all you like, fact is in the meanwhile, you're off the road.

All right. All right. Mark, it was like he was off the leash. Like they hadn't had that caper carrying Trouble down the stairs in his carpet. Like it had never happened. Like they'd done abracadabra to the lift and it started working just for them.

Not half an hour previous as if none of it had happened.

—You see what I'm saying, course you can appeal. Meanwhile however, Mark said.

None of it. Not twisting and turning down the stairs with a deadweight carpet. Not the old dear popping up in the doorway of the flats and smiling at them like they were good boys when Patsy K's pal was likely to start performing in his tube any moment.

—Hey Tony, you were brilliant, fucking brilliant. Oatmeal, I don't like the oatmeal, shows the stains too easy. Brilliant. I was shitting myself, the old dear in the doorway. I'm just waiting for the Invisible Man to throw a wobbler.

All right. All right then. It hadn't been that hard. He'd lifted a corner and shown her. Oatmeal, of course love, a Vodka and Orange, knock that over and you'll see it, stains easy. And she'd smiled at that because they were good boys and you could see, it was obvious, she'd had a Vodka and Orange in her time. So he'd said you didn't have to put up with what you didn't like, which was only right, and he was going for a red flocca.

—And that was a cracker, the flocca, you know, the hairy one. The hairy one, she loved it. Lapped it up.

Not bad as it happened, for the spur of the moment, and him shitting himself come to that. Tony leaned across and turned on the car radio.

—*Left with the feeling that NATO hasn't yet formulated its future.*

That was their diplomatic correspondent.

—*It has emerged tonight that squatting protesters in Clare-*

mont Road, Leyton, are about to spend their second night in makeshift structures above the dilapidated houses. The protesters are objecting to the extension of the M11 motorway into East London. A police spokesman said that the safety of all those involved was of paramount . . .

The mobile was ringing. One hand on the wheel, Mark took it up off the dash.

—Who's that . . . Are you taking the piss John, thirty minutes I was waiting, no forty . . . Yes, so . . . it so happens I've got other things to do in a day . . . No.

He turned to Tony. Cheeky sod, he said. He's only expecting me to take those kees off him.

—*In the run-up to the launch of the National Lottery. A spokesman for Camelot, the organisers, said . . .*

—Here you know what, we're up five grand apiece on the day, Mark said.

Tony didn't cotton on, you could see it in the oncoming dipped beams.

—He did have the money for his five, silly bollox did. You remember, Mark said.

Well well well. He had forgotten. Mind for what he'd been through, for what they were going through, you'd be wanting a few grand. Several. Walking out the door with 60G into who knew what; sweating over carpet; telling the old dear he didn't care for oatmeal. Several several grand.

Mark had taken the wad from his pocket, was telling him to split it.

On the other hand, a grand in the hand was worth a few on a promise.

—Did you hear him, that John, Mark said.—No one to beat him when it comes to a whinge.

He slowed down for an intrusion of cones in off-red and white hoops. Tony was tapping his feet to the Eric Clapton off of the radio. Cars were closing up ahead.

—A Car Supermarket, Tony said, pointing out to the left.—

It'll be a struggle pushing your trolley. Give little Davey a shock. Me, Me, I'm going to push it. I want to push the trolley.

—What is he, seven? Mark said. It was true, CAR SUPER-MARKET it said, and in all the windows, smaller type in red, AUTO HYPERMARKET.

Tony had nodded.

—I want to push it, he said.—And bosh, there's a chassis on the trolley. Ugh ... Shove. Ugh ... Shove. And he'll never admit it, never admit he's beat. He won't say nothing so there's the trolley just stood there in the aisle, if that's what they've got, aisles, and Davey stood there like pushing a trolley with a motor on top is the most boring fucking thing in the world he's just discovered, and why bother.

—Seven? So what's that make you, a proper grandad, Mark said as the traffic took a lurch towards the dual carriageway.

—It makes me feel old, Tony said.—Like this whole caper. I mean it makes you wonder, who the fuck can you trust.

Mark shrugged. The dual carriageway, it looked like the promised land. Tail lights hurrying away into the night.

—So the strength of it is, all he knows is you're Mark, your mobile number, and you've got a mate called Tony.

—Plus he's seen my motor. It's in Christine's name. Mind you he's such a div I can't see him remembering the reg, Mark said.

At last. On the dual carriageway. It felt private in the Mazda. And after his experiences of today he'll be doing well to remember his name.

—Mark, you said the flat was fucked. This afternoon. Whatever else, you said, the flat was fucked.

They slipped off the dual carriageway: along the slip road they slipped on to the motorway. Out, into a barrage of orange light and speedy cruising speeds.

—I did say that, you're right. But you know what, look, we've made it. So I don't know, just leave it for a month. Or clean it up and leave it for a month. Get Charlie Cook to walk past it now and then in the meanwhile. Was that true what you were saying, Charlie and the TV mob.

—Freaked them out, didn't know what had hit them.

—Here, do you think he's got any of those Premium Tranks spare?

The Mazda was going bump bump. Like it had hiccoughs. Bump bump bump. Like a flat fucking tyre. Just when you thought you'd done the hard bit, bosh, you were out on the hard shoulder with a jack in the freezing fucking cold.

—Look at it, Mark said.—And they call it a motorway. Slabs of tarmac stuck together with squirts of tar. That's if it is tarmac. As it happens, it's oatmeal. Look at it. Fuck that, BRING ON THE FLOCCA.

Mark was shouting, he was banging the wheel. Black on yellow signs were looming up to narrow his options. He could see the bulldozers ahead straddling the hard shoulder, surrounded by cones.

He spoke quietly, What matters Tony is we're away. Nothing terrible's happened.

—What about him in the carpet?

—That's what we're doing isn't it? Dump the cunt. Look for turn-offs after Newmarket. Dump him. Take him out of his carpet, tell him what's what and we fuck off. A forest, somewhere off the road.

—But still tied with the sheets. It's fucking cold out there. What if he gets exposure. What the old dears get, hypothermia.

—Let's have it right Tony, this is 1994. Naked and cold, if he can't handle that what chance has he got. He's getting a result, anyone else, and I'm not just talking yardies, anyone else and he's dead. Here, look, more fucking cones. They're taking over. The cone empire, see the way they're spreading out. Before you know it they'll have reached John O'Groats.

—John O'Groats, that's where they walk for charity.

—Is that right, Mark said.—For charity?

PIG!

Steven Wells

'Hold your fire!' barked top pig Frank Stank. Two hundred flak-jacketed élite combat cops reluctantly eased their twitching fingers off the hair triggers of their oiled and gleaming Heckler-Koch semi-auto slag-slaughtering submachine-guns. They were like machines, these men, tensed and turgid terrorist-terminators trained to take out the enemies of the state with extreme prejudice. Four hundred eyes squinted hawkishly at the dilapidated council house that contained their prey. Two hundred stunted libidos screamed for the subliminal sexual release that could only be achieved by the savage, slashing penetration of human flesh by thousands of titanium tipped explosive dumdum bullets.

'Fuck me, vers farsands of 'em,' chirruped cheerful cockernee costermonger-stylee rent boy cum judge stabber cum punk performance artist, Ricky Tickytimebomb as he twitched aside the dust-caked lace curtains to stare nervously at the assembled forces of Law, Order and Decency.

'Today is a good day to die!' spat anarcho-psychopath Justine Justice as she heaved a bandoleer of heavy duty crossbow bolts across her massive yet amazingly firm breasts. 'Hang on, what does *she* want?'

A mini-skirted woman with massive blonde hair was teetering up the drive clutching a cracked tea-cup. The top pig's megaphone spluckfustered and squawked like an electroduck spitting spunk into a 3-bar electric fire and spasming like a twat hatted techno raver at the very peak of an E laced with domestos overdose heart attack as the voltage thrashed its cyborg body into a pulsating shitfest of blood, wire and sparking metal feathers. The boss pig told the lurching leopard-skin-tighted and low-cleavaged lady that she was in great danger and ought, for her own sake, to retreat to a safe distance.

'FUCK OFF, COPPER!' shouted the heavily made up and come-to-bed-eyed woman, pivoting on a high-heeled foot and giving the assorted swine a Kes-style two-fingered salute.

Inside the knackered council flat the assorted besieged terrorists adrenally spasmed as the doorbell chimes rang in a chintzy versh of The Internationale.

'Oh bugger!' ejaculated black belt karate master and ex-army demolitions expert Aki Khan as he fingered the 560-year-old Himalayan throwing knife that his grandfather had bequeathed him with the wheezily requested deathbed wish that the youngster only use said weapon to slash the throats of fascists and bureaucrats.

'It's Mrs Harris from number 15!' explained Aki. 'She's a ruddy nutter who relentlessly pursues a lifestyle of stereotypical Northern slapperdom which mainly consists of getting off her face on gin every afternoon before attempting to shag her way through the 289 most sexually desirable men in the greater West Yorkshire conurbation. She's been after me for years!'

'Hmmm!' murmured Justine, stroking her Arnie-style steroid-swollen jaw. 'Is she the same Candice Harris who was rejected by the Turner Prize committee last year because her art wasn't middle-class, poncy and utterly fucking shit enough?'

'The same!' grunted Aki.

'Better let her in then! We could always do with more hostages!' laughed Justine, nodding over her shoulder to the corner of the room where the entire inner cabinet of the current Tory government sat trussed-up like the one-eared pig in Reservoir Dogs in stinking pools of their own shit, piss, blood and sweat.

It's really annoying the way Tories always void both bladder and bowel when you slash their throats open, thought Justine (who was a bit of a hygiene nut on the quiet) as she surveyed the pile of still twitching Tory corpse meat.

'Hang on, I'm coming!' shouted Aki as he ran down the stairs two at a time.

'You soon will be!' laughed Candice Harris, gingering her cleavage and feeling her clitoris stiffen in anticipation of the soon-come furious fuck-fest.

'What do you want?' yelled Aki as he threw the front door open wide in the cocky knowledge that the assorted heavily armed pigs wouldn't dare fire whilst they thought the crème de la crème of Tory scumbastardry were still alive and rescuable.

'Have you got a cup of sperm, I mean sugar?' purred Mrs Harris seductively, pushing her pert breasts into Aki's face.

'For fuck's sake, Candice!' screamed Aki, suddenly coming over all hysterically eloquent. 'Your behaviour is extremely inappropriate! Have you not noticed that we're engaged in a thrillingly tense hostage stroke siege scenario here?!'

'Oh shut up and fuck!' snarled Candice contemptuously as, in one fluid movement, she tossed the now redundant tea-cup over her naked left shoulder, pushed Aki down on to the doormat, whipped out his impressively proportioned and heavily veined purple headed yoghurt squirter, mounted him and proceeded to milk him with her incredibly strong vaginal muscles whilst slamming the door shut.

'Aaaaaargh! Aroooogah! HeeeeeYAH! AaaaaaRUMPH!' screamed Aki as he was brought to the very brink of mindmushingly intense orgasm again and again by the most incredible cunt in Christendom.

'My GOD!' wailed Stank as the inhuman hollering reached his hairy and mole spotted ears. 'They're torturing the poor woman! OK, lock and load everybody, we can't afford to wait for the SAS, on my command, we're going IN!'

'You're going NOWHERE!' roared a lean and muscular figure clad all in black with his face covered in sexy dark green camouflage paint (like Arnie in *Commando* and again in *Predator*) who appeared wraithlike at the top pig's side.

'Who the fuck are you?' squealed the boss pig as he stared into the clear blue eyes of this obviously well-bred apparition.

'Colonel Dan Daniels, Special Air Service!' woofed the man in black, threateningly fingering the knuckleduster-handled combat knife that dangled from his Sam Browne Belt. 'I'm taking over this operation before you flat footed plods make a pig's ear out of it!'

'Wha? Y-you can't just . . .' spluttered the king of the pigs seconds before Colonel Dan Daniels silenced his pathetic lower-middle-class whining with a snakelike strike on the jaw with his manly left fist that sent the blood-spurting pig flying back in slo mo to land with a sickening and spine-cracking thud on top of the roof of a panda car from whence he rolled to land with an audible flump in a crumpled heap of humiliated pigflesh.

'What's going on?' bellowed Justine Justice as she finished dipping her blowdarts into an old school style round goldfish bowl full of highly toxic buffalo-snake urine that she'd bought in a bulk order with a stolen credit card from a Chinese herbal remedy shop in London's Gerrard Street.

'Strewf!' spat Ricky Tickytimebomb as he leant on his blood-rusted genuine samurai sword and surveyed the bickering forces of corporate bastardry through the filth-smeared council house bedroom window. 'Wot appears to be h'occuring is that ver top rozzer is 'avin' is blinkin' noggin bashed in a no 'old's barred demarcational dispute wiv some SAbleedin'S geezer whilst, meanwhile, in the 'allway of this very cancil rat an'marse, our mucker Aki is getting 'is tubes cleaned by that bird from number 15!'

'So! The SAS!' snarled Justine contemptuously, as she rolled a stogie from side to side between her utterly seductive collagen-enhanced lips like Clint as The Man With No Name in all them cool spag Westerns. 'That means that they'll pretend to negotiate whilst planning a night-time attack with stun grenades where they'll shoot us in the back after we surrender . . .'

'Coo, larve a fackin' dack!' babbled the cheerful cockernee shitrouserdly. 'We're facked and no mistake! What we gonna dooooo! What we gonna dooooooo!'

KRAK!

Justine backhanded the fearful cockernee with a Mighty Joe Young style fist and started barking out orders.

'Bring up the catapult! Prepare the petrol bombs! It's time to cook some PORK! HAHAHAHAHAHA!'

'OK, Lieutenant, you know the drill?' inquired SAS Colonel Dan Daniels of the dapperly dressed posho with the mobile phone and the steel-rimmed Himmler specs who stood in front of him.

'Yes, sir!' said Pete Ringer, government hostage scenario negotiator-in-chief silkily. 'I keep them talking, make a few minor concessions and generally soften them up until it gets dark and you and your highly trained team of assassins can barge in, rescue all the hostages and shoot all the terrorists in the back after they've surrendered just like you did in the siege of the Iranian embassy way back in the good old days when Maggie was in power. *SIEG HEIL!!!!*'

'Make it so!' smiled Colonel Dan Daniels who modelled himself on Captain Jean Luc Picard out of *Star Trek: The Next Generation* except without the woolly liberal emotional blancmangeness.

BRUP! BRUP! brupped Justine's mobile phone.

'Hello, Justine Justice, terrorist she-wolf!' answered Justine, politely.

'Hi, Justine!' slurred Pete Ringer in his best let-it-all-hang-out social worker voice. 'My name's Peter Ringer, I work for the Home Office. Now, look, I'm sure we can work this out so that nobody gets hurt. Why don't you tell me what it is that you want and I promise you that I'll do my very best to . . .'

'DIE, PIG!' screamed Justine puce-facedly and broke the connection.

THWONGHAH! thwonghahed the catapult.

'What the bloody hell?' murmured Pete Ringer as he stared at the clumsy missile that was hurtled high into the air above him by the giant catapult that suddenly jutted from the bedroom window.

The slick-gobbed professional liar stared in horror as the missile broke up in mid-air and divided into a score or so of individual projectiles which, with their momentum lost, now crashed down on to the forces of piggery like the multiplied fists of an angry and righteous God.

'AYEEEAH!'   'AAAAAAAAAARHG!'   and 'FUUUUUUUUUUCK!' screamed a score or more of coppers as they were suddenly and spectacularly turned into fat spitting human candles by the deadly rain of napalm and white phosphorous Molotov cocktails.

The surrounded terrorists, surveying their handiwork, laughed their cocks and cunts off.

'Music . . .' roared Justine above the competing cacophonies of pig squealing and terrorist hilarity, ' . . . ON!'

The jovial sounds of the classic recording of the Laughing Policeman bellowed out from huge speakers in the council house living room. Watching TV crews pissed themselves with excitement. Burning filth plus top soundtrack! Ace footage! Arriba! Arriba! Sex on a fucking stick minus the fucking stick or WHAT!

'BONG! Death and destruction on a Bradford council estate! BONG! The cabinet hostage crisis takes a new and savage twist! BONG! Fifteen police officers dead and another twenty-seven injured, several of them severely! BONG! Good evening, we're going straight over to the scene of the cabinet hostage crisis in Bradford, West Yorkshire, where this already bloody conflict looks set to take another and possibly even more violent turn . . .'

Justine, Aki, Ricky, Candice and the gaggle of wild-eyed teenage scum known collectively as The Pudsey Posse were huddled around a tiny battery powered TV.

'OK!' roared Justine, her eyes alight with the bloodlust of

imminent battle. 'We can expect the trained killer dogs of the SAS to come blasting through the walls firing submachine-guns from the hip at any second! ACTION STATIONS! MUSIC ON!'

Outside, behind the barrier of armoured cars and tanks, the forces of the state felt their Jungian collective sphincter tighten as their Jungian collective ears were blasted with the defiant tones of Men Of Harlech.

'GO GO GO GO GO GO!' screamed SAS Colonel Dan Daniels.

KARUMPH! Huge holes appeared in the walls of the council house. BRAAAAKA! BRAAAAAAKA! BRAK! barked the snazzy fired-from-the-hip submachine-guns of the SAS troopers as they emerged wraith-like and running at full tilt from the surrounding murk. KARUMPH! BRAAAKA! BRAAAAAAKA! BRAK! KER-ASH! Tinkle tinkle! Ker-UMPH! BRAK! BRAAAAKA! BRAAAAAAKA! BRAK! OOF! AAAAAAAARGH! screamed Mars, God of War as yet more heavily booted abseiling SAS men smashed through the upstairs windows tossing stun grenades willy nilly and firing at anything that didn't look like a hostage.

Silence.

The front door of the spookily quiet and smoking council house flew open. Out walked an erect SAS trooper. HUZZAH! roared the watching pigs and squaddies spontaneously. SPLAT! went the body of the SAS man as it fell full length on its face to reveal a hideous array of home-made spears, crossbow bolts, knives and hatchets sticking out of its highly trained and utterly dead back.

'EAT HEAD, PIG FASCIST SCUM!' bellowed a blood caked Justine Justice triumphantly as (THWONGHAH! THWONGHAH!) her comrades in extreme direct action for its own sake catapulted the decapitated heads of the slaughtered SAS men straight back at the watching forces of repression.

'WOW!' ejaculated ITN cameraman Bruce Babbington as

he caught one of the oncoming SAS heads in a freak close-up and noticed that it gripped between its tightly clenched teeth a fizzing stick of red dynamite.

KER-BLAAAAAM! AAAAARGH! OH MY GOD! MY FUCKING LEGS!

NOOOOOOOO! AAAAARGH! KER-UMPH! AYEEEEEAH!

Chunks of white-hot machinery and even harder to replace expensively trained ragged ended bloody body parts whizzed through the air as the hastily improvised heads of death exploded savagely behind the piggish barricade.

'Coo, lumee!' chirruped Ricky Tickytimebomb, nursing a hard-on a cat couldn't scratch as he surveyed the spectac pork barbecue with relish. 'H'oive nevah seen so many pigs a-screaming in h'agony in all my blessed loife, blow me if it doesn't warm the cockles of yer blinkin' 'art, so it does!'

'OK, my babies,' murmured a similarly excited Justine Justice, 'let's get out there and finish the bastards off whilst they're still traumatised!'

'ZIGGER ZAGGER, ZIGGER ZAGGER!' chanted half the teenage scum the tabloids called The Peckham Posse.

'OI! OI! OI!' replied the other half, slamming the shafts of their crude but wickedly effective home-made spears into the carpet with gusto.

'Um, hang on a minute,' interjected Aki, 'you've got us all bollock naked and smeared in archaic scribblings done in red paint augmented by the blood of the Prime Minister. Are you sure this is going to make us invulnerable when we ton out of here in a hooting, hollering Lord Of The Flies style mob!'

'Oh ye of little faith!' laughed Justine, grabbing Aki by his ears and planting a huge slobbery kiss on his perfectly formed forehead. 'Look, I'll explain it all one more time. One of the more interesting features of nineteenth-century imperialism was that the fightbacks against the technologically superior Europeans invariably involved some attempt to use magick. The best-known example is, of course, the Ghost Dance of the plains Indians who thought they could make themselves bulletproof by ripping their nipples off and painting themselves with doo-lally doodlings, but other examples include the so-called fuzzy wuzzys of the Sudan and the Boxers in China. Now, then, those mugs bolloxed it up and got their heads kicked in. We, however, have got it sussed. When we go out there with our teeth gritted, waving our gleaming weapons aloft like fucking maniacs, the pigs will let fly with every gun they've got and the bullets will just spang off our magically invulnerable bods. And if you want proof, ask the twenty SAS muthas we've just offed without any of us getting so much as a scratch. Did that fucking rule or what!? With your bubbling teenage enthusiasm for gratuitous violence and my massive in-depth knowledge of arcane magick, we are unstoppable! There are psychopaths still abed in England who will rue that they were not here this night! Onward! My cherubs! Deadpigcity awaits! HUZZAH!'

'HUZZAH!' roared everybody else in the room suddenly frothmouthed and boggleeyed as the magick Viking berserker serum which they'd taken earlier was kicked into action by the code word 'rue'.

'IWANNAKILLEEPIGEENOW!' howled bollock-naked and wild-haired recent recruit Candice Harris as she leaped around the room like an electrocuted salmon on a hot tin roof whilst clutching two massive meat cleavers and pissing herself violently in a savage bloodlust frenzy of HATE!

'OK!' screamed Justine at a magickally enhanced head-in-the-bass-bins at a Motorhead gig style 456 decibels. 'Let's kick pig ASS!'

'AYEEEEEEEEEEEEEEEEEEEEEEEEEEEHAH!' screamed the terrorist collective as they threw themselves out of the window and hurtled to the attack.

It was just like the bit at the end of *Butch Cassidy and The Sundance Kid* where Butch and The Kid, surrounded by tooled up pigs, decide to go out in one final blaze of suicidal glory! With one difference!

'BUDDA! BUDDA! BUDDA!' roared the pig machine-guns.

'Don't shoot!' whined blood-caked Home Office negotiator Pete Ringer pathetically, 'they've got the PM with them!'

'Ha! Fooled you! I'm not really the Prime Minister,' said a figure who it had to be admitted did look an awful lot like the PM. 'Actually I'm teenage terrorist Carol "The Cat" Williams, leader of the so-called Pudsey Posse and I have disguised myself by flaying the PM's corpse and wearing his skin as a disguise. Eat spear, scumbag!'

'Urgle gurgle urgle!' grunted Pete Ringer bloodsplutteringly as the home-made assegai punctured his lily-white throat.

'Die, bitch!' giggled Colonel Dan Daniels who had been pushed to the brink of insanity by recent events as he levelled his snazzy submachine-gun at the horrific figure of the teenage lass dressed in the skin of the dear departed Prime Minister and squeezed the trigger, sexily . . .

'DAKKA DAKKA DAKKA!' shat the machine-gun.

'SPANG! SPANG! SPANG!' went the bullets as they ricocheted off harmlessly.

'Whoops, was that your cock?' queried Candice Harris archly as she smashed the top squaddie in the nads with a hefty meat cleaver, splitting the cunt in two and killing him instantly.

The rest of the battle went pretty much the same way. End result – Terrorists 567, pigs and SAS – 0! Live on prime-time TV!

Result or WHAT!?

TERMINATIONS 1

Roger L. Taylor

Waspish

FIRST VOICE (Austere, detached): Is there a dialogue with yourself, necessarily? You can only surmise how a life might be. And, as it ends. It might be: –

SECOND VOICE (Two voices, one Belfast Irish, the other, inside the one, occasional, Batman's Jack of Clubs): Howlin' down street. 'That's me, me, me, me . . . take that, bang! Bow-wow. Got 'im. Got 'im! Yeah!'

Hyper. Never stops. Even asleep, on the go, 'pow, pow, take that, if you can.'

He is the leather man. Black leather, scuffed skin. The jacket heavy, open, be-chained, like the doors to hell, and hell . . . purple and red pigment, raised scars, enormous exhaust-orifices, blasting.

I'm having a conversation with him, in his head, sometimes; inside the rock . . . hard man. Can't always quite keep up with himself, then I might ask my question or two, like 'Why don't you have a bike then?' or worse, 'Why can't you ride a bike then?'

'Stuff it. Broom! Broom!' He never replies. 'See that? Little tart, I'd lay my tawse on there. Hey you! Yes you! Red arse!

I'll make it red for ya. Fuck off then. Tight cunt! Self-annihilation for you in my esteem, cow!'

The boots, laced L's – antiparalleled clubs – rumble down the slabs of North Street, lashing out at light, holed Tangos and Pepsis, spiralling them into harsh percussion.

'I'm huge. I'm the exterminator. I'm in my mind and you can't get in. When I don't look at you, you're exterminated.' Shoves his face into someone who's trying to avoid him. 'You didn't say I smell, did you? Well you'd better not have. Fucking better not have.' Moves on. Relief to see him move on if you're not him, if he doesn't you're peeing yourself.

Got to have some Metallica. 'Got to, period!' Full vol' in the ears, pain in the tympanic membranes. 'Love it!' Through the ear into the mind, into a vast, empty warehouse.

'Is this where you live,' I say to him, 'electronically?' He stands still and blinks, several times, slowly a smile spreads across his face, breaks the rule and talks to me, 'I don't live out there with you cunts. I'm in here and no one's goin' to get me. I'm tight in here.' On the spot he pumps his knees up and down, into the air, boots thudding. 'Kalashnikov all of ya, pull out the pin, dump a grenade, artillery man above Sarajevo, multiple rocket-launcher, zap zap. I'll tell ya where I live, high up on that campus tower, remember? Pickin' 'em off, one by one. I'm the power, Mr Omnipotent. See me down the arcades, that's where I come alive, powin' them screens. Shag it! Shag! . . . It!'

His lucky day. Right opposite the urinal. The one with the hole in the frosted glass. 'Made it with me 'ead, done it several times.' Standing on the ledge, over the trough, 3-inch boot heels, he can look straight through the hole, log in hand, ready to shoot, and today there's an arse sitting on the wall outside, the sun bright on its bare legs, briefest of skirts. The loo's empty, forgotten, smelling stale, as though shitting is banned for the day. She crosses and uncrosses the highlighted legs, glinting. I could join him in this. Usually though he revolts me.

I let him have the life because he saves me from invasions I can't handle.

'Get off! Fucking insect! Fucking insect! Do you not hear me? Where'd you come from?' He might not have, but I noticed it as soon as we entered, flitting around the corner of the ceiling, as wound up and angry as my alter-ego. He swipes it as it takes an interest in his hair. It flies off and we resume. She's in no hurry to move on. But the wasp is back, yellow and black, abdomen full and bursting, breaking both our concentrations. 'I'll bite your fuckin' head off!' And then it's on his leg and moving upwards. He goes to squeeze it between finger and thumb, and does so, but not before the glans penis is stung. He kicks out at the porcelain causing a hair-line fracture in its surface and tosses the remains of the wasp, now wet and sticking to his fingers, into the swill at his feet. He calls out 'Shit!' and returns to pulling the log. For a while we are fine. We've never been stung before.

When it comes, the pain is quite intense, probably made worse by rubbing, frigging. As one swelling recedes another comes up, red, angry. 'Pain's no problem. I deal with pain. I'm an iron door, a safe, a bank vault. Fuck it! Only me can blast into me. Pain's not me.'

He's OK with pain. He's made us inured. First he went and got us holes in the lobes, then in the nostrils, then the navel, but for his fear of androgyny we'd have the nipples done too. And he gets himself chained up, through the rings, shackled ankle and wrist bones, by metalled and masked whores who teach him tricks with a bullwhip, like a dancing bear in a circus. He rehearses for the way of the world. We're prepared, practised, for the department of employment queue, the quotidian poverty, our one-room hovel for fitful sleep, and, fatally, a whole life to live without prospects. 'Shit face! Don't talk to me shit face!' No one wants to have a go at us. He makes them mess their pants. I can see their funk as soon as he's spotted in the line. A few toughies will try to stone face him, but when he pulls out the snot on his finger they know they're not going to fancy their tuna salad sandwiches in a fraught lunchbreak.

Asphyxiation we don't know about though. Breathing's how we survive, which is the only socially acceptable thing we do do. The rest is 'cause breathing's all we've got, all unacceptable. He's not sensitive to polluted air. He breathes it in like a rat drinks sewer water. He's no dysenteric rodent, no asthmatic, yet he's fighting for breath just because an insect's ovipositor has mistaken its function and injected venom into our blood stream. So, our mucous membranes are behaving like jumpy airbags. It's very sudden and permits no hostility.

Stripped of behaviour we become reflexes, on our knees, gasping, fingers playing riffs in puddles of misdirected urine. 'Oh! ass-hole,' he manages for me, as though some homophobic instinct protests at an insect wasp getting the better of us when he rolls for us, in the cause of international mugging, American tourists who are on the loose. In the next instant he's left me. If I could see outside which I can't, all I can see are some tiles wearing a red swastika coming at me in irregular pulses, I would see his little bit of arse moving off with a John. My actor, my representative, my proxy is not going to be with me to the end.

I'm saved though. What's revealed is not an angel with a key to the abyss, but it is socially recognised, acceptable, required, to be the Samaritan when the cost is, 'Hold on old chap! I'll have an ambulance here in a jiffy'? You do not have to breathe into his mouth, because it is his booted carcass, heavy and skinned on the floor, like a decked flat-fish, or open a hole in his/our enlarged trachea.

I can't make out my saviour. I heard him enter, he would say who has left me, 'like one looking for a faggot', shifty footsteps, unsure, exploratory, and I look up, damp with my own cold sweat and my urine, involuntarily down my leg, to black, patent leather and striped, immaculate, worsted turn-ups.

There must be a glance down at him, which I can't see. A

judgemental decision, followed by a sentence, executed by the sartorial feet. What did he represent to provoke quiet, calculated malice? First, the Walkman, shed, adrift from the collapse, goes under the leather heel, cutting off the lifeline, followed by a blinding of Samson, sharp, pointed toes into our bulging eye-balls, leaving blood spreading slowly across the whites.

As the cistern water floods, a torrent in a valley of waste, I wish he would return to heave apart those pillars supporting this disdain, but I am alone and slipping, unable, as ever, to split philistines in two. From slipping to senselessness to terminal suffocation.

FIRST VOICE (as before): Are there always two of us necessarily? One a means to the other?

THIRD VOICE (Two voices. One, inside the other, on the brink, like air in a hard tyre, the other funereal, a symmetrical tread, reliable unless the inside gets out, then breakdown): Business-like he walks from the toilet and inside I am seething, disturbed, trembling, exalted. He stops, pulls a paper-handkerchief from a pocket, raises his foot to a wall and polishes the shoe furiously, then the other one.

It's time one of them got it. Don't you think? They're such wasters, wankers. I wish I could tell Goldie about this. I wish I could tell her. Wankers! Aren't you just proud of yourself. Well done! He doesn't listen to me, much more direct now than when I entered the gents: bee-line back to the office. Gross faggot, probably the worse for drugs, not even a nice faggot, no Farahs, no Pringle. I hate Skins.

He is wonderfully composed. Every inch the MD. So polite, almost human with the client. 'Yes of course we will expedite without any delay ... we will give it utmost priority, if we don't deliver by the fifteenth you can have the staff's guts for garters' ... laughter ... then reassurance, totally professional ... 'you mustn't worry that's what we're here for . . . we provide quality service . . . our mission statement is – your satisfaction by our unstinting service.' He looks out panoramically from the MD's suite on the top floor. He can survey the whole of the Old Steine and beyond to the Royal Pavilion. These are magnificent offices. He brushes a speck of dandruff from the lapel of his expensive suit and straightens his tie, which is a little awry as if he might have just exerted himself. Hypocrite! The panoptic populace below convects warmth to his desire for business: on the move, pocketfuls of money and magnetic connections to bank accounts. He sees a courteous, luxurious future laid out for Goldie and himself and their brood of well-behaved children, none of whom will ever know of my existence, here, inside.

And then, before I am ready or can do anything about it, he disowns our life together. He unbolts the double-glazed doors, there is no balcony, and walks through them. I don't have time to remind him that our double-life is only appearance and reality and cannot be genuinely contradictory. We lose everything in the vertigo of rapid descent.

FIRST VOICE: As suddenly as that! You may surmise differently. All we know for sure is that bodies, deserted of lives, are found on pavements and in urinals and everywhere else, and that inquests reveal death by misadventure, manslaughter, murder, suicide . . .

LAST TRAIN HOME

John King

Annie was nervous taking the last tube back to Acton Town. She'd been to visit her aunt in the Archway and had lost track of the time as they talked, losing the thread in a soothing haze of words. It had been a nice evening, shut away inside the flat with the gas fire burning, talking about her mother, her aunt's sister; stories from childhood, looking at family photos. They'd had sandwiches and cake, and three cups of coffee each. A couple of glasses of sherry.

The flat was small and cramped, and the gas made a person tired and could bring on headaches, but with the wind screaming outside it was safe and comfortable. The evening had passed so quickly, and now Annie was outside pushing through the wind, past swaying men and a packed kebab house. London was drunk and her aunt wanted Annie to stay the night, but she needed to get home. She had to start cleaning offices early next morning and dared not be late. The atmosphere was so warm in the flat that she could almost lean back and go to sleep, stay in Archway safe and sound, but a job was a job and worth clinging to during hard times.

Archway tube station was grim and cold, the smell of ground-in dirt soaked in the spirit fumes of three men sitting on a bench. They took no notice of Annie, and she was glad, reminding herself that she was pushing middle age and ugly, that no man would want her. Deep down she knew she wasn't really ugly, not bad looking if she was honest, but the age bit was true, and drink could easily dim that particular prejudice.

Old or young, a woman was a lump of meat to some men when they were drinking. These three were arguing politics and she took them for union men and felt a bit safer, because to be in a union nowadays was a sign of bravery, a symbol of decency. It suggested minds that stretched a bit further than the sex equals power equation. Maybe she was being romantic. She could never be sure. The wind had made her head spin.

The tube arrived before Annie reached the end of the platform and was soon rattling its way through Kentish Town and Camden, filling the carriages with youngsters who were harmless enough, but loud and silly in their costumes. It wasn't until she reached Leicester Square that there was an ominous depth to the crowd which put Annie on edge. In among the tourists and kissing couples she identified the men who left their half-empty coffee cups behind for people like Annie to clean up, cold coffee that ran down her arms and soaked her sleeves, a total lack of respect for the cleaners.

These men were drunk and stupid, with creased suits and blotchy necks, after-shave that had turned rancid as the drink flooded their pores. They stared at Annie as she passed and she hoped none of them worked in the offices she cleaned, that nobody would recognise her and start a conversation. She would die from embarrassment, though the crowd around her meant it unlikely she would be attacked.

When the train for Acton Town arrived, the whole platform pushed itself aboard, Annie finding herself wedged against the door linking two carriages. She was sober with just those three cups of coffee to give her confidence. Two small sherries to give her strength. She closed her eyes and thought of her mother, piles of photographs set in her mind, happy memories of a woman dead and buried the past five years.

Annie's eyelids felt heavy and she was tired. The carriage reeked of fumes and she had to fight against her fear of dying underground, sealed in a metal casket, no escape possible as she choked on the smoke, flames lapping through the train.

The gradual flood of poison through her lungs. Gagging as she fell to the floor. Buried alive.

She missed her mother but knew death was the one constant. Time rolled on. She pushed the sadness away and watched the people around her, everyone packed so tight, groping hands ready to work their way into her coat, over and under her skin, ripping the lining away and raping her against the door, mute and unprotected, rib cage exposed. All these strangers breathing into each others' faces, a mist of sweat and dead alcohol, a lack of oxygen and heavy lungs. It only took one madman to insert his knife and twist the blade. One way or the other they'd soon be lowering her down to rest next to her mother.

By the time the train passed Earl's Court it was empty of tourists, and when it left Hammersmith there were few people remaining in the carriage. Annie relaxed and sat down, reminding herself that human beings were basically kind and considerate. Newspapers played on the basic fears of the population and exaggerated the worst cases of rape, murder, torture. She was no fool, no irrational misfit, so she smiled as she read the adverts for abortion and skin care plastered along the carriage, wondering how much companies paid to reach out and connect with bored and tired travellers.

As the tube approached Acton Town, Annie was up on her feet waiting for the doors to open. She walked briskly along the platform and gave her ticket to the skinhead on the gate, making sure she avoided his eyes, not taking any chances. Men had one thing on their minds. She veered right and turned down the street leading home.

Annie walked quickly, eyes straight ahead, not daring to turn when she spied a man urinating against the wall of an alley. He was just a harmless drunk and she didn't want to pry. If he had to go to the toilet, then he had to go to the toilet. Simple as that. And if there was no toilet available then thank God he was being discreet. She kept walking, her coat wrapped tight, ignoring the truth, aware of heavy footsteps behind.

It was a man. She'd known it would happen one day. It was the man in the alley. There could be no doubt. A man following her home. Tracking a defenceless woman. The hunter and the hunted. No, he wasn't following her, he was on his way to the warmth of his own gas fire, where he would lean back and watch the flames dance, the wind crying outside, safe and sound. On his way home to a loving wife and child. A family man who worked hard all week and had a quiet drink on Friday night. She shouldn't brand all men worthless because of the few. A man with a lovely daughter whom he loved and cherished.

She was walking near the tracks now, electricity sparking and lighting a train as it thundered past, its destination unimportant but the extra light welcome. The street lamps were dim and tired, and created more shadows than the illumination was worth.

Annie was seized by panic as she felt the hot breath of the rapist on her neck. Smelt a sour odour mixed with the hate of drink. Felt clammy hands reaching for her under a blaze of lights, her body paralysed. She wondered if she had been stabbed in the back, or her throat slit, a chicken hanging upside down bleeding to death. Hands around her neck. Forcing the air from her lungs.

As her eyes rolled she saw that the bricks and blank windows of the houses had reversed, the inmates sucked in on themselves as the light from the track cracked and popped, her nose filled with burning flesh, a popping of body gases a million miles from the happy family barbecue, her thinking distorted and misfiring.

Annie felt herself travelling down a tunnel, and for some reason she thought of her friend Doris. She imagined the two of them hoovering carpets. Emptying ashtrays and half-full cups of coffee. The cold liquid along her arms. But Annie was no dreamer. She was a realist. She saw memories judder in

newsflashes, her mother ahead balanced on the edge of a platform. A train was waiting for her and the faces pressed against
the window were smiling and happy. Annie felt the pressure
released.

There were no happy endings. Life was nothing special,
nothing to which she wanted to cling. Mum was dead and
gone and she had hated her dad. A worthless drunk. Come to
Daddy. She shouldn't have had the sherry. She hated alcohol.
The long winters and lack of money meant everything was a
struggle. Perhaps life was supposed to have a meaning, and
perhaps it was supposed to be enjoyed, but that was for the
men in the offices she cleaned. They had holidays and gardens
and confidence. She did not. They were privileged, and didn't
bother emptying their cups.

Annie was excited. She could feel the clammy hands of the
rapist fading. Her sensual perceptions were changing and she
was floating. Even the image of her mother was becoming
more subtle. She was experiencing different shades of colour
and her understanding of what was happening began shifting.
The tunnel became an impression without walls. There was a
bright light ahead and she had the idea that it was the driver's
signal. Acton Town full of saints and ghosts. An old tube
station packed with unseen memories. Crowds of people
passing through. Year after year. Fully illuminated for the
occasion. Then there was the close-up of the train, perpetual
motion, spinning in on itself.

Everything seemed right about her death. Annie would stop
fighting and accept her fate. She would kneel down in front of
the light up ahead and accept whatever imagery her con-
ditioning created. If she had to accept Jesus to see her mum
again, she would play the part. She hoped there would be a
hell as well. Was there a heaven?

Doubt stopped Annie still and she willed it to disappear.
The train was melting into a mass of gentle colours, mingling
together. She had fought against the injustice she experienced
all her life, forced to fight in her mind, deep inside, but she

had never surrendered. She was quiet as a mouse. Nervously smiling and doing as she was told.

But Annie didn't care any more. She had been ground down and spat into the gutter for a sex beast to grab and strangle. A monster feasting on her flesh in the low wattage streets of West London. She didn't care. They could have her body. She didn't need it now. She was free and on a journey. Just get rid of the last doubts and she would escape.

Annie felt a sharp pain in her throat. There was a loud bang and she was being sucked back up the tunnel. The train was leaving without her. She screamed but no sound came. She had been trained to be quiet and obedient, to stand in the corner and face the wall like a good little girl, lovely little girl, but though the chords were frozen the mind kept rebelling. She didn't want any more. The train was solid now and moving away, doors shut tight, friendly faces blurred and lost as it picked up speed. She couldn't see her mum. Had to get home.

She was being dragged back past a drunk father standing in an alleyway, back into Acton Town station, and then she was retracing her journey, racing now, faster and faster, and she wondered whether this was the final flashback and how far it would go, whether she would have to watch Mum being buried again, she didn't want that, back to childhood, she didn't want that either, and then Annie was in Archway hearing those deep whisky voices embedded in concrete. The voices were playing at the wrong speed and she was looking at three men waiting for their train, and then there was the cold of the escalators, freezing steel and the wind up above hitting her in the face, as though someone had come into a room and opened a window, letting in the freezing night air, breaking the spell, shattering the glass.

Annie felt another bang and she was gagging. A man's mouth was pushing against hers and she shuddered, felt sick. She thought of the photos of her mum on Brighton pier. Annie as a child. Fists battering her body, some kind of perversion driven by what a sick old man pretended was love. She was choking, coughing, crying through gas-filled lungs, her aunt on a stretcher being carried from the flat, the window smashed and a fireman leaning over her, his mouth working to resuscitate the dying woman, fists shocking her heart.

Annie watched the men fighting for her life and wished they'd just leave her alone.

A NOTE ON THE CONTRIBUTORS

John Barker has contributed stories to *Edinburgh Review* and worked as a removals man. He lives between North and East London.

Steve Beard is the author of the ambient novel *Digital Leatherette* and the surrealist book *Perfumed Head*. *Logic Bomb*, a collection of his lifestyle journalism, will be published shortly by Serpent's Tail. He lives in East London.

Bertholt Bluel is the pseudonym of a young and iconoclastic architect. His non-existence often manifests itself in several places at once.

Ted Curtis has contributed stories to a number of anthologies and received requests for a book from several agents and publishers. To date he has brushed off these advances. He lives in East London.

Robert Dellar is the editor of *Gobbing, Pogoing and Gratuitous Bad Language: An anthology of punk short stories* and one of the seven authors of the collectively produced novel *Seaton Point*. He works in the mental health sector and lives in East London.

Simon Ford is a curator at the Victoria and Albert Museum whose published works include *The Realization And Suppression Of The Situationist International: An Annotated Bibliography 1972–1992* and *Wreckers Of Civilisation: The story of COUM Transmissions and Throbbing Gristle*. He lives in South London.

Naomi Foyle is a mystery wrapped in an enigma. She was born in London, grew up in Canada and lives in Seoul.

Barry Graham's novels include *Of Darkness & Light, Before* and *The Book Of Man*. He grew up in Glasgow and lives in Phoenix, Arizona.

Hilaire's stories have been published in various places and *Time Out* have tipped her as a future literary megastar. She grew up in Australia and lives in South London.

Stewart Home is the author of several novels including *Come Before Christ & Murder Love, Slow Death* and *Blow Job*. He divides his time between drinking Islay single malts and Adnams Suffolk ales. He was born in South London and lives in the East End.

John King is the author of *The Football Factory, England Away* and *Headhunters*. He lives in South London.

Jerry Palmer runs Outer Spaceways Incorporated, a legendary psychogeographical outfit. He lives in North London but longs to return to his native Essex.

Neil Palmer fronts the Fire Dept., whose last album was *Elpee For Another Time*. He grew up in rural Cambridgeshire and is in the process of relocating from Brighton to his beloved East Anglia.

Bridget Penney is the author of *Honeymoon With Death*. She grew up in Edinburgh and lives in East London.

M. Stasiak was raised among the spruce budworm in New-foundland. She lives in North London and works as an editor.

Simon Strong is the author of an experimental novel, *A259 Multiplex Bomb 'Outrage'*. He is a computer programmer who grew up in Sheffield and lives in Melbourne, Australia.

Roger L. Taylor is a former Sussex University philosophy lec-turer and the author of *Art, An Enemy Of The People* and

Beyond Art: What art is and might become if freed from cultural élitism. He lives in Brighton.

Ian Trowell edits the journals *Communist Headache* and *Autotoxicity*. He is a librarian with young children who lives in Sheffield.

Tommy Udo is a freelance journalist who contributes to *New Musical Express*, *Esquire* and other magazines. He grew up outside Glasgow and lives in Central London.

Steven Wells writes for the *New Musical Express*. His first novel, *Tits-Out Teenage Terror Tottie*, will be published shortly. He grew up in Yorkshire and lives in South London.

ALSO PUBLISHED BY SERPENT'S TAIL

Mind Invaders: A reader in psychic warfare, cultural sabotage and semiotic terrorism

Edited by Stewart Home

This collection comprehensively samples the resistance culture of recent years, featuring innumerable utopian protest groups dedicated to attacking the very foundations of 'Western Civilisation'.

In London, the Association of Autonomous Astronauts is expanding the terrain of social struggle, launching an independent proletarian space exploration programme. Future ventures shall include raves in space. In Italy, the Bologna Psychogeographical Association is helping to levitate government buildings and playing mind games with prime-time TV. Meanwhile their London counterparts are busy exposing the macabre occult practices of the British Royal Family, and Decadent Action plots to bring capitalism to its knees through a programme of exorbitant shopping sprees leading to hyperinflation. Break out the champagne and canapés!

'Stewart Home curates the fistful of mercury that is the commonwealth of the "mind invader". Texts so crazy you have to trust them ... A dazzling anti-anthology.' – IAIN SINCLAIR

'In the 2090s *Mind Invaders* will be revered as the roots to the creative paranoia that has corroded our once mighty civilisation. Read this book and die.' – BILL DRUMMOND, KLF

ALSO BY STEWART HOME AND PUBLISHED BY SERPENT'S TAIL

Slow Death

A gang of socially ambitious skinheads runs riot through the London art world, plotting the rebirth and violent demise of an elusive avant-garde art movement. Taking genre fiction for a ride, *Slow Death* uses obscenity, black humour and repetition for the sake of ironic deconstruction. The sleazy sex is always graphic and all traditional notions of literary taste and depth are ditched in favour of a transgressive aesthetic inspired by writers as diverse as Homer, de Sade, Klaus Theweleit, and '70s cult writer Richard Allen.

Praise for Stewart Home:

'It's an exercise in futility to complain that Home's novels lack depth, characterization or complex plots: that is the whole point. The project operates within its contradictions, subverting the spirit of redundant industrial fiction, while honouring the form ... Home's language feeds on metropolitan restlessness, movement, lists of trains and buses, gigs in pubs, rucks outside phone kiosks, the epiphany of the grease caff.' – Iain Sinclair, *London Review of Books*

'Home is a serious "wind-up" artist emerging from a high-culture, oppositional tradition that started with Dada and descended to the street in the 1970s with punk. His main theme is that so-called uncontrollable desire for sex (and maybe violence) are in fact highly artificial, constructed by social convention in general, and by the modern state in particular.' – *New Statesmen and Society*

'... The skinhead author whose sperm'n'blood-sodden scribblings about the insaner fringes of pop culture make Will Self's writings read like the self-indulgent dribblings of a sad middle-class Oxbridge junkie trying to sound "hard."' – *New Musical Express*

Come Before Christ and Murder Love

Kevin Callan is running away but the past keeps catching up with him. That's the price he has to pay for using the occult to get his sexual kicks while manipulating everyone around him. Sometimes Callan claims to be the victim of a state-sponsored mind control programme, at others, the man in charge of the whole operation. The thing is, Callan has a thousand different identities, and a range of London apartments, disciples, lovers, and possibly murder victims to go with the lifestyle.

Come Before Christ and Murder Love is a tale of mental disorder, magick, London, food, thought control and human sacrifice. Stewart Home's outrageous new novel explores sex and the occult both as ideologies and ways of organizing 'knowledge'. Here, the traditional distinctions between novelist and critic, truth and fiction, authors and their audience are visibly eroded.

Blow Job

As the leader of Class Justice, Steve Drummond has the London anarchist situation in his pocket, until Swift Nick Carter makes his return to the political scene. Unlike Drummond, Carter believes there's more to starting a revolution than claiming the credit every time trouble breaks out on the rundown inner city London estates. Soon Drummond finds himself drawn into a local conflict between a crew of anarchists and a fascist fringe where events start to get murderously personal. As the tempo of bombings and assassinations speeds up all across London, from Whitehall to Brixton, it becomes increasingly difficult to distinguish the warring parties. Finally, as the plot races to its cataclysmic conclusion, anarchism and fascism are revealed as mirror images of each other.

Stewart Home's ongoing satire of urban sub cultures has never been so fierce, furious or entertaining.